STILL OUT THERE

STILL OUT THERE
By Laurie Holbrook

Still Out There is a work of fiction. Names, characters, places, and incidents are the product of the author's imagination or are used fictitiously. Any resemblance to actual events, locales, businesses, or persons, living or dead, is coincidental.

Published by Frisson Publishing
Print ISBN - 978-1-7335609-0-0
Ebook ISBN - 978-1-7335609-1-7

Cover Design by Book Design Stars, www.bookdesignstars.com
Interior Design by Kimberly Peticolas, www.kimpeticolas.com

Library of Congress Control Number: 2019900840

STILL
OUT
THERE

LAURIE HOLBROOK

For my love.

ONE

DECEMBER 1998

IF ANYONE WOULD HAVE BOTHERED TO ASK Mabel where she wanted to live, she would have said California. But no one asked. Portland would take some getting used to. If it rained again, it'd be the eleventh straight day. The sun-filled days of Denver were no more. Mabel wondered if Portland got three hundred days of rain a year.

She finished the last of her homework and began writing her new name sitting crisscrossed on her bed.

Mabel Peters. Mabel Peters.

She struggled with the *b*. At this point, she'd be surprised if she ever got the hang of it. Two pages, three across, twenty-seven lines down later, she stopped, chewed on the tip of her pen, and started up again with her grandparents' names.

John Peters.

Kathryn Peters.

John was easy to write, but sort of boring. Kathryn was fun. She liked writing the K and y in cursive. She made it all loopy.

It didn't take long for her mom and Pete to pop into her head. A single tear fell on Peters. She watched as it soaked through the paper and Peters became P . . . s.

Mind your Ps and Qs, her mom used to say.

She wished they were there. Mom and Pete.

Dad too. She'd cried every day and night for a month after her dad died in a car crash a year ago. The pain in her chest ached so bad she thought she'd die.

But right now, she wanted her mom and little brother more. Thinking of them brought a different kind of pain.

Every time she opened the wooden shutters, particles of dust flew in her nose. The smell reminded her of the old library Mom used to take her and Pete to. She thought of cleaning the layer of dust, but what was the point when Grandpa said their stay there was temporary.

"Ready?" Frankie asked, tapping the door frame with his big hand.

She smiled. Frankie had that effect on her and more than anything she wanted him to fill the gaping hole in her chest.

"I am. I've been thinking . . ."

"You have? Hopefully not too hard." He lifted an eyebrow.

She gave him an eye roll. "I wanted to ask you if . . . I can call you uncle?" Her heart beat faster. She couldn't look at him. "You know . . . since you're kind of like an uncle anyway."

Nothing. No comeback. The man always had a comeback of some sort. Maybe she'd stumped him and now he felt sorry for her.

Yup, she'd stumped him alright.

His mouth hung open. She imagined a fly disappearing into

the dark hole of his mouth. It can happen. Dad told her that a big bug flew into his mouth once when he was running. From then on, she ran with her mouth closed. She didn't know what she'd do if it went up her nose.

He blinked and rewarded her with one of his enormous bear hugs. "I would love nothing more," he said, squeezing the air out of her.

"I can't breathe," she muttered

He let go.

"What are you teaching me today Uncle Frankie?" It rolled of her tongue with ease. Her dad had been an only child and her mom had had a sister who'd died before Mabel was born. She always wished for an aunt or uncle. Now she had one. She found it hard to fight her excitement.

Frankie told her a few weeks back that he'd teach her to fight. So far, all she had done was cardio and strength training. Nothing new there. She'd done that stuff with her dad all the time. But Frankie did let her hold a variety of weapons. The guns didn't have bullets in them—he'd said she wasn't ready. And he had watched her like a hawk with the knives. She didn't dare touch the sharp side. Once, when she was younger, she'd cut her thumb on a knife that was hidden behind the spoons. It bled a lot. Dad used super glue to close the cut. She thought it odd, but he said Grandpa did it all the time and showed her the scar on his leg. *Super glued*, he'd said.

"Doc said we can take it up a notch." He waggled his eyebrows.

Doctor Melvin gave Frankie strict orders on what she could and couldn't do. He and his wife, Donna, had followed them to Portland until Mabel was in the clear, medically. The two of them had returned to Colorado last month.

"Really!?" She had already watched hours of videos and

read book after book on self-defense, Tai Chi, Jiu-Jitsu, Krav Maga, Kung Fu, and so on. Frankie knew most of them. She couldn't contain herself. "Teach me!" Mabel said, jumping up and down. Then she took it too far. "Teach me how to beat the hell out of—"

"Mabel." His voice firm. "What have we been talking about?" He shook his head in disgust and her face flushed. "I'm teaching you this so you know *how* to protect yourself. Always remember—it's about having confidence and discipline. Don't ever abuse it."

"Sorry."

"How about I let you beat the hell out of me?" He gave her a deep belly laugh.

She followed him through the kitchen, down to his basement. There were two distinct areas. One with weights, a heavy bag, a treadmill, and a stationary bike. The other side was completely open with mats covering the floor. This is where she would learn to fight.

She loved him more than she thought she might love an uncle. Not quite like her grandpa and dad, but darn close. Frankie was the one who'd given her and her grandparents their new identities. She didn't know how it all worked, but he'd chosen her name.

Mabel Peters. *Ma* from Margaret after her mom, *Be* from Ben after her dad—Mabel. And *Peters* from Peter, her brother. How clever. He'd given her a piece of her family in her new life.

You are no longer Melodi Stucker. Melodi Stucker died in the creek. The man in black killed her. They never found her body. . . .

Two months ago, her entire world changed.

It started the year earlier when her dad died. How many kids lose one parent only to lose the rest of their family the following year. That's right. Her life took a path only possible in horror films, the ones her mom never let her watch because she'd have nightmares.

She had lived it.

Before, she was known as a talker—*yap, yap, yap*—her dad always said. She never stopped talking. Silence made her uncomfortable.

In the three days following her real-life nightmare—more like five, since she was knocked out for two of them—silence became her friend. She didn't want to be Mabel. She wanted Melodi to die in the creek. Her existence no longer made sense. Everything she knew—gone. If she had died, as intended, she'd be with her family. She'd thought of nothing else in those three days.

The nightmares her mom had once successfully kept her from now came anyway. She believed she was being punished for living. And fighting sleep only lasted so long, her body eventually betrayed her, falling asleep at awkward moments. Like a baby. Like Pete as a toddler. He once fell asleep at the table in his bowl of mashed potatoes. Another time, he fell asleep on their hardwood floor—butt naked. Not sure how that one happened.

Then Frankie gave her something to look forward to. He gave her a reason to go on living. Just the thought of defending herself gave her the strength she needed.

Grandpa found a house after all. *It's only a fifteen-minute drive,* he'd explained. Fifteen or five, she didn't care. What she wanted was to stay put.

She sat on the couch and watched the men go in and out of the house, waiting for Grandma to yell at them for leaving the door open.

"Mabel, sweetie, help the men load the truck," she said instead.

"Me? The men do the hard labor and the women stay inside."

"Ha! Who told you that nonsense?"

"No one, but you're not helping."

Sounded logical to her, but Grandma gave the look. "Do you cook? Do you clean the house? Do you go shopping? Do you wash laundry? Do you—"

"Grandma, Grandma, okay. I get it. I don't do anything. Geez." Mabel slouched her shoulders and headed for the stairs. She chanted to herself, *I don't want to move, I. Don't. Want. To. Move.* A word for each footfall, because if she helped move, they'd leave sooner.

"Mabel. Get back here," Grandma said in her, *don't mess with me* voice. Grandma had *the look* and *the voice.*

She stopped with three more steps to go. She had two choices. Storm off to her room and shut the world out or face her grandma and apologize for being selfish. She chose the latter.

"I know you don't want to move, but . . ."

Here come the buts.

"But you need to learn respect and help around the house more. You think you can do that?"

She nodded.

"I know you can. You can do anything you put your mind to." She kissed Mabel on the forehead. "And I know you helped your mom all the time."

She swallowed the lump in her throat. "I miss her."

"It's okay to miss her. Your mom would want you to keep doing the things she taught you. She told me all the time how proud you made her."

It was hard to believe adults when they said things like that. Mabel wasn't there. And she'd witnessed firsthand adults saying anything to avoid conflict. Mom called them *white lies* and she only told them to spare someone's feelings. Like when Pete drew a picture of their family and Mom had told him how perfect it was. It wasn't. Not even close. Mabel told him so and got in trouble. After that she spotted white lies from everyone around her. It made her wonder, if everyone told white lies then how does anyone learn the truth?

"She did," Grandma said, sensing her uncertainty. "She'd go on and on about what you did or said at home and at school. And I can see why. You're a pretty spectacular girl."

White lie.

"Who needs to be more respectful," Mabel added. *Let's not forget the original lesson here.*

"Sometimes you forget. Everyone needs a reminder. I'll help you load up your room and you can help me make lunch."

"Okay," she replied, to make her grandma happy. Does that count as a lie? Saying you'll do something when you really don't want to?

As she loaded up each box the tears began to fill her eyes. Mabel kept her face turned so Grandma wouldn't see her crying. She felt the snot roll down her nose, nearing her lip. At any moment she'd have to sniffle—or lick it off. If she sniffled, Grandma would know. Deciding she didn't want to sniffle or lick her snot, she set the box down and scurried to the bathroom to blow her nose and wipe her eyes.

Knock, knock, knock.

"Mabel. Are you alright?"

She didn't answer and thought about lying. She'd often lied to her mom, convincing herself they were just white lies to avoid conflict. But the night her mom and Pete were murdered, she didn't lie, she told her mom exactly how she felt.

Grandma opened the door. She should have locked it. "Oh, sweetheart. What's wrong? Why are you crying?"

"I don't want to move again. I want us to stay with Uncle Frankie."

"Sweetie, we aren't moving far." She pulled Mabel in for a hug and stroked her hair. "You'll see Uncle Frankie all the time. He loves you."

She responded with a sniffle.

"Come, sit down." The bathroom was closest to her grandparent's room. It was bigger than the bedroom Mabel used, but there were curtains instead of blinds and the bedspread had a floral print as opposed to the bright blue one on her bed. "Tell me what else this is about."

Mabel put the hair she'd twirled with her finger into her mouth. A bad habit Mom told her to stop hundreds of times. "I'm afraid," she said, looking down.

Grandma pulled her chin up so Mabel's eyes met hers. Now they both had tears.

"I don't want to think about what happened. And my training helps keep my mind off what happened," Mabel explained.

"I'll talk with your grandpa. Don't you worry, Frankie will keep training you. And if I know your grandpa, he already has a plan in place to build you a workout place of your own."

Mabel's face lit up. "Really?"

"Oh yes. And if he wasn't already planning on it, he's doing it now." She smiled and kissed Mabel on the forehead.

"Thanks, Grandma."

"Don't thank me child, thank your grandpa when it's done. Now let's go lend them a hand."

"I'll help him build it, too."

"That's my girl. Your dad used to help your grandpa build things all the time."

"He did? Like what?"

"His tree house for starters." She laughed recalling a memory.

"My dad had a tree house?"

"Oh yes. Your dad insisted he have one for him and his best friend Ryan to hang out in. They slept in it on many occasions."

"That would be cool."

"Grab that box," Grandma directed. "You'll have to ask your grandpa to tell you the stories someday. He was usually the one pulling your dad out of there late at night."

"Do you think he'll build me a tree house?"

"Oops. I shouldn't have said anything. You'll have your own gym, I think that'll be enough."

"What will be enough?" Grandpa asked when they stepped outside.

"Grandma said you're building me a gym."

Uncle Frankie let out his big belly laugh.

"She what?" Grandpa asked.

Uncle Frankie laughed louder.

"What's so funny?" Mabel asked. "I need somewhere to practice, and I'll help build it."

"Damn straight you will," Grandpa said, "and so will Grandma . . . and Uncle Frankie."

"Wait—what?" Frankie asked.

"Yay! It'll be fun." Mabel jumped up and down, gave everyone a quick hug and ran back inside to grab more boxes.

She'd show them she could work extra hard. Anything to keep busy. Grandma was right, she needed to help more.

TWO

FRANKIE DOWDY HAD MET HIS SHARE OF degenerate criminals, sociopaths, psychopaths, trouble-makers, and downright sadists in his line of work over the years. But never had it hit so close to home. Who could have foreseen one of them would have come for Ben's family?

Melodi . . . Mabel (he still had problems with her name) had seen more and lost more than any person should. Her mom and brother murdered in cold blood and she, left for dead. Then she's expected to go on living, knowing that the killer is still out there, somewhere.

The first time her grandparents left her with Frankie, she fell asleep on the couch watching *Scooby-Doo,* only to wake up in pure terror. He could only imagine the wretchedness she suffered in her dreams. Her body spasmed as if she was having a mild seizure. Face sweating, fingers gripping the sofa, head jerking—screaming, *No Daddy. No. He didn't do it. Over and over.*

It's just a dream, he had told her.

Her killer kept coming back and he'd never stop. Frankie had to give her purpose. He talked to her grandpa, John. It was time to train her. Martial arts, combat fighting, meditation, discipline, learning to protect herself—moving her attention from being a victim to being strong and healthy. Living again. Never would she be put in a situation where she could not protect herself. She needed something to build her confidence again.

It worked. He wouldn't go as far as to say it saved her life. John and Doc did that. John especially. He was her glue and still is. *God help her if she ever lost that man.*

Frankie was not one for negativity. He did not lose control. He did not stress. There were only three things that mattered to him; family and friends, health, and his work. He lumped family and friends together because to him they were one and the same. If he considered someone a true friend, you were family.

Bottom line—he got shit done. Frankie was no saint. He'd come close to death more times than he would like to admit, and that didn't include his time in the Army.

He didn't like to think about how many lives he'd taken. He didn't enjoy it. He guessed no one did in his shoes. But he didn't worry whether he was as bad as the scum that killed families and left little girls without a mother. He knew that wasn't him. He knew when he did it—when he took a life—he had no choice. Absolute last resort, like an officer protecting the streets and cities we live in.

Life or death.

Him or the bad guy.

When it came down to it, he chose to live every time. No question. He chose the innocent every time. He chose the kid he just rescued, every time. No question.

He would give Detective Ryan Cross three months. Not because he was a detective, but because John had faith in Ryan. And he had faith in John. But that didn't mean he won't go hunt the demented fuck that invaded the lives of the people he cared about.

THREE

PRESENT DAY

Y*OU HAVE TO PAY FOR WHAT YOUR FATHER DID.*

Her eyes flew open and quickly scanned the room, settling on the darkest corner—on a shadow of a man dressed all in black. *He came back to finish the job.* Trembling, Mabel squeezed her eyes shut. When she opened them again, the man remained, watching. She reached for her 9mm Springfield XD with a mounted tactical light that was tucked away in her nightstand—her favorite. As she took aim and flipped the light the man vanished. Reality crept over her—another bad dream. She's safe. Yet Mabel couldn't shake the feeling he was lurking in the shadows, repeating the words . . .

You have to pay for what your father did.

Mabel hated the feeling of waking from nightmares, of her mind playing tricks on her. Her hand found her chest as if she planned to pledge allegiance to the flag. No allegiance, but maybe stop her heart from exploding and tearing her ribcage open.

The same heart that once dodged a bullet.

Her t-shirt, completely soaked, stuck to her skin. Kicking the covers to the bottom of her bed, she took a few deep breaths. What good is therapy if she couldn't get rid of the demon—or the man—who haunted her?

It's decided, no more therapy.

The green light beside her bed displayed five thirty-four. Lucas grumbled and rolled over, his arm hanging off the bed. He didn't wake, he never did. He'd sleep through a hurricane. Mabel's heart slowed to more of a *thump, thump, thump*. She closed her eyes, forcing the dreadful images out, and counted on an hour of dreamless sleep before her alarm demanded she get up.

An hour later and wide awake, Korn's "Coming Undone" blared on the radio. Mabel made no attempt to move.

How fitting, she thought.

Lucas, still asleep, snored softly.

Maybe it was time. She had gone from her grandparents straight into college and back to her grandparents. Then, five years ago, she moved in with Lucas.

It was time—Mabel needed to be on her own.

Mabel backed into her usual spot—closest to the exit, ready for anything—just like she'd been taught. Part paranoia, part second nature.

Richard crossed the lot, briefcase in tow. A somewhat slender man with a protruding gut. If he were pregnant, he'd be in the middle of his second trimester.

A garbage truck rolled by, stopping at the end of the street.

A policeman drove the opposite direction, looking at Mabel as he passed. She probably looked suspicious—parked, watching. That's what she did now. She watched everything.

Grandpa thought she'd be asking for trouble if she moved back to Colorado "Why would you put yourself in danger?" he'd asked.

Who am I?

Am I Melodi, daughter of Ben and Margaret Stucker, sister of Peter Stucker? Melodi who lost her father in a freak storm and a year later her mother and brother were shot and killed by a monster?

Or am I Mabel? The girl who lost her entire family in a car accident, raised by her grandparents, and is now a fifth-grade teacher?

She's both. And she's stuck.

Mabel moved back to Colorado to find her way. And as each day passes, she becomes Melodi—more and more. The girl who had shitty things happen to her. The girl who will stop at nothing until the killer is either six feet under or sentenced to life without parole.

Better yet, the death penalty.

I'm back asshole, come get me.

At twenty-seven, Mabel is no longer an eleven-year-old helpless girl. She sipped her coffee as her phone buzzed sending her cup flying, spilling coffee all over her and her car.

Crap!

Using the napkins from her glove box, she sopped up the mess. Reaching for more, her phone buzzed again. Again, she jumped.

What's the saying about making the same mistake twice?

Mabel was wound tight. Ignoring her phone, she used her sleeve to wipe the steering wheel. When done, she discarded the soaked napkins in the pocket of her door. The phone buzzed for the last time.

Fuck me!

No jumping, just an exaggerated eye roll. Mabel grabbed her phone, answered without looking, ready to yell at whomever had nothing better to do but annoy her.

"Oh, hi Grandpa . . ." A hint of guilt in her voice.

"Good morning, Mabes," he said. "Did I catch you at a bad time? You sound a little frazzled."

"It's been a rough morning. I didn't sleep well."

"Sorry to hear that." His voice softened. "I was calling to invite you to dinner with Grandma and me."

"I'd love to. Only . . ." Thinking of Lucas, she already knew she didn't want him to join her, ". . . it'll be just me."

His voice, no longer soft. "If you don't want to be with the man—let the poor chap go." His words were true, but she was in no mood to discuss Lucas.

"Yeah, yeah, so you've said. Thanks for the invite. I gotta run."

The overpowering aroma of coffee filled the car. How can something so good, delightful, stimulating, and gratifying smell so bad when she wore it? Thank goodness for her weird habits. She reached for her change of clothes in the back seat.

"I know, dear. Plan for five if you're up for a few rounds—that is, if you think you can take on an old man," he joked.

"You're on!" Something to look forward to.

"Love you, Mabes," he said, and the line went dead.

Principal Strom's coming. *What did I do now?* Mabel thought, as she stepped out of her car.

It was stupid to naturally assume she was in trouble. As a student once, a principal meant trouble. Grandma had home-schooled her for two years, through sixth grade, then Grandpa sent her to public school. It took some getting used to.

Mind you, this was two years into Mabel's combat training. Combine that with anger issues, new school, puberty, and mean kids. Disaster. Disaster meant visits to the principal's office.

During her first week Mabel punched a boy in the face. Doug. She tried to explain Doug started it. Doug, a pimple-faced boy, had nothing on her new friend Patricia. Someone needed to put him in his place. Why not her?

No one listened to Mabel—her pleas or her reasoning.

She even warned him. *Leave her alone. No one finds you funny. Back off.*

Mabel's only regret that day was a teacher witnessed her brutality. Where was this teacher not two minutes prior when Doug the bully was in Patricia's face, calling her bad names? Talk about terrible timing. Mrs. Baker sure as hell made her presence known when Mabel's palm struck Doug's big nose. He had cried like a baby when he saw the blood.

Not so tough anymore.

Mrs. Baker hauled Mabel, now the bully, off to the principal's office like a criminal. She's surprised the handcuffs didn't come out.

She's acting out. Kid who lost her family and all. Maybe it'd be best if Mabel saw a counselor and talked about her feelings, learned to control her anger . . .

It took three visits and a short suspension for Mabel to learn her lesson. Why three visits? She wanted to be kicked out.

And there were plenty of bullies around to take her anger out on. She wanted to be home schooled. But Grandpa had other plans for her. He insisted she learn to be around kids her own age. Eventually Mabel learned to control her anger—most of the time. Part of her training, after all, was about discipline. The hardest part of all.

"Good morning, Mabel," Janet Strom sung, as she sashayed Mabel's way with a huge fake smile. "Do you have a few?"

Few what? Issues? Yes, I have those.

Mabel considered the small petite lady, who looked far too young to be a principal and carried herself like a ballerina. She had a perfect, pale complexion with a delicate blush of pink across her cheeks.

Mabel closed her car door. "Good morning, Janet. Sure, a couple anyway. As you can see, I'm wearing my coffee and need to change before class." She smiled weakly and glanced toward the school anticipating how long it would take her to get to the front door. That's how long she'd have to listen to Janet. Mabel hastened her step to get there faster.

Despite Mabel's sour mood, Janet remained in good spirits. She scurried to catch up. Mabel could feel Janet analyzing her as she kept stride. "I was going to ask how you were doing, but it looks like you've had a bad start," Janet suggested.

Is that all she wanted to do was state the obvious? "I'm good. A little tired this morning is all," Mabel said.

Janet placed her hand on Mabel's arm to keep her from reaching her destination. "I've been watching you. Wait, that sounds creepy," she laughed. "What I mean is—you've seemed a little distant recently." Janet's green eyes watched for a reaction. When she didn't get one, she continued. "Like something might be going on. Are you okay? Everything good at home? You know I'm here if you need anything."

"I'm sorry?" Mabel protested, because how dare Janet think she knew her. "I don't think I know what you're talking about. Can you be more specific?"

Thoughts raced through Mabel's head. *You're not my therapist. You're not family, nor do I consider you my friend. What gives?*

"I didn't mean to offend you, Mabel." She looked offended herself. "I know we haven't been very close and I'm sorry for that. But I do care about all my teachers. You're great with the kids, and by no means am I implying that you're not. I just want you to know if you ever need anything outside of the classroom, or in, I am here for you."

"I appreciate that, Janet. I really do. I'm fine. I just haven't been sleeping much recently."

"Offer still stands. We should grab coffee soon." She put her hand on Mabel's forearm.

"Sure, sounds good."

"I'm sure there's fresh coffee perking in the lounge. I can bring you a cup. I'm heading there myself."

"No thanks. I think I've had my share this morning." Mabel laughed, hoping her day would get better.

Janet joined in. "Okay then. Enjoy the rest of your day." And turned on her heels and greeted Maria Wilde, the school administrator, with the same enthusiasm she graced Mabel with.

Mabel had the feeling Janet put on a front, like a totally fake person. Someone entirely different than she let on. Or it could be her wild imagination and trust issues in general. After all, Mabel was someone totally different than she led others to believe.

For heaven's sake!

Mabel stopped by the teacher's lounge to change, took a

quick peek in the mirror and noticed dark circles under her eyes. She cursed her nightmares and lack of sleep. She should have spent more time on her makeup.

She made herself another cup of coffee before heading to her classroom.

FOUR

OCTOBER 1997

DESPITE THE BELOW-FREEZING TEMPERATURES, Jimmy Dumel woke in an unusually good mood. His body felt the minimal hours of sleep he managed to get, but he didn't care. Jimmy had something to look forward to.

William is coming home. Holy fuck, he missed him.

It'd been a year since he saw his big bro, felt like a lifetime. A lifetime of hell. Jimmy was seventeen when Will had gone and joined the Army. He wanted to go with him, but Jimmy was no soldier; never mind the fact that he'd been too young at the time.

He spent most of the morning playing Final Fantasy VII to pass the time. The less time around his pops the better. What he really wanted to do was go to the airport to pick up Will, but Pops said snow was coming and his Corolla would never make it. Jimmy needed to find a damn job to buy his own car. A truck.

Pops told him time and time again he wouldn't amount to anything. William was his pride and joy, while Jimmy was the focus of his pops' beatings. When Pops wasn't inflicting physical pain on him, he criticized him. Then the day came when Jimmy grew into himself, gained enough muscle to defend himself. It only took one punch to the face of his old man—one time fighting back. Jimmy could have beat the living shit out of him. He wanted to. But he didn't. His pops wasn't worth it. Still isn't. His pops never again laid a hand on him.

The one thing his pops taught him, that was worth anything, was to take care of his family. Funny, coming from a man who didn't know shit about taking care of his own.

Someone knocked on the door. Four knocks. He didn't answer because he didn't feel like it. The four knocks told him what he needed to know. His pops was at the door. Always four knocks. Every single time. A predictable son-of-a-bitch.

Knock, knock, knock, knock—harder this time. "Jimmy—open up. It's your brother . . ." he paused, correcting himself, ". . . about your brother."

Jimmy rose, panic taking him over. He opened the door. "What about Will?" His voice gruff.

Pops grabbed Jimmy by the shoulders and pulled him in close. The hug getting tighter by the second. Jimmy couldn't remember the last time his pops had hugged him. Never? Jimmy's arms dangled at his sides.

Jimmy squirmed to free himself. "What the hell, Pops?" he asked, both furious and shaken. He had a good three inches on him. His pops rested his head on Jimmy's shoulder. Jimmy could smell the alcohol seeping from his pores. The smell made him nauseous.

"I think William was in an accident—"

Before he could finish, Jimmy shimmied his arms in between their bodies, pushing with all his might to create space. "What do mean, I think? What accident? Where? How do you know?"

His pops stood there, head down—shaking it—as if saying 'no.'

Blood rushed to Jimmy's face. "Pop!" he shouted, grabbed him by the shoulders and shook him. "What accident? How do you know?" He looked out the door. "Where's Mom?"

"Just Stop! Stop with all the questions. Give me a goddamn second," he said, running his hands through his thick wild hair, stopping midway. He looked like a man who belonged in an asylum.

"Don't come in my room and say my brother's been in an accident and stand there like a fucking mute idiot." Jimmy scowled at him, but he'd checked out again. *Fuck him*, thought Jimmy.

He bumped his mute pop on the way out, not finding his mom in the kitchen baking for Will. "Mom!" he shouted.

No one answered.

"Mom!" Not in the living room. He went room to room, panicked, like a ticking time bomb. She vanished. Reluctantly, he went back to find his pops where he'd left him.

His pops sat on Jimmy's bed, staring at the wall wearing his crazed expression.

Maybe a softer approach. "Pop, please tell me what's wrong."

He looked right through Jimmy as if he were translucent. Closing his eyes, tears rolled down his face. "I'm sorry . . . I just can't believe it. The news said three dead at the scene from a thirty-car pileup. I think one was William."

The walls closed in. Jimmy replayed what he said. *Three dead, William one of them, he thinks . . .*

"What the fuck Pops? Are you kidding me? You *think*? Are you fucking kidding me right now?" He desperately wanted to punch him in the face. How could he say such a thing without knowing with absolute certainty?

"It's true. I know it, with everything inside me. I don't want to, but I feel it."

"No, No, No," he said over and over.

"Jimmy, stop. I saw the crash on TV—"

"Shut the fuck up! Shut up!" he screamed. "I don't want to hear another word." He stormed out and planted himself in front of the TV, watching the man and lady talk about the crash. By their enthusiasm, he'd bet no one they knew was caught up in there. Maybe they should have been on the road, in the middle of it.

His eyes glued to the TV, he couldn't see his pops standing behind him, but he felt him there. His presence gave him goosebumps and he shivered. Was it possible to shake your father from your life?

Breaking News. I-25 shut down. Thirty vehicle pileup, northbound lane by US-24.

Fuck! His brother would have taken that route.

At least three fatalities assumed, many others injured, some taken away by ambulance. Drivers lost control, low visibility, whiteout conditions, icy patches, blah, blah, blah . . .

He saw nothing to prove his brother was one of the corpses. Hell, he may not have even been in the accident. He didn't even know what fucking car his brother was driving. He said an SUV, but more than half the people on the road drove one. It could've been any unlucky bastard.

The time on the lower left corner of the screen said 2:33PM. His brother should have been home by now—even with the snow. But the roads were bad and maybe with the accident he took a different route—out of his way.

"I don't believe it," he whispered. "No fucking way."

"He should have been home by now," Pops said.

He threw daggers his way and picked up the phone.

"I'm calling about the accident, the thirty-car pileup," Jimmy said to a male voice from the police department. "Can you tell me if my brother was involved? He should have been home by now." The man told him he didn't have information to release. "I just want to know if he's injured or . . . or at the hospital." Growing more impatient, Jimmy repeated himself. "Please. His name is William Dumel. He was on his way home from the airport. I can give you my number."

And to that, the man offered to give him the number of the hospital, where they had taken the injured people.

He grabbed a pen and paper out of a drawer. "Go on." He scribbled the number down, ended his call and called the hospital. No William Dumel had arrived. He didn't know if he should be happy or scared.

Mom.

"Where's Mom?" Jimmy asked.

His pops leaned against the wall. "She's upset. She knows we can't get anywhere in this weather but isn't listening to reason—she went out on foot."

"What? Are you crazy? And you let her?"

"Did I have a choice?"

"Yes, Pops, you did. Just like you—don't care about anyone but yourself."

Jimmy opened the front door and a blast of cold air and snow pounded him in the face. It was colder than balls. Turning back, he grabbed his thickest coat, gloves, and hat hoping his mom had done the same. When he returned to the door, two men in black coats approached. Their heads were down, shielding the wind with the top of their head. One removed his hat.

"Pops," called Jimmy over his shoulder. He dropped his coat by the door. "We have visitors." Jimmy noticed the stripes on one of their coats and hat. His heart fell into his stomach.

"My name is Officer Andrews and this is Captain Hollinger. Are you the family of William Grant Dumel?"

"Yes," Pops said, his voice quivered.

No pleasantries. Get right to it. Why would there be when you're delivering bad news? Jimmy's ears rang, his body went numb. He could see the man's lips moving but couldn't hear his words.

His pops fell to his knees.

Jimmy couldn't move.

"Son, son . . ." one of the men repeated and the other helped his pops to his feet.

Jimmy didn't have to hear the words. He read their face, their lips. *William died, William died, William died.* The image now entrenched in his head.

"Are you certain?" asked Jimmy. It didn't sound like him. Somehow, he became a kid again.

The snow fell in huge snowflakes. The wind whipped the flakes around. The men were an unlikely duo. A policeman from the city and an Army sergeant or captain who probably lived nearby. Should he thank them for coming out in the blizzard to tell him it killed his brother?

"Yes," the officer said.

"Did they even try to save him? Like Flight for Life or something?"

"He was pronounced dead at the scene. Most likely he died on impact," he said.

"He was almost home—he was almost home," Jimmy murmured.

"We're sorry, son," the Army man said. "Your brother was a fine soldier."

Soldier? He was a fine brother, the best. A good person to everyone he met. Jimmy walked away. He didn't want to talk to them anymore. He went into Will's bedroom and stood by the door.

William Dumel, the perfect son—the most popular kid in school—straight As, a scholarship to play baseball in college but turned it down to join the Army because that was Will's way. He put everyone before himself. Save the world kind of shit. He didn't deserve this.

Jimmy became aware of his limp body and tightened his fists. Negative thoughts ran through his head and a familiar feeling took over. His heart pounded and he wondered if he might have a heart attack.

That'd be fucked up. Or a blessing.

Blood rushed to his face, every muscle tensed, he felt the anger steaming—like a bull getting ready to attack. His pops walked past Jimmy and sat on Will's bed. Jimmy looked at him as pressure spread to every part of his body, pressure he needed to release.

At six-foot-one and 180 pounds of muscle, he could have given his pops one hell of a beating. Just like he'd given Jimmy before he could defend himself.

"NO!" he screamed at the top of his lungs, punching the wall with all his strength. The pressure remained, and he threw his other fist into the wall. Plaster crumbled to the floor. The pain in his hands felt good.

His pops hadn't moved.

"I want to know how," he said, working to keep his voice steady. "I. Want. Every. Detail."

"What are you talking about? There's a blizzard outside. He probably didn't even see it coming."

"It started somewhere—now didn't it, *Pops*," he said through gritted teeth.

Thoughts of his mom drifted in his head for the third time. Outside, frozen. Would he lose the only two people he cared anything about on the same day?

Bundled up, he stepped out into the deathtrap that took his brother. The wind whipped like a bat out of hell and her footprints were long gone. The snow looked a foot deep, deeper in the drifts—

He thought of Will. He wanted to go to him, see for himself. He didn't believe. He didn't want to believe.

"Mom," he shouted, thinking he'd lost his mind. She couldn't hear him if she stood two feet away from him. He could barely hear himself. He'd probably lose his mom today. Why on earth would she go out in this blizzard by herself? Better question, why in the hell did his stupid ass pops let her?

He recognized the Corolla, buried, like every other car on the block. So she didn't drive anywhere—and she couldn't have gotten far if she walked.

Where is she? What would Mom do?

He trudged through the snow, leaving a path in his wake, stopping half way. Branches hung low, ready to snap free from the tree, the weaker ones already had. He spotted his neighbor's blue Pathfinder under a tree, half buried in snow. What a mess. *Serves you right!* he said under his breath. The tree died a few years ago and his neighbor, Dan, was a prick. He shoved his gloved hands in his coat pockets and continued down the driveway toward his Corolla.

Inspecting the Corolla, he made out a figure on the driver side. Wiping the window with his glove, he peered inside. His mom had her head on the wheel.

Stupid woman.

He slid into the seat next to her. She didn't move or say a word. The car felt like a freezer, but it protected him from the wind. The key sat in the ignition—the piece of shit car probably didn't start. Though, not many probably did on this sub-zero day.

"Mom . . . it's cold out here. Come inside with me," he said, breaking the silence. His breath made a smoky cloud as he spoke.

His mom didn't respond. She wore a thin coat. She wasn't shivering, but she had to be cold. He nudged her and she sniffled.

Not dead.

He put his hand on her knee and said with a firm tone, "Mom—let's go inside where it's warm."

She didn't answer.

"Mom."

Nothing.

He removed his gloves and touched her cold hand. "Come inside. You're freezing."

"What happened to your hand," she asked, her voice flat.

He looked at his hand and remembered punching the wall. The blood drying, his knuckles red, swollen and now throbbing. "It's nothing. Come inside."

"He's gone, Jimmy."

"I know, Mom." The rush crashed in. "We don't need to lose you too, out here in the cold . . . Will wouldn't like that."

They sat there for another ten minutes, without talking. When he couldn't take it anymore, he got out and dragged her with him. He needed to think, and he couldn't do it in a freezer of a Corolla. Inside, he put her in bed and covered her up like a child.

What did he do to deserve such torment? The worst he'd ever done was steal his pop's car and run it into a ditch. He got a good beating that night too, not that his pops needed a reason to slap him around or tell him how worthless and stupid he was—

"Men aren't that stupid, son," he'd said.

It was stupid, but he was only thirteen.

His pops sat on Will's bed. Jimmy had some words for him but decided it could wait. He didn't want to see or talk to him the rest of the day.

Jimmy lay on his bed thinking how he hated everything and everyone growing up, but not Will.

Will—a goody-two-shoes for sure, but Jimmy loved his brother. The only person in the world he could say that about. Will always had his back. He protected Jimmy and stood up to Pops on several occasions. He got Jimmy into lifting weights.

You have to protect yourself, he'd tell Jimmy. He knew Will meant from their pops. Then he up and joined the Army. Up until now, that had been the worst day of Jimmy's life.

He'd learned long ago not to expect much from this fucked up world. Not when his life consisted of a father who, for some unknown reason, detested Jimmy.

There was a time when the younger, dumber version of Jimmy wondered why. Stupid little Jimmy wanted to be good, do right by his father. Stupid little Jimmy thought he was cursed. Maybe he had some demon deep inside him that only his father could see.

Why else would his father hate him so much?

And his mother didn't do a damn thing to stop him. So much for maternal instincts to protect their young. Instead, her words of wisdom were, *Maybe you shouldn't have provoked him. You know how your dad is.*

Is that what you did, Mom? When Pops beat you? Provoke him?

Jimmy didn't like how the pain in his chest felt. How his thoughts drifted into a void—*No good Jimmy. You're nothing without your brother.*

With no one to turn to, he replaced it with rage and hate. He knew exactly what he needed to do. He stood on the outskirts of his brother's funeral and watched. He couldn't bring himself to stand by Will's grave as they lowered him into the ground.

The uniformed men carried Will with little effort. The flag covered his casket. He'd never been to a military funeral before, although he'd seen them on TV. His heart beat faster when the men fired three volleys. When Taps played, tears welled up in his eyes for the first time.

His mom cried hysterically, and his pops reeked of booze. He couldn't stay sober even one fucking day. Was that asking too much? The men folded the flag carefully and handed it to his mom. She accepted it between sobs. At the end, Jimmy didn't want any part of accepting condolences. His pops caught his eye a couple times. He couldn't care less what his pops thought. He didn't control him. Not anymore.

A stream of cars coming down the drive interrupted his thoughts. *Was it that time already?* He had another funeral to attend, and Jimmy couldn't be late. He needed to get a closer look.

An older man dressed in uniform, the driver, stepped out and opened the back door. He was Army, Jimmy guessed. A slender lady dressed in black, appeared next to him, wiping her eyes. She reached into the car and a small boy appeared, clinging to her waist. The older man pried him away and held the boy in his arms. Jimmy watched, absorbed, taking the scene in.

Their pain warranted, but he felt no sorrow for this family. He continued eyeing the family as the production unfolded.

One more. A little girl. Did she come?

There she is.

The dark-haired girl, ten years old, popped her head out and decided she wasn't going anywhere. She sat there with her hands on her lap. The lady said something to her and the girl shook her head. *Stubborn little shit, isn't she?*

After a minute of the little girl and the lady going back and forth, the girl got out and wrapped her thin arms around the man's waist.

The older man looked right at him and Jimmy flinched, ducking behind the tree.

Did the old man see him watching?

FIVE

OCTOBER 1998

MELODI STUCKER DREADED THIS DAY, YET here it was. Time passed by—day by day, hour by hour—without her permission. If she had powers to roll back time, she'd go back 365 days before her dad left for work. She'd make some excuse, pretend to be sick, cry, anything—something that would have kept him home that day.

She peeked out her window expecting a blizzard. The kind that took her dad—a white blanket of death—the kind where time froze.

No snow.

Not one stupid snowflake.

As a matter of fact, it hadn't snowed at all so far. Once upon a time, Melodi loved the white fluffy stuff. She found it beautiful, inviting, even breathtaking.

She was pretty sure she hated snow now.

Melodi plopped herself down on her unmade bed and tears spilled over her eyes. She didn't want to forget her dad but thinking of him hurt. It hurt her heart, her head, her eyes—

"Melodi, you up?" Mom called from outside her bedroom door.

She should have been ready by now. "Yeah, Mom. Give me a few." She tried to sound normal. Her mom cried all the time and did her best to act normal. If Melodi acted normal, her mom wouldn't make her see a therapist.

On her way to the bathroom, Melodi touched her chest making sure it was safely in place. A little bear necklace her dad had given her. On their last camping trip together, they came across a black bear. Melodi took a step forward. It was beautiful. A huge, brownish-black, beastly thing with a light brown snout. The bear looked directly at her, with gentle brown eyes. It sounds crazy, but she would swear it meant no harm. It stood up, put its nose in the air, sniffed and huffed as it fell back on all fours. Melodi's heart pounded, not from fright, but excitement.

Her dad said, "Put your arms up Mel." She did, without taking her eyes off the bear. He kept saying something like, *"Hey bear, hey bear."* She thought she heard fright in his voice but couldn't be sure. The bear never attacked. It looked at Melodi for a few seconds—it seemed like an eternity—then turned and walked the opposite direction. Her dad had said they were lucky it didn't have cubs. She couldn't stop talking about it. The following weekend her dad had surprised her with the necklace.

As she went downstairs, she saw her mom making breakfast. "Good morning, my sweet girl," her mom said, kissing her forehead.

Melodi looked forward to visiting her dad's grave but

wouldn't exactly call it a good morning.

"I hope you're hungry. I made you some waffles," Mom said, pouring batter into the waffle iron. The sweet smell filling the air.

"I am. Where's Pete?" Melodi asked, sipping her orange juice.

"I'm right here, Mel," he said, giggling like only a seven-year-old can. The turd snuck up behind her.

"Where did you come from? You're like a ninja."

He giggled even more as he climbed onto the chair next to her. When Melodi realized what he was wearing, she smiled and raised one eyebrow.

"What?" he asked, puzzled by her face.

"Nothing," she replied. "You look amazingly cool like usual."

"Thanks . . . so do you," He looked her up and down.

He'd dressed himself in his Woody costume mixed with his Buzz Lightyear outfit, because he liked them both equally. He wore Woody on the bottom with his holster, boots, and spurs; then Buzz Lightyear on top with the chest guard, wings and hood. He topped it off with Woody's cowboy hat. He looked hilarious. That was Peter. He marched to the beat of his own drum, like Daddy. That's what their dad always said. *You make your own path, Pete. No reason to do what everyone else is doing. That's boring.*

"Oh Pete, you look incredible today!" exclaimed Mom as she set his waffles in front of him.

"Thanks, Mommy."

"Would you like me to cut your waffles for you?" Mom asked.

"Nope, I got this." He struggled with the fork. It didn't work the way he planned. Melodi leaned over to help. "I said I got it," he insisted, pushing her away.

"Fine. I was just trying to help you . . . Buzz, Woody . . . whoever you are. Who are you supposed to be anyway?"

"I'm Pete, duh."

"That's right," she said, rolling her eyes.

After eating every bite, Melodi put her plate in the sink. She watched her mom move from room to room getting everything ready to go. Her eyes were puffy, more than usual. She cried when she thought Melodi wasn't looking, mostly at night after she tucked them in and thought they were asleep. Melodi's room was at the top of the stairs, her mom's downstairs, and still she heard her crying.

Her mom looked out the window. Her eyes distant, far away.

"Mom, we're ready."

She didn't answer.

"Mom," Melodi repeated, standing behind her.

"Hmm." She turned slowly.

"I love you." Melodi hugged her. She did love her mom very much. Why she didn't say it more often, especially over the past year, was stupid of her. Come to think of it, she couldn't remember the last time she had told her she loved her.

Tears formed in her mom's eyes. "My sweet girl," she exhaled heavily. "I love you, too." Her mom laid another kiss on Melodi's forehead, leaving her lips there a few seconds longer. Her hands were soft and warm on Melodi's face and she smelled of plums. She always smelled of plums. It was a good smell.

"He's here," Mom said. "Let's go."

"Ryan!" Pete shrieked, running out to greet him.

"Hey buddy. Did you grow since I saw you last?"

Pete looked from his legs back to Ryan. "I think so," he said, grinning.

"I think so, too." Ryan ruffled his hair. "Jump in and buckle up," he told Pete. "Melodi, how's my favorite girl?" he asked, kissing her cheek.

"I'm okay," Melodi shrugged and wrapped her arms around his waist. "Happier now that you're here."

She loved Ryan Cross, her dad's best friend.

"I wouldn't want to be anywhere else" He smiled and turned to her mom. "Margaret," he said, hugging her. "You look lovely. Thank you for inviting me."

"As much as I'd like to take credit, it was Melodi's idea."

Ryan ducked his head into the back seat. "Thanks, Mel." He winked.

Melodi smiled. Ryan came around weekly after her dad died to help Mom with yard work and play with her and Pete. He had a son, Jackson, a couple of years older than Melodi. No girls. He told her stories about her dad. She looked forward to their time together.

At the cemetery, Melodi closed her eyes. She didn't want to look at the mound of gravel that smothered her dad's body. She knew enough about death to know his body was in there somewhere, but his spirit was in heaven. Melodi knew it because he was a good man.

She didn't need to visit his grave to talk to him. Visiting the grave of a loved one, on the anniversary of their death, is overrated. Everyone said it was a good idea. Melodi even looked forward to it. But it didn't bring her any closer to feeling anything but pain and confusion. Truth is, she didn't know what she expected or what she should feel.

Her mom cried, Ryan consoled her, Pete played, and Melodi stared at the ground until she couldn't take it anymore. She turned and walked back to the car. On her way, she bumped into a lady.

"Sorry," Melodi uttered.

The lady looked dazed. Blonde hair, blue eyes, older than her mom. "You visiting someone?" the lady asked.

"My dad." Melodi knew not to talk to strangers, but this lady appeared upset. She looked harmless enough. Being at a cemetery, Melodi guessed the lady lost a loved one too. And her eyes were puffy and red-rimmed like her mom's.

"I'm visiting my son. He died last year," the lady said.

"My dad too."

"Brought him flowers."

"Us too. Me and my mom," Melodi said, pointing to her mom. "And my little brother." A small glimmer in the lady's eye flickered when Melodi said brother.

"You have a brother?" the lady asked.

"Yup. Your son—did he have a brother?" She liked talking to this lady. Even if they did talk about their dead family.

"Yes." She looked so sad.

"I'm sorry."

"Did you know my boy?"

"No." Melodi looked for her mom, who was now kneeling beside the grave, where her dad's smothered body lay.

"Oh . . . I thought . . ." The lady wept, her racking sobs shaking her whole body.

Without thinking, Melodi put her hand on the lady's arm. "Don't cry. He's in heaven now." Her attempt at helping made matters worse.

Grief gushed out of the lady's eyes, like the breaking of a dam. She was loud enough to make her mom look over.

"Melodi!" Mom yelled out.

"I'm coming," Melodi assured her. "I have to go," she told the sad lady. "You okay?"

"It'll be alright. I'll be with him soon," she said, a strange look crossing her face.

A sudden rush of fear ran through Melodi and she ran back to the safety of her mom and Ryan. There was something odd about that lady. It gave her the heebie-jeebies.

"Mom, can we go?" Melodi begged, not wanting to be there any longer.

"In a minute," Mom said in a low voice.

Ryan pulled her close, keeping her from running off again. Melodi turned to watch the sad lady walk down the path. She lost sight of her when a bus pulled up. When it drove off, the lady was gone.

She spent most of the day in her room. Her mom said they were having dinner at Grandma's. Melodi didn't want to go. She loved spending time with Grandpa, but today she just wanted time alone. She read a book to pass time and then went through some old pictures of the family—which turned out to be a bad idea.

She decided to see what Pete was up to. Melodi found him in his room playing—of course. "Hey, Pete."

He looked up from his pretend game of Toy Story. He had the crew strategically laid out across his carpet. Buzz Lightyear, Sheriff Woody, Bo Peep, Mr. Potato Head, Rex, Hamm, and Slinky. He begged Mom daily for the green Army Men. How he didn't have them yet was a mystery.

"Hi, Mel. Wanna play?" he asked with a cheesy grin. He lost his first tooth last week. Since then he sticks his tongue in the empty hole. The tooth next to it is loose, so it's crooked when he does it. He's such a goof.

"Sure, for a little while."

"You can be Hamm or Bo Peep, since you're a girl."

"You need more girls in your party, Pete."

"Whatever. Which one do you want to be?"

"Can I be both of them?" she asked.

He shrugged. "I guess."

Melodi played with him till it was almost time to go. She enjoyed playing with him. He had her dad's eyes and his personality. A happy-go-lucky way about him, nothing seemed to bother him. She wished she had that, instead she felt bothered by everything. She over thought all the details, things she shouldn't be worried about, but they bothered her anyway. Her mom and grandpa told her that all the time. Her dad said he admired her for it and said she just hadn't learned to use her superpowers to their full potential yet. Her dad always said stuff like that.

She noticed the room getting darker. It was time to go. She could feel her heart beating faster. She didn't want to fight with her mom, but she knew not wanting to go would lead to one. Melodi was a total daddy's girl. Her mom said it all the time, she'd gone everywhere with him.

She and Pete cleaned up and went into the living room.

"Oh good, I was just about to go get you two. We're leaving in five minutes."

"Mommy," she called her this when she wanted something, "I don't feel like going anywhere tonight. Can we stay home?"

Her mom sighed. "Melodi, I told you already. Grandma and Grandpa are waiting for us. They've made dinner . . . we have to go. Just for a while."

Melodi had tears forming in her eyes. She tried to hold them back. Her mom looked upset.

"Mommy!" exclaimed Peter from across the room. He fought to fit his last truck into his overfilled bag.

"You ready, buddy?" Mom helped him rearrange his toys and zip up his bag.

"Now I am," he replied.

Her mom glanced at her watch. "Melodi, we have to go—now," she said, getting to her feet.

Melodi slammed her glass on the counter making Pete jump. Her mom was by her side in no time flat. She has her attention now. Melodi faced her mom, squaring her shoulders to gain courage, and glared. She didn't want to look mean, she was trying to think of what to say.

Her mom's eyes rolled ever so slightly. Melodi got in trouble for rolling hers.

"I'm not going," Melodi insisted. She stomped off into the living room and fell into the big, bulky, brown recliner that was once her dad's. "I've told you—," she couldn't finish. The stupid crying started again. She tried to gain what little composure she had, but the words just came out broken between her sobs. "I can't . . . be there . . . today. Not today. Why can't you . . . understand that?"

Her mom reached out to touch her, but Melodi flinched her shoulder away. She didn't want to fight. She wanted to be left alone, she curled up in a ball, as small as she could, so her mom wouldn't touch her. The leather recliner squeaked as she did. If she wasn't so mad, she would have laughed. It sounded like she farted.

She wanted her dad and that would never happen.

"Grandma and Grandpa miss you and Pete," Mom said in a soft voice. "And they miss your dad, too," she whispered. "We all do. Please Mel. It'll break their hearts if we're not with them."

What about my heart? It's already broken. Why can't I have this day to myself?

Her mom walked to the window looking out at the sun settling in for the night. Melodi could see the orange glow as it dropped behind the mountain peaks, the view was incredible. She thought her mom was admiring the view as well. Her mom talked about moving after her dad died. She asked Melodi and Pete what they wanted. They both said no. Even though the house had memories of him, Melodi didn't want to forget. Her mom said the same thing and they stayed.

After a while, her mom turned to her. Melodi looked away. She felt horrible for being mean. She knew her mom was right, but that didn't change the pain she had in her chest. Seeing her grandpa today would be too much. She loved him, but he reminded her too much of her dad. Just an older version of him. They both served in the military. Daddy in the Air Force and Grandpa in the Army. Daddy grew his hair out after, but Grandpa always kept his short until her dad died. She didn't like that. It made her sad and mad at the same time.

Her grandpa was still her favorite person in the whole world—now that her dad was gone. It's because he is so much like her dad. But on the day her dad died, she didn't want to see anyone—that included her grandpa. She didn't care if she were grounded forever.

Melodi licked her lips and bit down on her bottom lip, gearing herself up. "Go without me!" she yelled and darted up the stairs. In her room she slammed the door shut. And locked it, for good measure, to keep her mom out. She leaned against the door with a heavy sigh of relief. There was an eerie darkness in her room and she flicked the lights on. Holding her ear to the door she waited for her mom's footsteps.

Nothing. It was quiet. She may have won the battle.

With her back to the door, tears streamed down her face.

She fell into a heap on the floor and grief poured out of her in uncontrollable bursts. She allowed herself to let go, something she hadn't done before.

Why God? Why did Daddy have to die?

It's not fair. Her mom told her accidents happen—but why him? He was a good dad.

Knock, knock, knock.

She scampered away from the door. *Holy cow!*

"Melodi . . . sweet girl?" her mom called out, wiggling the door handle. "Can I come in?"

"No!" she yelled, her heart pounding.

"We don't have to go. Just come down stairs. We can watch a movie together. How does that sound?"

Still breathing heavy. "Go away, Mom. I just want to be alone."

"Mel, it's not good to stay alone. You should be with fam . . ." she paused. "Come watch a movie with me and Pete. You can pick."

"Not now, Mom," Melodi pleaded. The hurt in her mom's voice ripped her apart. "Just leave me—okay? I'll be down later."

"Fine. I'm starting dinner soon—love you. . . ."

Melodi didn't answer.

She spotted her favorite blanket sprawled out on her bed. A gift from her dad on their last vacation together in Aspen. He planned to teach her how to snowboard. Pete was just a toddler. She'd had her dad all to herself. Then she ended up getting sick. Her dad bought her a magic blanket to get better. And he was right. Melodi woke up feeling a hundred times better—no fever, lots of energy. They went snowboarding the next day, against Mom's wishes. One of the many days she'll never forget.

Scooping her blanket up and holding it tight, she curled into a ball and wished she was seven again.

Her eyes were getting heavy. Giving in, she closed them.

SIX

IT'S AMAZING WHAT ONE YEAR WILL DO TO a man's psyche. It had been an unforgiving, downright treacherous experience. As each dark, rotting day passed, Jimmy Dumel counted down the days he would avenge his brother's death. That—in and of itself—was the only thing that kept him going.

Jimmy woke to the sun shining, no snow in the forecast, a bit chilly, but no freezing temperatures like that miserable day a year ago. This day would be magnificent. He lit a cigarette, sat back and relaxed. Everything was in place. The gun he stole during a burglary lay next to him. He had felt dead for so long and the burglary gave him the rush of adrenaline he needed. He let his buddy Randy take everything. All he wanted was the gun. He figured, that way, Randy would keep his mouth shut.

Jimmy had got a job, had wheels, and no longer lived in the deplorable conditions that only brought bad memories.

All this was good, but none of it mattered to him knowing his brother would never walk through his door. He only had wheels because Will left him his truck, which then motivated him to get off his ass. Even when Will was gone, he took care of Jimmy.

Now it was Jimmy's turn. Today, the anniversary of his brother's death, would be his day of redemption. Jimmy had waited a long and agonizing year for this day to come. He had planned every detail. It didn't take much digging to find out who had been responsible for his brother's death.

Ben Stucker killed his brother.

He learned Ben left the airport the same time as Will, taking a different route. Their routes merged onto the interstate at different points. Will's before Ben's. This put Will on the interstate first and as Ben merged onto the interstate he lost control of his car. Witness after witness verified this. The fucking moron caused the thirty-car pileup.

He pictured the scene over and over in his head. So many different scenarios could have happened. A late flight, going to the bathroom, a different route, stopping for a drink, stopping to talk to someone . . .

He drove himself mad thinking about it. But in the end, it always came back to Ben. Plain and simple. Ben killed his brother—any way he looked at it.

To make matters worse, if that was possible, Ben had been a pilot. Seeing that word, pilot, sent tremors through his body. William's dream was to become a pilot. He had just graduated as an official Army pilot. When he returned from his break, William would have finally lived his dream.

Ben took that from him.

Ben took William from Jimmy.

You live . . . well, you lived . . . in Colorado asshole. If you can't drive here, get the hell out! And don't take Will with you. For this, he would never forgive. He would never forget.

Ben Stucker put a hole in Jimmy's life and shit in it.

The fucking moron needed to pay. Jimmy would see to it. And since Ben died—due to his own stupidity—the Stucker family would pay the price.

Jimmy was busy preparing when he got the call. His pop said, "Mom's missing."

"What do you mean, she's missing? Did you actually look for her this time?" Jimmy said sarcastically.

"Can you not be a smart ass for once and listen to me?"

"Whatever you say, Pop. I'm kind of busy today. Can you be more specific? I mean, like did she finally get fed up with you and leave or what?"

"Like I'm worried, dumb ass. She was talking nonsense, half of it I couldn't understand. I made an appointment for her on Monday—but she's gone. She's not here."

"Maybe she just went out for a walk." He thought of his mom, how she usually just sat there staring at the damn wall. She went batshit crazy after Will died. When she wasn't staring at the wall she wandered around the house like a zombie. The doctor put her on meds, but Jimmy didn't think she took them.

His pops' voice got louder. "You don't understand. Your mother doesn't go anywhere. She's always home. I just ran out to refill her prescription and when I returned she was gone."

"Calm the hell down." He was about to tell him to check the car, where Jimmy found her last time, but his pops had the car.

"Jimmy, I'm scared. I think she's going to hurt herself."

"Why would you say that?"

"I told you. She was rambling. The only thing I could make out was her saying she wanted to join Will. She'd been talking that way for the past few days."

"Oh hell, Pops," He was tired of his shit. "You think you could have said that? Did you call the cops and report her missing?"

"Not yet. I thought we could go looking for her first."

"Where? I don't know where she would have gone. Do you?"

Wilbur didn't answer right away. "No. I've got no goddamn idea where she went."

"Fine, if you haven't already," he said it because he knew his pops, "Search the house completely—inside and out. Check the garage, neighbors, her old friends, anyone and everyone you can think of. Even if she's no longer in contact with them. I'll be over in a few. *Then* we call the cops if nothing turns up."

Jimmy ended his call thinking, *It's half past eleven—plenty of time to get my own shit done.* He just needed to be back by four. He locked up, hopped in his black Toyota Tacoma—the departing gift from his big bro. He kept to the speed limit, the last thing he needed was to see flashing red and blue in his rearview mirror.

Funny how his mom didn't pay two cents worth of attention to him over the last year, but today, of all days, she chose to make his life hell. He would probably find her in some random place staring off into space.

"You only have four damn hours lady and I'm out," he said under his breath.

He pulled up next to the police cruiser in the driveway of the house that brought unwanted memories.

That man can't listen worth shit.

Wait. Just wait a goddamn minute. This is good. With what

he had planned, it's good to be seen with his pop and the police. Maybe good old momma is helping him out after all.

He played nicey-nice with the two Chips look-a-likes and his pops, pretending as if he gave a half a fuck. He learned how to be a good actor over the years, with his temper and all.

His pops told Ponch he already searched the house and called everyone. No one had heard or seen her. Jon was busy searching the house. Ponch asked Jimmy when he last spoke to his mom. Thursday, and she acted the same as usual. Pops told him that she'd been on meds for depression ever since Will died. Ponch asked to see the pills. Wilbur returned with the bottle he had just had refilled along with the empty bottle dated nearly two months ago. Looks like his mom wasn't taking her meds after all. Figures her good for nothing husband wouldn't notice.

Jimmy got bored and stopped listening, his mind drifting to his plan and getting the hell out of there.

Jon joined Ponch in the living room and told the two of them to stay home in case his mom came back or called. Ponch would call if they found or learned anything. Jimmy watched as they drove away in their cruiser with no plans on spending the rest of his day with his pops.

His pop paced the room with an unsettled look on his face. He looked guilty.

"What's up Pop? What aren't you telling me?"

"Nothing. I'm just worried. I just don't feel right . . . something's not right," he responded, talking to himself mostly.

"Did you do or say something to her?" Jimmy asked.

"No!" He flinched. "How can you even think that?" He looked away in disgust. "I told you, and the police, she seemed off and kept talking about being with Will. I think . . . I think she's going to kill herself. That's the feeling I get."

The blood rushed out of his face. His dad said the same thing about Will—he felt it—and it ended up being true.

"What's wrong with you?" asked Pops. "You look like you saw a ghost."

"Nothing," he mumbled and turned away.

That's stupid, he told himself. *She'd been messed up for years.* Jimmy couldn't think.

Her nonsense was screwing with his day.

And if she killed herself—

His mom may not have been cursed by the bottle, but she certainly had her own issues. In her sick mind, her motherly advise sounded something like this; *You don't need to be tough or manly. I love you no matter what,* she'd say. What the hell is that supposed to mean? *I love you, but why don't you join the Army like William? Why don't you play sports like William? Why can't you get a scholarship like William?*

He hated her sometimes.

That familiar rage surged through him. He could almost feel his inner self blackening further, if that were possible. Sometimes it scared him. Then he reminded himself his brother didn't do a damn thing wrong in this world and look what happened to him. People needed to pay for their stupidity.

With his head up against the wall, the ugly thoughts he tried to keep back poured in. *I'll be damned if I let you mess this day up for me. If you want to die, then kill yourself . . . Mom.* His eyes glossed over at the thought and went dark.

She never gave him a chance. She was gone a long time ago. He realized she'd died the day William died. That was the day she decided Jimmy wasn't enough for her. The day she decided not to live.

SEVEN

THE LONG HAND ON THE CLOCK TOOK ITS sweet, agonizing time—*tick, tick, tick*. Jimmy Dumel sat upright in one of his two worn chairs, taking a long drag of his cigarette. His foot thumped the floor uncontrollably. Dressed head to toe in black, he stared at the clock willing it to move faster. When the stupid clock hit six, he could leave. He needed it to be dark. This time of year, it didn't get dark till just after six and the drive would take twenty minutes.

Five more minutes—*tick, tick, tick.*

His mind drifted to the hellish day he had. He'd done a damn good job not thinking about it so far. He skipped out on his pops at four-thirty. His pops called soon after, to say a woman stepped in front of a train, her body too mutilated to identify. His mom's purse had been found by the tracks, her driver's license inside.

His mom ended her miserable life after all.

It infuriated him that she could be so self-centered. He had no room for grief for that woman. Just pure rage—almost beyond control. Hell, screw her! She didn't love Jimmy. Nobody did. Not anymore. Not since he lost William.

There were very few times she went against his pops. He had given Jimmy the worst beating on his thirteenth birthday, and she stepped in and stopped him. She tended to Jimmy, like he imagined a loving mother would. He remembered her touch. The touch he longed for. The touch he seldom received.

He wondered what the last thought on her mind was before she stepped in front of that train. It sure as hell wasn't him.

Chicken shit! he thought, shaking her image out of his head.

Six o'clock. Time to go.

If everything went as planned, this would be too easy. Jimmy planned it for a year, waiting patiently for this day to come. It had to be this day, even though patience was not his virtue. He did it for his brother.

As he turned onto the dirt road, total exhilaration rushed through him. He glanced left, then right, double checking his rearview mirror—no room for mistakes. He'd waited so long—the day was finally here. He heard something. Partially rolling down his window, he realized it was his tires snapping branches. Halfway to the house, he parked behind trees—perfect cover to hide from unwelcome visitors.

Ski mask on—check. Gloves on—check. Gun in jeans—check. He'd walk the rest of the way. *This family couldn't live in a better place for what I have planned,* he thought. No neighbors, tree cover—no one to hear shit. He loved it. Thank you, Ben Stucker idiot family.

The house, his final destination, came into view. He paused, noticing the unnerving silence. His heart quickened. Excitement? Fright? A little of both.

He'd never killed before. Could he do it—when it came right

down to it? He closed his eyes to gain strength. A memory of his pops went through his mind. His father's words shot through him like a lightning bolt.

You'll never amount to shit!

You're worthless, weak, no good. No girl in her right mind will want you.

You'll never be able to defend your family.

He shook his head and whispered, "Not worth my time."

Most of the lights were off in the big house, except one upstairs and one downstairs. Bedrooms, shining like bright beacons. Using his gloved hand, he punched the glass watching it shatter. Reaching in, he unlocked the back door, letting himself in. *Too much noise,* he thought, holding his gun up, ready to shoot whoever he may have startled. The fresh smell of marinara filled his nose. A platter of spaghetti lay covered on the kitchen counter. He hadn't eaten, and his stomach growled.

No time.

After a few moments, he crept toward the sounds coming from the first-floor bedroom. Like he said. Too easy. His heart thumped faster.

Jimmy stopped short of the open door, stepping on a squeaky board. Patience. Listen. A quick peek in the bedroom. Both asleep. He brazenly walked inside. Mom lay peacefully—the boy sprawled across her. Both lifeless on the bed . . . nearly—he'd see to it. She was prettier than his mom. Dark silken waves of hair nestled around her cream-colored perfect face. Much lovelier in person. He wanted to see her eyes . . .

He crept, step-by-step around the bed, to get a closer look at the angel that lay before him. He almost felt bad for her—knowing her husband was responsible for her death. He reached out to touch her flawless face, running the back of his glove along her cheek.

Suddenly, her eyes popped open, startling him. Catching him off-guard.

POW!

He shot her in the head. He felt as if his heart recoiled. Not at all what he expected. The small boy moved, jump starting it.

POW!

He shot the boy in the back.

Jimmy let out a breath, hands shaking. He stared in disbelief at her empty brown eyes. What had he done? Jimmy inhaled deeply.

No regrets.

He looked up, and there she was.

EIGHT

A SOUND RAN THROUGH HER HEAD. *WHAT WAS that?* Her eyes shot open and she listened closely. After a few minutes of silence, she decided she'd been dreaming. Immediately she regretted how she treated her mom. She wanted to be good, but her mom always found a way to irritate her. This is how it went with them. They would fight and one of them would end up apologizing to the other. This time it wasn't her mom's fault. It was Melodi who needed to ask for forgiveness.

The light from her room illuminated the dark hall. Melodi was the worst at leaving lights on. Her first instinct was to flip the switch. Not wanting another reason to fight with her mom, she walked down the stairs with only the soft light of her brother's turtle night light. Her mom bought it for him when he fell down the stairs in the middle of the night. If he woke up next time, he could see where he was stepping.

As her foot left the last step, she heard a loud bang. Her

grandpa and dad took her shooting once and taught her all about gun safety. The bang sounded just like her grandpa's Smith & Wesson "Shorty Forty", loud and deafening.

Knowing her mom had a gun in her room, she ran to her mom's door just as another bang filled her ears.

Mom . . . Pete . . .

She froze. She blinked hard to make it go away. Make him disappear. He didn't. It couldn't have been more than a few seconds, but time seemed to have slowed down. There stood a man next to her mom's bed—a man wearing all black. Black ski mask, plain black turtleneck, black jeans and black shoes to top it all off.

The man in black, Melodi whispered.

The monster liked black. Even his eyes appeared black. Her dad's friend Ryan had really dark brown eyes—she thought his eyes were black—he told her no one had black eyes.

"Where do you think you're going?" the monster asked, his black eyes staring into her soul. He raised his gun and she ran. Up the stairs, into her room, door locked, and into her closet.

She heard him coming—*rrrrr, rrrrr*—each step creaking as he climbed the stairs. She thought if he'd stepped on the edges, like she always did, the stairs wouldn't cry out with his weight.

Next—*thud, thud, thud*—a knocking sound, muffling the sound of the squeaky stairs. Followed by murmuring—singing maybe?

Her mind, muddled, as she struggled to make out the words. She couldn't, the image of the monster in her house, standing over her mom . . . and her brother . . .

The monster reached the top of the stairs, paused and continued down the hall. Her room was the first door at the top of the stairs. He walked past her door. Why?

Knock, knock, knock.

By impulse, her hands found her mouth to keep noise from escaping.

The knocking continued. Door to door. The footsteps and banging got louder as he once again neared her room.

Her small closet, dark and claustrophobic, felt as though the walls were closing in. She couldn't breathe. She willed her arms and her body to move. They didn't respond. Her heart pounded in her chest, too loud to think. Tears formed in her brown eyes. Her lip quivered uncontrollably.

What did he want?

She wanted her mom. She wanted Pete.

The footsteps came to an abrupt stop in front of her door—pausing momentarily. Her creaky doorknob turned—followed by jiggling and banging. The locked door denied him easy entry.

The banging turned into a thump. Followed by another thump. She yelped.

I don't have much time. You can do this—get help.

She wiped the tears from her eyes and ran for her window. All the torturous lessons her grandpa had put her through, took over. He always said, "safety first". It sounded like such a cliché at the time. The window opened easy enough and she climbed out.

POW!

The deafening sound caused her to flinch and turn. The doorknob—no longer visible—was replaced by a huge hole and shattered wood. The door flung open. At that moment, Melodi knew the monster, the man in black, came to kill her. Deep down, she knew he killed her mom and Pete. If they weren't dead yet, she had to get help.

Melodi's small frame sidestepped the shot and she nearly fell off the roof. She reached for the side of the house to steady herself. The night air, cold on her face. She blinked, opening her eyes wider to see better. The moon offered little light. Digging her feet in for traction, she hurried toward the back of the house. Another gunshot rang in her ear as she turned the corner. Hunched over, she felt around for blood. Not feeling anything wet, she bent over and covered her ears waiting for the ringing to pass.

Down below she eyed the porch she needed to get to. She eased herself on to her bottom, sliding down the roof like her grandpa taught her. Not wanting to look back, she kept going.

Wooden planks lay before her. *Easy-peasy. I'm walking a beam,* she told herself. Never mind the porch was three times higher. Steading herself, she jumped down to the porch and gracefully crossed the planks. Not over yet, she peeked over the edge. It looked higher than she remembered. Before chickening out, she climbed over the edge and swung her body to gain distance. She let go, praying—*Please God, help me land on grass and not the deck.*

Landing in the grass, she fell back on her tailbone, catching herself with her hands. It hurt, but not too bad. Nothing broken. Melodi eyed the tree line behind the house.

She loved where they lived. Far out, away from the city. She played outdoors every opportunity. Sometimes leaving in the early morning and not returning until dinner. She'd pack a lunch and pretend she was a voyager, discovering new land. At that moment, she wanted to live near civilization.

The woods were darker than she anticipated. In the dark, she didn't know where she was going. She hadn't thought that far ahead.

A door slammed in the distance. He was coming. She maybe had fifty yards on him.

She ducked behind a tree to stay out of sight and gain her bearings. Up ahead, to her right, she spotted the trail she had taken many times. The trail led to the creek. Maybe she could hide, and he would give up. She didn't like the thought of going out in the dark by herself, but what choice did she have?

She started running, aware of all the obstacles in her path. Branches reaching out to grab her, wanting blood, like the monster who chased her. Her chest hurt from running, or maybe from fear. Her breathing—fast and hard.

She looked back, hearing a noise, and tripped on a rock. She went flying head first into a fallen tree. Her hands flew out to prevent her from smashing her skull. Her hands took the brunt of the impact and she landed on her stomach, skinning her knee in the process.

Melodi picked herself up, inspecting her bleeding hands. *They're fine. I'm fine.* If she said it, it had to be true. A tingle in her left knee prompted her to lift her foot up onto the fallen tree and examine the damage. Her pants were torn—her mom would be upset. They were one of her new pairs. She could hear her mom now, *What did you do all day Melodi? Crawl around on your knees?*

Sometimes she did. This was not one of those times.

The big gash in her knee oozed blood. It hurt. She wanted her mom. Her mom would take care of her, clean her up, and make it all feel better.

Tears filled her eyes. Sniffing, she blinked back the tears, took another deep breath and stood up. Her mom couldn't save her this time. Despite her left knee hurting bad enough to stop, she ran. She had to keep going.

As Melodi reached the creek, she stopped to listen for the man dressed all in black. All she heard was the rushing water from the creek.

Not aware he was gaining on her, she hunkered down no more than thirty feet away from him, taking cover behind a tree to catch her breath. Scanning the ground, she noticed dead trees and branches carpeting the forest floor. None of it looked familiar. She must have taken a wrong turn.

Disoriented, Melodi stepped out to find her path, colliding into something hard. Losing her footing, she fell back, nearly falling into the creek. It took her a moment to realize what happened.

The man in black.

His black eyes, now a bottomless pool of darkness as he towered over her.

She screamed.

He flinched, looked from her to the ground.

He dropped his gun! she thought. *RUN!*

Melodi jumped to her feet, spun around to make her escape, and to her surprise the dark rushing water blocked her path. Without thinking, she bolted to her left, dodged trees, hopped logs, diverted anything in her way. In the woods she'd once played in, she never had imagined her life ending. She pretended the insects, rodents, lizards, and birds were a hundred times their size—and even then, none of them tried to kill her.

The gun went off and a bullet sliced through the air, hitting a tree. It took everything for her to keep going. She didn't want to die.

"Your mother and brother are dead," the Man in Black yelled, "and you're next. You have to pay for what your father did."

Melodi stopped short.

Everything moved in slow motion. Suddenly the world stopped turning, the night stopped living, everything at a stand-still. She no longer heard life—the river or the night creatures. All her feeling and senses were gone.

Except for the man in black. The man who wanted her dead.

He took a threatening step in her direction, but she couldn't move.

He laughed, raised his gun and fired, hitting Melodi in the chest. She dropped like a rag doll.

It was cold and wet. She was drowning.

NINE

JAMES STUCKER HAD JUST WOKEN FROM A NAP, feeling refreshed. His grandkids were coming to visit, and he looked forward to seeing them. It's one the great pleasures in life. If you already have grandchildren of your own, you are well aware. You're no longer the enforcer in the family, but the person they run to with arms wide, smiles on their faces, giggles and secrets to share.

You're everything to them.

Children are a reminder of how sweet and innocent life can be. A reminder to not take life so seriously.

He heard Libby in the kitchen banging pots. She had made lasagna, Melodi's favorite. A little green blinking light caught his eye. A voicemail. He clicked it and listened to Margaret's voice, "James, sorry but we had a long day and the kids are tired, I think we have to cancel. Hope that's okay with you and Libby. Bye."

She sounded tired, nothing new there. But there was

something else in her voice. Since Ben died, she hadn't been herself. And being the one-year anniversary of Ben's death, he could relate. But James really wanted to see the kids.

He made up his mind—he would go to them. He thought of calling but then thought better of it. Margie would talk him out of it. They'd make it easy on her and bring dinner.

"Libby, pack up the lasagna. Change of plans," he called out.

It was dark out when he pulled up to Margie's house. The first thing he noticed was the front door had been left open. In all fourteen years he'd known Margie, she never once left a door open. He told himself not to jump to conclusions. The kids could have done it and Margie didn't notice.

Margie noticed everything.

No broken glass.

No—he would not be crippled by negative thoughts. He and Libby would walk through the front door and be greeted by their two grandchildren. Margie would be relieved to see them, and they'd sit down to a delicious meal.

But he couldn't help preparing for the worst. "Stay in the car and keep the doors locked," he told Libby in an even tone.

Libby's face told him all he needed to know. She was imagining the worst possible scenario. He placed his hand on her knee for a brief second. He met her eyes, and she nodded.

Taking his gun and flashlight from the glove box, he opened his door and scanned the area. The clouds covered the full moon offering little light. It gave off an eerie essence.

He shook off the feeling.

When his son bought the house, he'd been proud of him. Now that he was gone, and Margie and the kids were left to live here all alone, he didn't like it one bit. Their closest neighbor lived a half mile away. At night—this far out from the city—even with a full moon, you couldn't see much of anything at all.

His heart quickened as he walked toward the half-opened door, gun drawn, pointing toward the ground. The last thing he needed was to shoot one of the kids by accident. Focus, he reminded himself. If Frankie was with him now, he'd tell him to keep an open mind and not to let anything specific take his mind off the task. Target blindness, Frankie called it. *Look for anomalies,* he would have said.

As he approached the front steps, he saw his first sign. Footprints.

Anticipate your target's intentions.

He took a deep breath. Open door. Roughly guessing, the footprint was bigger than his own and he wore a size ten, the footprint belonged to a male. He followed the tracks out as far as he could see, sweeping his flashlight left to right and right to left. He didn't see any other prints. Only one set leaving the house. By the impression, he guessed in a hurry.

He hoped he was being ridiculous, but his gut told him he had come too late.

Without any footprints leading toward the house, the target entered the house another way. *But why?* He knew why.

Careful not to contaminate the area, he moved toward the open front door and glanced inside, his gun ready.

Toss him overboard. No, no, no. Hurray! So long, Woody . . .

"Margie?" he called out.

"Melodi? Peter?" he yelled.

Nothing, but the sound of Toy Story coming from down the hall.

He sniffed. Marinara sauce filled his nose. His gun in sync

with his eyes, he scanned the room from left to right and right to left. He saw nothing.

He walked slowly through the living room and into the kitchen, a plate of spaghetti lay on the counter.

Crunch.

He looked down, broken glass. He had found the entry point. His heart quickened. He hurried back through the living room and then down the hall.

Ahhhh! This is the part where we blow up! Not today . . .

Light flickered from the TV into the hallway. Before checking Margie's room, he cleared the bathroom.

He paused by the door to the bedroom.

Buzz, you're flying! This isn't flying, this is falling with style. To infinity and beyond . . .

A quick look inside.

Jesus Christ Almighty!

Tears sprang to his eyes. He blinked them away quickly. As he approached the bed, he looked around—in the closet, under the bed. He settled himself on the edge of bed, head hanging between his knees. He couldn't breathe. The image would be burned in his head forever.

Margaret shot in the head, between the eyes. Little innocent Peter, shot in the back, as he lay across his mother's chest. They were watching *Toy Story*, Peter's favorite movie, together.

Who would do such a thing?

Melodi? Where is she?

He sprang to his feet, darting down the hall to the stairs. If the killer was still inside the house, James no doubt would've been shot. He wasn't thinking clearly. All Frankie's training, out the window. He no longer protected himself. All he could think of was Melodi.

Is she safe? Where is she? Did she get out? She's a smart girl.

Half way up the stairs, he found her door open, doorknob gone.

Oh, God!

He searched—under the bed, in the closet—no sign of his granddaughter. The curtains flapped with a small breeze, as if dancing to a song he couldn't hear.

"Melodi," he whispered, hope running through him for the first time since he had stepped foot into their house. She got away. After Ben died, they practiced getting out of the house, in the event of a fire. Out the window. He never imagined she would need to escape from a killer.

He stuck his head out the window and heard the distinct sound of a gun firing in the distance. His heart plummeted.

"Melodi!" he yelled, his voice cracking.

No response.

He raced down the stairs and out the front door—*like the killer,* he thought.

Libby opened her car door. "Was that a—"

"Yes. Call Ryan and Doc. Melodi is out there. I have to go to her."

Libby gasped.

His mind going a million miles a second, "Don't go into Margie's room."

"Peter?" she asked, her voice shaken.

"Margie and Peter are gone. Now go inside and lock the doors until Ryan gets here. Take your gun, it's in the glove box." They both turned their heads toward the woods. His heart sunk. Another gunshot. "I have to go," he said. "Go inside, now."

She did, warning him to bring back her granddaughter and

be careful. He noticed she didn't say alive. He would gladly give his life for Melodi's.

As he stepped through the tree line, he had the overwhelming feeling he'd been there. Déjà vu. He'd experienced it before, like being in the twilight zone. This time, his mind was recalling a past memory.

When Ben was a boy, thirty something years ago, he'd wandered off from their campsite. He was in search of the perfect marshmallow roasting stick. James believed in giving kids freedom to explore, letting them fail, and allowing them to make their own decisions.

Libby, back then very much a helicopter parent, disagreed. Ben insisted on doing this big boy task on his own. The boys won, and James watched as Ben walked off, the woods swallowing him up.

Stay close, where I can see you, James had told him.

After five minutes, Libby ran off to the outhouse, and James turned his attention to the dying campfire. Adding more tinder, he blew on the smoke waiting patiently for a small orange glow. When Libby returned and asked for Ben, he panicked. He'd lost track of time—and his son.

It's one of the worst feelings a parent could have. Giving your child wiggle room to learn and grow, experience life. And then all your most vile thoughts come true.

They found Ben, twenty minutes later, not a scratch on him, with his stick. He sat on a dead tree with a dead squirrel in his hands. He wanted to hug him and beat the holy living shit out of him at the same time.

Why hadn't he called out? Why hadn't he responded when they called him? What was he thinking? Did he even know how much he scared his parents?

All the questions in the world wouldn't change what happened. So he hugged him instead, told him he loved him, and helped him bury the squirrel. When they had eaten, had their s'mores, and were safely tucked into their sleeping bags, he talked to Ben about safety. From then on, he reviewed safety with him twice a year—every March and November.

When Americans were springing forward or falling back and putting fresh batteries into their smoke alarms, James was teaching his son about added safety. Dangers in the home, out in public, at school, in the mountains, with friends. He taught him to trust his instincts, how and when to call 9-1-1, weapons, fire, first aid, online safety, secrets, and so on.

You never think it will happen to you, until it does.

He followed the footprints into the woods.

Even in the quietest and most isolated area of the woods, there was action going on all around him. Frankie taught him to see it. *What didn't belong? What disturbed the natural environment?*

He could have used the big man now. But Frankie wasn't there to do the work for him and he didn't have much time.

With a keen eye, his flashlight, and gun drawn, he kept going. The breeze picked up again and he shivered. His breathing was ragged and fast, and his left knee argued with him.

Within a couple minutes, he found Melodi's footprints, along with the killer's. His heart sunk. Her tracks told him what he already knew but refused to admit. She made it out of the house, the killer was on to her, and the gunshots he heard were most likely her getting shot.

"Melodi! Melodi . . ." he yelled.

Nothing.

Melodi, where are you?

Fear ran through him as his thoughts darkened. *Had he been too late?* He had to find her. He couldn't move fast enough.

The trail curved, and James followed the prints through the tall pine trees.

"Melodi, Melodi . . ."

His voice echoed. Leaves rustled, and he pointed his light at the culprit. A fox, watching him closely. His phone rang, jump starting his heart. An owl screeched in disagreement.

Damnit! He placed his flashlight in his right armpit, angling it toward the ground. He grabbed his phone from his pocket. "What?" he snapped, out of breath.

"It's Ryan. I'm almost there. Have you found her?"

"No Ryan, I haven't. I haven't fucking found her. I know she's here. I just have to find her."

"We're sending a search party. And the cadaver dogs. We'll find—"

He tuned Ryan out, moving his phone into his left armpit and once again shining his light on the ground.

"Something happened here," he yelled in his armpit.

James could hear Ryan yelling into the phone.

"Hold on," he yelled back. Stopping he surveyed the area spotting the killer's footprints mixed with Melodi's. *A struggle?*

The creek bubbled up ahead. His granddaughter was out there, afraid, possibly hurt, and nature didn't seem to care. The crickets chirped, singing their love song. Birds whistled. A dog howled? A wolf, coyote, or man's best friend? He hoped for the latter.

He hoped Melodi to appear, intact, beautiful as ever.

He followed the footprints and a bullet shell casing flickered under the light of his flashlight. A flicker of gold.

"I found something," he said. He put the phone back to his

ear. "Something happened here. I found a bullet casing."

"Don't touch it!" Ryan screamed into the phone. "And watch where you step. Can you wait for us?"

"No—I don't see Melodi. I have to keep looking." He walked along the creek. "Heavens no," he choked up, "there's blood," he added, dropping to his knees.

"I'm pulling up to your house now. Don't move," Ryan demanded. "You're stepping all over—" James hung up.

Nothing was going to keep him there, not until he found Melodi. He stepped into the swollen creek, water rushed by, not strong enough to take him, but it would certainly whisk a small child away.

He kept searching within a fifty-yard radius of the blood. Everything appeared whole. No trampled grass, no shoe scuffs, no broken branches or overturned vegetation.

He froze. Drawing his gun, he pointed it toward a loud cracking sound. It could have been a damned rodent or the same fox he'd seen earlier—hell it could even be a mountain lion that roamed down from Pikes Peak.

"James, it's me," called Ryan, holding his hands up.

He spun around ready to pull the trigger. "Shit, Ryan, I almost blew your goddamned head off," James scolded him. He seemed to appear from nowhere.

It was good to see his familiar face, but James didn't have time for his bullshit. He could see the wheels turning in Detective Ryan Cross's head, the steam coming out of his ears. James stomped all over his crime scene.

"I know. And you know I'm not leaving. I'm going downstream . . . As part of the search team," James added in response to Ryan's unspoken rebuke.

Ryan frowned and scratched his head. If it were anyone else but James, Ryan would have stopped them. James met Ryan the day he was born. Ryan slept at his house, ate his wife's cooking, and went on vacations with them. Ryan could not stop him from doing what he would have done in his place.

He was about to turn away, when Ryan said, "Be careful. And call me the moment you find anything at all."

TEN

ALL HIS YEARS IN THE VIETNAM WAR DIDN'T prepare James Stucker for what he found along the creek on that chilly October night. He was twenty when he carried his first wounded soldier to safety. Twenty when he held his first dying soldier in his arms as he took his last breath on the battlefield. Twenty-two when he saw the first innocent child killed in the crossfire—blood splattered everywhere.

But seeing Melodi's small body at the edge of the creek, brought back images he tried hard to forget. And goddammit, at fifty-seven, he had found her mother and brother shot to death.

He nearly tripped over her, as he crept along the side of the creek. He was trying to stay ahead of the police. He thought the dogs had to be out by now. He wanted to be the one to find her. He'd walk forever if he had to. And by God, there she was.

Her tiny body sprawled out on the rocks. Her gray t-shirt

gone, except for the collar that caught on a branch. Her jeans ripped, both shoes gone, and her beautiful brown hair unrecognizable, tangled in knots. His heart faltered as if it stopped beating momentarily. If she was dead, he could die right there with her. He would never forgive himself for not making it to her sooner.

He recalled holding Melodi for the first time at the hospital. An itty-bitty being in his giant hands. Immediately he noticed her lips, like his dear Kat's, and he smiled. Her skin was fair with rosy cheeks. She wore a white knitted hat on her head which he lifted to expose a mess of dark hair. He fell in love. Suddenly his world was perfect. He never dreamed he could feel the way he felt that day. It was different from having your own. Dare he say it—even sweeter. His own child having a child, this creation in his arms.

The daughter he never had. He hated himself for thinking it, but he couldn't help himself. He would never take his son's place as her father. But he would be the best damn grandfather there was.

He stepped closer, reaching down to lift her—that's when he saw it. Blood—dark red oozing from her chest. He shouldn't have been surprised, after all, he heard the gunshot, found gun casings and blood. But the sight of Melodi, shot, made him sick to his stomach. His eyes fixated on the scarlet red puddle forming on her pale skin.

Oh Mel. My sweet girl.

His first and only granddaughter—and now his only grandchild. The thought brought tears to his eyes.

As horror coursed through his veins and his hands trembled, he pulled his handkerchief out of his back pocket and covered her wound, pressing to stop the bleeding. He gently laid her down flat and leaned over to see if she was breathing. He could see slight movement. He put his ear near her chest. A faint heartbeat. If she lost too much blood, her heartbeat would be rapid before she died. Feeling a ton of bricks lift from his shoulders, he let out a breath.

Oh, thank you Lord! Thank you, dear Lord!

He removed his jacket and carefully wrapped her in it. Her skin ice-cold. He snatched his phone out of his pocket and called Doc.

"I found her. Meet me at the turnout, before you take BUS 23 South." He hung up before Doctor Melvin argued about the location being right off the busy highway. He didn't care. He only cared about Doc getting to Melodi and doing what he does best—saving her life.

He slid one arm under her neck and the other under her knees. One quick look around him and he took off. He knew the trackers would be on his heels. *Time to move your ass, James,* he said under his breath. And he did. He moved fast through the trees, being vigilant not to trip. He saw the one gunshot wound and hoped to God there weren't more. The poor girl was already banged up enough.

"Where is he?" James whispered. Never mind it had only been ten minutes since he hung up with Doc. He held Melodi close to him to keep her small body warm. It was cold out, but he didn't care about himself. He was anxious to get Melodi medical help.

Seconds later, he spotted Doc's Beamer circle around—*there's my man.* You drove like a maniac, didn't you Doc? Doc flicked his headlights off as he drove into the circle and threw his car in park. He jumped out of his car, medical bag in tow and moved past him without saying a word. The eye contact said, "I got this. Time is of the essence." James couldn't have agreed more, and he gave his friend an approving nod.

Doc listened for her heartbeat, displeased he said, "She needs blood and she needs it now."

"I know. Let's go. We're both type O."

"No—we're doing it here. Now."

James was about to argue. He wanted to save his granddaughter, that was his primary concern. But, he didn't want anyone else to know she was alive. Not yet. He looked at Doc, opened his mouth and shut it.

"Give me your damn arm Stucker. Let's get this girl some blood—,"

Doc didn't have to finish, he had his arm out before he could spit the words out. James hated needles, but at this moment the thought didn't even cross his mind.

After placing the IV line in Melodi he poked James and the much-needed blood made its way into Melodi's little body. "Now we can go," he said. He picked her up, "Watch the line and stay close." At the car he ordered James to get in and proceeded to give him the limp girl to hold. "Hold her in the back with you."

Doc, bossy as ever, called the shots.

James didn't mind one bit.

Doc jumped in the front seat and stepped on it. His house, a twenty-minute drive, took ten minutes with Doc's crazy driving.

He stepped out to call Detective Ryan Cross, preparing himself for a lecture that didn't come. It would come soon enough. Doctor Melvin barked orders, just like the old days, and James Stucker did everything asked of him. He was relieved when Donna, Doc's wife and certified physician's assistant, took over.

Libby watched, white as a ghost but didn't say a word.

He paced the hall feeling useless. He would never forgive himself if anything happened to Melodi. What a stupid thought. Something did happen to her, and he wasn't able to protect her. He should have been there—to protect her.

Hell! He couldn't protect Ben . . . and now, a year later, he couldn't protect his family.

He jumped when Libby's hand touched the middle of his back. She put her arms around his waist and he pulled her small frame in, burying his face in her hair as he took in her sweet scent. She was crying. He wanted to cry, but he had to be brave. His wife needed him and soon Melodi would too.

"What are we going to do James?" she asked, breaking the silence.

He took her in for the first time since they pulled up to Margie's house a few hours earlier. He watched her lips move as she spoke, red and full. Her brown eyes, catlike, now red and swollen. She wore her hair off to the side, in a braid, with wispy strands surrounding her beautiful face. "We wait, we pray, and we stay strong for our granddaughter," he said. They were the only family she had left. Margie's parents died before she and Ben married. "We're all she has now Libby." When she wasn't satisfied, he added, "We protect her, we do what we have to . . . to keep her safe."

She offered a brief but sweet smile.

I know my sweet Libby, I know.

Ben had been an only child and it devastated Libby when they lost him. She wanted a house full of kids. Libby made that clear to him on their first date. She wasn't about to waste her precious time on someone who didn't. Her dreams were crushed when they found out two years after Ben was born that she was infertile. It didn't make sense. She'd already given birth to one child. Why on earth could she not get pregnant again?

Unexplained infertility said their doctor. As well as the doctor after that and the one after that. They ran so many tests on her, she finally had enough. *You're lucky you had Ben,* one young doctor said. James thought he saw the devil in her eyes that day. He'd never seen her so angry. That was the last straw. They never went back. If they were meant to have another, they would, she said.

Donna poked her head out. "Melvin wants to talk to you both."

They looked at each other. He grabbed Libby's hand and walked into the room where their granddaughter fought for her life.

"Bad news, she needs surgery to get the bullet out. It didn't go through, as you already know, it stopped centimeters from her heart." He pointed to the x-ray. "She's lost a lot of blood, thanks to you, we got her some, but she needs more. I have an old friend from the hospital dropping some off. Don't worry, he doesn't know why and doesn't ask questions."

John swallowed hard. "There's good news?"

"I don't see any other serious injuries on her. She skinned her knee and hands and bumped her head, could be from falling in the woods or from the creek. I don't see any fluid in her lungs, but I'd like to check her further when she's under. I'd hate to jinx the whole damn thing, but she's a lucky girl to be alive at this point. I'd like to think she's meant to live. She's a tough one."

"Yes, she is. Do it Doc. Save our granddaughter," he said, squeezing Libby's hand.

James Stucker gave himself a once over in the bathroom mirror. What a mess. He ran his fingers through the hair he let grow after his son died. He couldn't say why. He'd kept it short, even after he left the military. He'd cut it first chance he got.

The realization he may never see Melodi alive again came over him.

He splashed water on his face to get the ugly thought out of his head.

He joined Melodi in her room, as Doc and Donna prepared another room for surgery. He looked at his watch for the umpteenth time wondering what was taking so long, yet, taking comfort in knowing she was in Doc's hands. Hearing commotion in the hallway, he met Ryan at the door.

Ryan Cross held out his hand toward Doc, who flew past him bumping his shoulder. "Does that man ever slow down?" Ryan asked, shaking his head.

"Just like Doc. I'm thinking of changing his name to *The Flash.*" James said it half-joking. He gave Ryan a hug. "Thanks for coming." He needed to make more time for Ryan. He'd treated him like a stranger a couple of hours earlier. He'd always been proud of the fine man Ryan had become.

James observed the man as he stepped into Melodi's room, closing the door behind him, glancing around as he did. Ryan's eyes briefly rested on Melodi. "I'm sorry this happened." He paused. "But, you know I need to call this in."

And . . . Ryan let him down. Ben's best friend. Melodi's second dad, after her own died. James hoped he wouldn't go there—but he did. "No. No, you don't Ryan. You know, as well as I do, it'll be leaked to the news immediately. The son-of-a-bitch is out there. He killed her family and left her for dead." He pointed at Melodi. His voice getting louder as he spoke. He cleared his throat, trying to calm down. "He thinks she's dead. What do you think he'll do when he finds out she's alive and can ID him?"

Ryan's face turned red, his hands were buried in his pockets. "Sir, I hear what you're saying, but you're not thinking straight right now." His voice shaky, trying to keep his composure.

"Oh, I guarantee you—I have thought this through. I've thought of nothing else for the past couple of hours." He put his hand on Ryan's shoulder. "I know you have a job to do, but Melodi is like a daughter to you. How about you treat her like one."

Ryan looked at the floor, paused, then back at James. "I know you don't mean that. This is tearing me apart too. I had to make up some bullshit story just to get here all while there's a search party going on. The resources involved . . ." He looked at Melodi. "If I don't give them something, they'll spend hours, days, people's lives out there searching for nothing. When she's here safe . . ."

"I know exactly what I'm asking. But whoever did this," his voice cracked, "thinks that little girl is dead." How many times did he have to say it? "He left her out there, like an animal! Hell—she may still die." He looked away, ashamed that he even thought of it. He couldn't think that Melodi could die right now. Doc will save her, he knew he would.

"Sir—,"

"Call me James. Good grief son, you're a detective now. I've known you your entire life." He shook his head thinking of his own son, Ben.

"I will do everything I can for Melodi."

"What does that even mean? You're either with me or you're against me. Which is it?" James asked, searching Ryan's eyes.

Ryan's eyes widened, his breathing became heavier. His eyes settled on Melodi. Ryan walked over to her bed and sat on the side holding her hand. He held it for several minutes, kissed her on the cheek and whispered in her ear, "I'm sorry Melodi.

Get better soon sweet girl," He took a deep breath, turned to James and said, "I'm with you, one hundred percent. I brought Detective Bill White with me. Before you say anything, I trust him. He's with us. We'll take care of it." Ryan got up and turned to him as if waiting for direction.

"No one knows we found her. Do what you must," he stated.

ELEVEN

TWO DAYS LATER

MELODI TRIED SITTING UP—*OWWW* . . . SHE strained. The pain threw her back down.

"You're awake," exclaimed her grandpa, hurrying to her side. "Don't move." He touched her arm and gestured to the unfamiliar man.

She supposed he might be a doctor, he had a stethoscope around his neck, although he sure didn't look like a doctor. Come to think of it, this room didn't look like a normal hospital. It had all the equipment you would find in a hospital, but the room looked more like a bedroom.

"Oh darling . . ." her grandma said. Her hand found her mouth, tears streaming down her cheeks.

Why is she crying?

"Whe . . ." the words wouldn't come. Melodi cleared her

throat and tried again. "Where . . . am I?" she managed, her voice low and raspy.

"You're in an infirmary—it's like a hospital," Grandpa said. "Doc here is going to look you over and ask you some questions. I'll tell you everything when he's done."

Her grandpa looked like he did after her dad died. Maybe he was coming down with something. And Grandma didn't look so good either. She's crying . . .

Am I . . . dying?

As she became more aware of her body, her heart quickened, and a rush of dizziness took over. The machine next to her bed beeped loudly. She looked from her grandma to her grandpa and back—then her eyes settled on the doctor. A surge of sudden pain blasted through her chest.

"Where's my mom? Where's Pete? Why am I here?" she asked, her voice rising with each question.

And the damn machine wouldn't shut up. It seemed to get louder by the second. She closed her eyes tight—she couldn't think. Her head hurt. Her body hurt. Her ears hurt from that stupid machine . . . *make it shut up!* She opened her eyes to find the bearded doctor granting her wish. Grandma looked just as relieved.

"Hi," said the bearded doctor. "My name is Doctor Melvin, I'm a friend of James . . . your grandfather." He looked at her grandpa and back. "I'm going to look you over and ask you a few questions. Is that okay with you?"

Melodi shrugged, watching him intently.

He didn't look like a doctor. If it hadn't been for her grandparents by her side, she never would have let this man near her. Most doctors she saw were—doc-like. This man was not. He looked bigger, brawnier, and needed to shave. No doctor she ever saw had a bushy beard—

That's it! He looked like Anthony Hopkins in *Instinct.* Her first Rated R movie she ever saw—Grandpa let her watch it with him. She wondered if he thought Doctor Melvin looked like him too. Melodi smiled at the thought.

Doctor Melvin pulled out a light and flashed it in her eyes. "What's your name?" he asked.

"Melodi . . . Melodi Stucker." What a stupid question.

"How old are you?" he asked, stealing a glance at her grandpa as he continued to check her.

"I'm eleven."

"Do you know who these two folks are?" he asked, motioning toward them.

He pulled the cover and untied her gown, exposing a big white bandage wrapped around her chest. She puffed out air, realizing she had been holding her breath. He asked her to move to her side, so he could check her back. She cried out from the movement. He carefully helped lay her back down.

"Sorry about that. I promise I'll get you something for the pain," he said. "Do you know these folks?" He pointed to them again.

"They're my grandma and grandpa," she whimpered, wondering if he planned on asking her any questions he didn't already know the answers to.

"Do you know why you're here?"

Melodi thought about it for a minute, not sure how to answer. She searched her memory.

Nothing. Blank.

Now that was a good question. Why am I here? She's in the hospital, she hurts all over, has a bandage around her chest, and it hurts worse than when she fell out of the tree her mother told her not to climb. Ended up getting a concussion and breaking her left arm.

"I'm guessing I was in an accident—and I'm hurt," Melodi said, sarcastically.

Doctor Melvin gave a half smile, "Yes, but do you remember what happened? How you were hurt?"

"No—," Melodi's pulse quickened and the stupid machine started up again. Tears filled her eyes and rolled down the side of her face. "Did Mom and Peter get hurt too?" She looked at her grandpa. "Are they here?"

"You're going to be okay," the doctor answered, no comfort in his voice. "Your grandparents will talk to you about what happened. But first I'll give you something for the pain and then give you some privacy."

TWELVE

WHEN JAMES STUCKER SERVED IN THE military, he saw more death than he had ever imagined. It had been hard to put the images out of his head. His family had been his salvation. Aside from his wife, this little girl was all the family he had left. He would do anything for her.

He looked at his granddaughter who was watching him. This is by far the most difficult thing he had ever done. Losing his son last year in a car accident ripped him apart, and this was his son's only daughter. He'd be damned if he'd let anything else happen to her. She'd look to him now; her life would depend on it.

He spent the last two days going over what to say to her. How would she react when she came to? He couldn't imagine this poor child losing everything and going through what she did.

There was still a triple homicide to be solved. He had so many questions for her, as did the detectives assigned to the case, two of them he would be forever in debt to. The thought never occurred to him that she wouldn't remember.

How do you tell an eleven-year-old that her mom and brother are dead? That she herself was shot, was supposed to be dead, and the murderous lunatic was still on the loose? He couldn't decide if it was good news that she didn't remember or worse. He knew one thing for sure, he would do whatever it took to keep her safe.

He studied his wife. She looked frail and distraught. She had been crying non-stop for the past two days. He knew she didn't get much sleep—he knew because he didn't sleep at all.

Libby will be mad at me and I may pay for this later, thought James, but she can't be here when I tell Melodi. It will break her heart.

"Libby, my love, would you mind going to get us something to eat. I'm sure Melodi's starving."

"But . . ." Her beautiful russet brown eyes coming to the realization that he wouldn't ask this of her, unless it was an absolute necessity. "Alright, I'll be back soon," she said, her voice reluctant. Looking down at the fragile, ghostly girl lying in bed. She added, "My dear girl, I love you—don't be scared—we're here. I promise, I'll be right back." She squeezed Melodi's hand and placed a soft kiss on her cheek.

James waited for his wife to leave, turned to Melodi and said, "Mel, my sweet girl . . ." He fought the lump in his throat.

"Grandpa, you're scaring me. What's wrong?"

Get a grip, he told himself, fighting back the tears. He didn't consider himself a wuss, but he sure felt like one. Look at her, how could he not? He knew it would be hard, but he wasn't ready for this. Would anyone?

"Mel, I have a lot to tell you. First, how are you doing?"

"I'm scared."

"I know." He didn't think he could feel any more defeated. She looked so innocent, fragile. But also, beautiful, even as she lay there, paler than usual, dark circles under her eyes. She was lovely. Her brown eyes full of . . . life.

Thank you, dear God, for allowing my grandchild to live. He stared at her, his face desperate, emotional. His heart full of love.

"And my chest hurts," she continued, "but not as much since the doctor gave me some pain stuff."

"Okay, good," He managed a smile. "You did get hurt—but it was no accident."

Melodi gasped, as panic shot through her.

He knew he was scaring her but didn't know how else to tell her. Careful not to move her, he sat next to her, grabbed her small hand, and squeezed. "I found you and brought you here to Doctor Melvin's house. Doc and I served in the military together. He was our medic and he's the best damn doctor I've ever known. He will take good care of you. He has everything here you need. I trust him with my life, which he saved more than once, along with many close friends."

"Grandpa, where's Mom and Pete?"

"I'm getting to it," he wished to God they were right next to him. "There was a break-in at your house. Do you remember anything?"

"No," she whispered.

"You were shot. . ." His eyes explored hers.

"Why don't I remember?" Melodi asked softly.

"It's okay. Doc says it's normal that you don't. You've been through a lot and your memory may come back over time."

"And Mom and Peter—were they shot, too?"

James closed his eyes and took a deep breath. He couldn't hide his shaking hands and the tears burning his eyes. When he opened them—he saw his sweet girl weeping quietly. "Yes, they were both shot. Only . . . they didn't make it. I'm so sorry . . ." he said, shaking his head, wishing it weren't true.

She closed her eyes, tears pouring down her sweet young face that had already seen too much. Her body shook as she lifted her hands to her face. His first instinct was to scoop her up and hold her. But he settled for nestling his head next to hers—pulling her hands down and replacing them with his. His hand on one side and his head on the other, as he wiped away her tears.

They stayed that way for a long time crying together. Not in a million years did he imagine he or his grandchild would be at this unlikely juncture. He didn't believe in fate or destiny. If such things existed, what did either one of them do to deserve such an intervention into their happy lives? Had he not paid his dues? Had Ben not paid his?

"Nooooo!" Melodi Stucker gasped for air.

James Stucker had been asleep in a chair next to her bed. His eyes shot open.

"Grandpa! Grandpa!" she shouted.

"Melodi! What is it?"

"I had a dream . . ." she said, sobbing like a baby. "It was awful Grandpa . . . except . . . except, it was real. I mean—I think I remember what happened that night. He shot me. I saw him. I saw him. I saw the man who shot me . . ." she continued rambling.

"Oh Melodi. It's just a dream," he comforted, hugging her.

"Grandpa," she ignored him, "he said that I had to pay for what my dad did," Her eye's panicked, searching for answers. "You have to believe me. It was real, I know it was. It happened.

I remember now. I remember . . ."

She stared off into nowhere in particular, talking to herself, as if the night unfolded before her—short flashes in her head—like an old film rolling. "I had a fight with Mom," she sighed. "It's my fault. We were going to visit you that night. I threw a fit and went to my room. That's when it all happened. I saw him, a man in black. He had eyes . . ." she paused and shivered, suddenly paralyzed with fear. "His eyes were black and dark and evil. I stared straight at him. Then he came after me. He shot me, he shot me! I was drowning. I should have died. Why didn't I die? I should have died . . ." her babbling becoming incoherent.

"Melodi. Melodi," he gripped her shoulders. She stared off, visualizing the horror, over and over again. She'd been shot once, but her mind was on replay.

"Please Mel, you need to calm down. It's not good to get yourself worked up. I'm getting Doc." He rushed out of the room.

When he returned with Doc by his side, she said, "It's true. Why don't you believe me? I saw him. He was dressed in black—the man in black. He shot me, and he killed Mom and Pete. It's all my fault," she whispered. "It's my fault they're dead . . ."

"Melodi, I'm going to give you something to help you relax," Doc said.

She looked at him like he had two heads.

"Why do you want to drug me? Why is no one listening to me?"

James Stucker sat in an old leather wingback chair, his elbows on his knees, his head hanging low. He stared through the hardwood floor, deep in thought. He just watched his granddaughter have a near breakdown at eleven years old.

"Melvin, we need to talk," he said gravely.

Melvin couldn't remember the last time James used his name, it had always been Doc—even in combat. "I'll send Donna in," he said. "We can talk in my office."

Absorbed in Melodi, he didn't see Doc scurry out of the room.

He heard a low tap on the door. "Come in," James said.

Donna poked her head in. "Melvin sent me. He said you two need to talk," she said quietly. "Don't worry James, I'll take care of her."

"Thanks Donna. Come get me when she wakes."

She nodded.

James liked Donna, she was good for his friend. Doc was shattered when his first wife died of cancer nine years ago. It wasn't until he met Donna four years later that he had a new spring in his step. She was fifteen years his junior and exactly what he needed. They fell in love and hadn't spent a day apart since.

The light of the sun peeked through the blinds onto the row of books that lined the wall of Doc's office. It provided enough light for James's taste, but Doc flicked on the switch anyway. He did it every time. They argued many times about it, something James did just to bust his balls. Today was not one of those days. So he let it go.

Doc retired fifteen years ago, bought this house and turned it into a private infirmary not long after. He started caring for his first wife when she became ill. He was a good man, always had been.

"What's on your mind," Doc asked. He sat in his chair, leaning forward.

James stood, too wound up to sit. "You were in there."

"You believe what she said?"

"You don't?" He scrutinized. "C'mon Doc, her memories are coming back. You saw it in her face, just like I did."

Doc let out a breath, pursed his lips and said, "Look, all I'm saying is that you need to give her a little more time. Let's have her see Jill—"

"No," he cut him off, "Jill's a nutcase."

"I'm only suggesting she see her a few times. And Jill may be a nutcase, but she's good at what she does."

James looked at the picture of Doc and Donna. No children. Did he fully understand? "I'm not waiting. There's no time to wait. We wait, she dies."

"What on earth would Ben have done that would make someone want to kill his family?"

"I don't know," James shook his head.

"And he's been dead for a year. Why wait till—"

The blood drained from James's face. "That's it! The anniversary of Ben's death. Whoever did this, chose that date for a reason. Melodi *is* remembering. The killer thinks Ben wronged him. This isn't random at all."

"You need to call Ryan."

He could only imagine how that conversation would go. Detective Ryan Cross had already put his career on the line by not reporting a missing child as found when the public demanded answers. He lied. They all lied. Now he had to ask him . . . no, demand he make another call.

"Later," he decided. Ryan may never speak to him again, he

might as well have all the pieces in place. "First step is getting Melodi safe—the only way I know how is to reach out to our old friend Frankie."

"How did I know you were going to say that?" Doc asked.

"We've spent a lot of years together Doc. Enough to read each other's mind. We're like an old married couple."

"You wish," he chuckled. "You can't move her, James," his tone serious. "Who's going to take care of her medically? I know I'm stating the obvious, but you need to know what you're dealing with. The shooting was only two days ago. She almost died. We're fortunate the bullet missed her heart and stopped in her pericardium. Fortunate is a terrible word though. She's still not in the clear—"

"You're not telling me anything I haven't already considered." When James's mind was made up, it was made up—end of story.

"Good. I'm coming with you," Doc said bluntly, standing up as if they were leaving right then.

"I can't ask you to do that." Doc never failed to surprise him.

"You didn't ask—I told you."

"You know what I mean. What about Donna?" Doc wasn't budging. "You know I would love to have you by Melodi's side, but I just can't—"

"Stop being a stubborn old fool, James. I didn't ask your permission. I'm coming with you, and so is Donna. At least until Melodi is in the clear."

James attempted a bro hug, pulling his friend in, holding on longer than usual. This meant the world to him. He owed Doc big time.

"You're the man, Doc. How could I ever repay you?"

"You were there for me when I needed you most, I think this is the least I can do. I'll go look in on Melodi. Help yourself to the phone."

James watched his friend shut the door. Doc may think he owed James, but, truth be told, James would do anything for that man. It's a nice reminder that he would do the same. The thought occurred to him that Doc was starting to look like a taller version of Anthony Hopkins as he got older.

It reminded him of the night Melodi slept over—after Ben died. One of the rare moments she let him in. It took some convincing, but she finally agreed. They had watched Instinct with Anthony Hopkins.

She said "What's it rated Grandpa? Mom won't let me watch rated R movies."

He had told her, "It's a good movie and a shame if you can't watch it with me. But if you can't, you can't. Just go learn to crochet something with Grandma while I watch it."

She looked at him like he was nuts, but she had a wild side to her and he knew she would give in, after all, Grandpa said it was okay and there was no way in hell she was going to crochet anything. So they watched it. Him sitting in his usual spot—his large recliner—and her eventually making her way over to squeeze in with him.

James parked himself behind Doc's big wooden desk. He stared at the tattered card he pulled from his wallet. Once he made the call, there was no turning back. Melodi's life had already changed, but it would change more than she ever thought possible.

He dialed the number and held his breath as it rang. "It's James, call me at this number," he said hanging up. Frankie would know something was up, he'd only called that number once before.

Franklin Dowdy—friends knew him as Frankie—was a six-and-a-half foot, two-hundred-and-sixty-pound black man cut like Rambo. He served with James and Doc back in '77 and '78 before joining the Special Forces. He retired and opened his own side business. The man had connections. Connections with skills. Skills James needed. Not to mention his own skills that would come in handy.

James stood up, pacing the room in anticipation for the phone to ring. It didn't help he looked at his watch every ten seconds.

The phone rang and James dove for it, knocking over Doc's pencil holder in the process. "Yes?" he said into the phone after the first ring.

"Stucker, my man," Frankie shouted into the phone, "It's been too long. Good to hear from you man."

"Frankie—if it were normal times, it would be good to hear your voice too."

"You're calling my private line, which could only mean one thing. What can I do for you?"

"It's my family," he said, exhaling loudly. "Some madman broke into my son's house and killed my daughter-in-law and grandson."

"Ah fuck, James." The line went silent for a few seconds. "I'm sorry man. What do you need? Anything—you name it. Want me to kill the fucker? I'll do it—you know I will."

"I would love nothing more. Problem being, we don't know who it is—yet. But I have a possible lead. He shot Melodi too," James could hear Frankie swearing on the line, "she landed in Columbine Creek where he left her for dead. The water carried her body downstream where she got stuck in an embankment. That's where I found her half dead. I took her to Doc's."

"Bastard!" He paused, making grunting sounds. At last, he added "You're with Doc? How's that son-of-a-bitch?"

"He's Doc. Saved another life. My granddaughter's this time."

"Of course he did. I'd expect nothing less. So what can I do? We going hunting?" he said with too much excitement. At forty-three years old, Frankie was tough as nails and ready to fight.

"Not yet. I need to get her safe and out of Colorado. She's remembering everything," he said thinking back to her near breakdown. "She thinks it's her fault . . ."

"Oh shit, that must be rough. How old is she now?"

"She's eleven. We need new identities too. For my granddaughter, my wife, and myself. And Frankie—I need them now."

"You got it," Frankie assured him with no hesitation. "You said you need to move, where you thinking?"

"Damn Frankie. I don't know . . . I didn't think that far." He thought he had a plan, he had more thinking to do. He didn't care where, as long as it was far away.

"You're coming here then. I can help."

"Frankie . . ." his voice crackled.

"Yeah, man?"

"I'm not sure if the description will be much help, he wore a mask, all black . . ." He paused. "But she said one thing I can't get past."

"What's that?"

"She said he told her she had to pay for what her dad did."

"What the hell does that mean?" Frankie asked, surprised.

"Exactly. It occurred to me—this man may have chosen this date to kill them for a reason."

"I'm not following."

"The asshole went after Ben's family on the twenty-fourth of October. This was the anniversary of Ben's death. He told Melodi she had to pay for what her father did. In his twisted mind, he thinks Ben did something to him and killed his family to make him pay." James paused. "I don't know. Everyone loved Ben. I just don't know who would do such a thing."

"Hell, man. It could be anyone with a chip on their shoulder. Someone from one of his flights, a co-worker, hell maybe even from the crash he died in. Where are the police in all this?"

He didn't think of that. The crash. That would make sense, but so would someone from a flight. A canceled flight, delayed flight, someone who missed an important meeting, date, deadline—hell, who knows. "Nowhere. No fingerprints, he wore gloves. I know a couple of the detectives working the case who have already bent over backward for me. You know Ryan Cross, he was Ben's best friend. After Ben died, he stepped up and helped Margaret. He's sort of a fatherly figure to Melodi. He would do anything for her. And Detective White. I guess he owes Ryan big time. Ryan has him wrapped around his pinky. Not sure what he has on him and I don't really care."

"If you need me to go down there, just say the word and I'm there. I'll hunt that mother fucker down."

"I know." He loved his enthusiasm. "Right now, I need your help keeping Melodi safe, away from Colorado. I trust Ryan will do his job."

"Has Melodi been reported dead?"

"Not yet. Still missing. Ryan's my next call. He doesn't know her memory came back yet, and I need to let him know we're moving."

"So Oregon?"

"What?"

"The IDs, you need a state. You're moving to Oregon. I want you all close to me."

"Sounds good. Oh, by the way—Doc and his wife are coming too. Not for good, but to help until she's feeling better."

"The old squad is back together!" he said with gusto.

He liked the idea of the old squad being together, though he didn't like what was bringing them together. They hung up and James ran their conversation through his mind trying to recall if he missed anything.

It was time.

How was he going to tell Melodi she had to start a whole new life? Not only one that didn't include her father, mother, and brother, but one where she walked away from everything she knew as Melodi Stucker.

THIRTEEN

DECEMBER 1998

THE POLICE CAME BY. AN OLDER MAN WITH A cowboy hat—looked like a Texan, with the accent and all. Said he was investigating a triple homicide in the area.

Jimmy Dumel replied, "That's why I keep my doors locked."

"We're questioning all the folks that had any connection to the thirty-car pileup in '97." Jimmy's heart pounded, his breathing labored. The Texan watched Jimmy closely. "We think there may be a connection."

Jimmy couldn't speak. He noticed the man's eyes drift down to his clenched hands. Jimmy relaxed the tight balls and let out a breath.

"I'm sure you're aware my brother died in that accident, officer."

"Detective. Bill White's my name."

Who gives a shit?

"I'm also certain you're aware that my mother committed suicide when the murders took place. So if you don't mind, if you're not here to arrest me, I'd rather not talk about the worst day of my life."

"I spoke to your father," the Texan said in a thick drawl.

Jimmy remained impassive, everything eating him up inside. His pops had a big mouth. Never knew when to keep it shut.

The cougar from down the hall walked by with her teenage boy, making eye contact with Jimmy as she did. She was old enough to be his momma and here she was flirting with him. She winked at him and blew her cigarette smoke at the detective's head.

The Texan turned to see who Jimmy was looking at. "Howdy, Ma'am," he said, as he tilted his hat.

She smiled and kept on going.

The detective turned his attention back to Jimmy. "He said you were with him the day your mother died, the day of the murders. Is that correct."

No response.

"I could bring you in for further questioning—if that suits you better."

"Am I under arrest?"

"No, you're not. I'm trying to solve a triple homicide, son—and I'd appreciate your cooperation."

"Yes," Jimmy replied, impassive.

"Yes, what?" He pulled out a small pad and wrote on it.

"Yes, I was with my father."

"What time did you leave his house."

"I don't remember."

"Can you think? Was it still light out?"

Jimmy knew what he was doing. If he didn't answer his questions, he would look like he had something to hide. "No. It was dark. Late. I don't recall the time. But it was night out."

The detective looked over Jimmy's shoulder, into his apartment. "Can I come in? Have some water or something. I've been out all day."

"I was just heading out," Jimmy lied.

The detective lit a cigar, "Want one?"

"Nope."

"Here's the thing—" he said, taking the cigar out of his mouth, "you want to know what I think?" he asked, eyes narrowed, flicking his cigar. "I think your daddy's covering for you because he's afraid."

"You can think whatever you want Detective. This is a free country. As a matter of fact, I may just write to the city about how one of their detectives is accusing an innocent man of murder on the day his mother committed suicide because he thinks his dad is afraid. Now unless you're taking me in, I suggest you leave."

Jimmy shut the door in his face.

"We'll be in touch." He heard the man say from the other side of the door.

He leaned against the door with his eyes closed. The blood drained from his face. He grabbed a cigarette, his hand shaking violently.

He was a murderer. If caught, he'd be sent to prison, most likely for life.

He finally got the redemption his brother deserved. It should have been Ben, but someone had to pay for his stupidity.

He had no regrets.

And his pops covered for him. He couldn't believe it. The old man came through. Finally, for once in his life, he did something for Jimmy. His pops hadn't had a single drop, to Jimmy's knowledge, in the last couple of months. Not since the day his mom killed herself. He'd like to give the man credit for doing something good, but he couldn't help but wonder if his drinking led her to jump in front of the train.

FOURTEEN

PRESENT DAY

JIMMY RIPPED THE CURTAINS BACK, THE LIGHT barreling through engulfing the bed in its harsh unforgiving glow. His cruel way of getting Robin's ass out of bed so he could get to work and she could take Isabel to school.

Robin flinched like a vampire, pulling the covers quickly over her head.

"Oh no you don't." He yanked them back down. "Get up!"

"Knock it off Jimmy," she said, reaching unsuccessfully—settling for a pillow over her head.

"I said get your ass out of bed. I have to go to work and you need to take Isabel to school."

"I can't. You take her."

When did his life get to this point? He didn't sign up for this.

The fighting, her drinking, the hangovers. The bottle took over his childhood and now it was taking over his marriage. He once thought marrying Robin would fill the dark hole in his chest and heal the wounds of his past. He'd been with many women in his life, all of whom he didn't care a rat's ass about. Robin was different. Yet here she was. No longer serving her purpose.

He looked at her, disgusted. Passed out like a drunk. The smell made him sick to his stomach. What a waste.

He opened Isabel's door, only to find an empty room. The toilet flushed and she came out of the bathroom.

"Morning Daddy. Aren't you going to work?"

"Yeah, after I take you to school."

"Mom can take me."

"No." He clenched his jaw thinking of Robin lying drunk in bed. "No, she can't. She's not feeling well."

The booze got her again.

"Mom hasn't been feeling well since she stopped working. Maybe she should ask for her job back."

"Did she tell you that," he snapped.

"No," she whispered.

"Go get ready. I'm already going to be late."

"K."

He leaned against the door frame, staring a hole in the back of Robin's head. Quiet, reserved, sweet Robin. She batted her long eyelashes at him reeling him in. No man had her before Jimmy. He was her first and would be her only, till death do them part.

Yes, till death do them part. He couldn't help but imagine her dead. He pointed his finger to mimic a gun.

Phew! he said under his breath.

Late to work, just like he knew he would be. To make matters worse, he ran into the prick—Jamison had always been a prick, and an ass, and a dweeb—but on this special occasion, he crossed the line. Jimmy was already on edge because his wife stayed in bed passed out. The dweeb pushed his buttons at the wrong time. If he had a gun, he would have blown the prick's head off.

Jamison, in his grating tone, said, "Dumel, get your ass to work."

He had literally just walked through the fucking door. "Go fuck yourself!" Jimmy replied.

Jamison screwed-up his face in surprise that Jimmy would talk to him like that. It wasn't the first time. "What crawled up your ass, Dumel? Robin finally decide to leave your dumb ass?"

The whole room, men getting ready to head out for the day and a couple of secretaries, fell silent. Jimmy could have sworn they all stopped breathing.

"What the fuck did you say about my wife?" Jimmy asked, as the blood rushed to his face. His breathing slowed, his chest puffed, his heart pounded. He knew Jamison was dumb, but today took the cake.

With an all-knowing dumbass smirk on his face, Jamison replied, "Ahh, c'mon Dumel. You gotta know she's out of your league. She—"

There was a sharp gasp from one of the ladies before . . .

Smack!

Jimmy went ape-shit. In a frenzy, he attacked Jamison like a wild animal. He let it all out—the anger, compacted over the years—hit after hit, blow after blow. It took two guys to pull him off. Jimmy didn't have a scratch on him. The prick laid there, bloodied, eye swollen and shit. Jimmy found out later he gave the guy a concussion and broke his nose. The prick should count himself lucky. Like Jimmy said, if he'd had a gun, he'd be dead.

It brought back feelings he had locked up. It felt good to release. He felt free. That is, until they locked his ass up for assault. He learned some valuable lessons that day. First, letting his anger build got him in trouble. Second, he got caught when he didn't finish people off. Third, don't leave witnesses.

He remembered what it felt like to protect his family.

His wife, his family, his property.

"Jimmy, what did you do?" asked Robin the following day after his pops bailed him out.

He warned her to keep her big mouth shut. He thought about it while in jail and decided this was her fault.

"What did *I* do?" he asked.

She looked at him like she had no goddamn idea what he was talking about.

"Don't give me that look Robin. I told you to stay away from Jamison and those other men," he accused. "But did you listen to me? No—you didn't. Instead, you flaunted your cute ass around," he gave a little demonstration to make it sink in, "turning them on—and a year later they think they have the right to disrespect me? No one disrespects Jimmy."

He had made the dumb bitch quit her job there a year ago. She'd become too friendly with Jamison. Jimmy was no fool—all the men took a fancy to Robin. She was good to look at, but she was his to look at. She said he had an overactive imagination. She didn't love anyone but him. Everyone there knew rudeness wasn't in her nature.

She had tears in her eyes, "I don't know what you're rambling on about. I got you that job. I didn't . . ." she cried, "I never . . ." She paused. "Jimmy, you could have killed him," she whispered.

"Prick is lucky I didn't have a gun on me, or I would have blown his brains out," he blurted out. "And it wouldn't have been the first time."

She inhaled sharply, eyes wide. "You're just saying that. You don't mean it."

"I don't?" His eyebrows rose. "Ask the Stuckers. Oh wait—you can't—because I killed them," he mumbled and walked out.

He regretted the words as soon as they left his mouth. He didn't turn back to see her expression. He turned on the TV, put his feet up on his favorite recliner and fell asleep.

FIFTEEN

THREE MONTHS LATER

W*HY ARE PEOPLE IN MY LIFE ALWAYS FUCKING up?* thought Jimmy.

He watched Robin, taking note of the unusual change in her behavior. Up early, no hangover, sketchy as a teenage boy after watching his first porno. She had been acting that way ever since he beat the living crap out of the asshole Jamison. She was cheating on him. He knew it. Only it wasn't with Jamison. Jimmy finally had some luck come his way with that one. His lawyer told him he could had done some time after assaulting him. No one cared that Jamison deserved it. But in the end, the charged had been dropped from second degree assault to a misdemeanor and Jimmy got probation. Maybe the asshole got Jimmy's message and was afraid he would come and finish the job. Either way, he wanted nothing to do with the asswipe.

Robin was meeting with some dweeb named Ryan Cross.

The lyin', cheatin', simple-minded whore thought he wouldn't find out. Guess what? He did. She'd get hers. Oh yes.

No one disrespects Jimmy!

He played along, just like she wanted him to.

Play along, Jimmy . . .

She kissed him on the cheek before he left for work. He tried hard not to cringe.

Steady, Jimmy.

"Bye Jimmy. Love you," she said.

Sure you do—Bitch!

"Love you, too . . ." he sang, forcing a smile on his face. He should have been an actor. Turning to Isabel, he said, "Bye sweetheart. Have a good day in school. Love you." He meant it. He kissed her on the head.

"Bye, Daddy. Love you more."

He left for work without looking back.

He went through his normal routine at work. To anyone who cared, he packed his truck with the necessary supplies with every intention to head out for a hard day's work. It was a dirty job, but someone had to do it. After he got fired from his last job, he was ineligible for another city job. Suited him just fine. He settled for a small company doing landscape. He didn't mind. He mostly worked by himself and didn't have to worry about some dickweed looking over his shoulder. And no assholes, like his last job, with too many egos measuring their dicks.

He took his time loading up, knowing a call would come in

any moment . . .

"Jimmy," yelled Sammie, their secretary. She ran out the back door screaming his name as he put his last load into his truck.

"Yeah?" he said, holding back a smirk.

"Call," she said, waving the phone in the air. "I think it's your wife." She smiled ear to ear. Miss Sammie thought she was prettier than she was. He guessed she was pretty in her own way. Her teeth were too big though. And he didn't like redheads.

He took the phone. "Thanks, doll."

She blushed.

"Robin—everything alright?" he asked for show, turned and walked out of earshot.

"No. I need my big man to come home and fuck me right now. Me so horny," said a male voice, trying to sound like a woman. Laughter followed. "You owe my girl big time," Anthony said.

"Hey fucktard. Tell her I said thanks," Jimmy replied, looking back over his shoulder. He was alone. "When she thinks you're cheating on her, she can call me."

"Fuck you—and hell no! I'd have to hand her the phone now."

Like he said—Fucktard.

"I thought as much—Bitch." Jimmy said, disgusted. What was he thinking asking Anthony, the whore, for help with his whore wife?

"Sorry about your wife. I hope you're wrong."

"Me too," he lied. "Catch you later." Jimmy hung up, went into the garage and told his fat boss he had to leave. His wife wasn't feeling well and he had to check on her, he worried that she didn't sound like herself.

His boss, an older, fatter, Pillsbury Doughboy—and just as freakishly jolly—bought his sob story. Jimmy liked him. And he liked Jimmy.

So far Jimmy's plan was working to a T. Robin was meeting Ryan Cross at noon. He'd pay a visit to Ryan first. After watching his house a few times, Jimmy knew he worked later hours most days. He guessed since Ryan was meeting someone else's wife for lunch, he'd be home this morning. Of course, Jimmy never fucked around before. What the hell did he know?

All he felt is anger and resentment. If he was supposed to feel anguish, depression, or heartache—he didn't. Nothing close to it.

When he first found the note in her purse, with Ryan's name and number on it, he about shit a brick right there. He searched her phone with no luck. He decided to follow her. Twice she drove to a nice neighborhood. Somewhere she didn't belong. She sat there, watching.

A man.

The man opened his front door to pick up a package the delivery driver dropped off. The moment the man shut his door, she sped off. Jimmy followed her to a hotel where she made a call from a payphone. She pulled out the same paper, dialed and put it back in her purse. That night he checked her purse again, just in case. He was right. Same note. Same number.

He searched who lived at 1368 Berth Circle and her boy Ryan Cross popped up. His wife had Ryan's number, watched him, and called him from a payphone at a hotel. He wondered if that was where they met up and fucked. He had half a mind to blow her head off. He had to look deep inside himself and call upon a more patient version of Jimmy. The patient version who waited a whole year before he carried out his vengeance.

He did it once. He could do it again. He made his mind up that day. He would put an end to her bullshit.

He parked a block away. The neighborhood—quieter than expected—was in a ritzier part of town. Probably had a neighborhood watch. He'd shoot them all if they got in his way. The time of day wasn't his first choice—but the fucknut would not have his wife.

He grabbed his backpack—filled with gloves, mask, hoodie, and gun. Just a normal person, going for a walk. He could pull this off.

Wait—he threw on a baseball cap and sunglasses—better.

He waited for the couple who were walking their dog to pass. Goddamned people and their dogs. Always out walking.

Witnesses, he thought. The nosey kind too.

He could hear it now—we were out walking little Fido here and there was a black truck parked where it shouldn't have been. The Parkers don't have a black truck and their son is away at Harvard . . .

Rich assholes!

Too late now. The couple and Fido were two blocks away before Jimmy got out. He strolled along the oversized sidewalk toward the house and around to the back path—it really was a nice area. He let himself into the backyard and ducked behind the bushes. You can always count on rich people to have lots of bushes for hiding. He changed quickly—ready.

He listened for any noises. No Fido here to shoot. He hoped there wasn't one waiting for him inside. He didn't want to have to shoot one. Not that he minded shooting Fido, he didn't need the gun going off and announcing his presence. Should have brought a knife, he thought. Next time.

He checked the back door, optimistic it would be unlocked. It wasn't. He busted the window with the butt of his gun and let himself in.

The house from long ago flashed before his eyes. He blinked, taken back to that night for just a moment. Darkness, the sound of the TV, the smell of tomatoes, hint of garlic and basil. The aroma made him hungry. After all these years . . . he remembered every detail.

His hand came to his face. Was he losing his mind? Focus Jimmy.

The house was quiet. You could hear a pin drop. The furnishing was modest, in a tranquil, serene sort of way. The fucknut's wife knew how to decorate. Rich folk usually went over the top with their décor. He'd been in many homes, this was not like the rest. He decided he liked the wife. He would spare her if she was home. After all, her husband was cheating on her.

He prowled throughout the first floor, checking each room.

No one.

He stopped dead in his tracks, in the hallway, next to the stairs. A noise came from up above. Walking. Someone was up there after all.

Please be the fucknut.

Jimmy set one foot on the stair and looked up. Damn good house. No creaky steps. He hurried up the stairs stopping short of the door the sound came from. The door was slightly open.

Standing next to the door, holding his breath, he snuck a peek. It was him. The Stuckers ran through his head again. His heart beat faster.

He'd never shot a man before and Ryan wasn't sleeping . . . and he wasn't a kid.

He let out his breath and stepped inside. Ryan turned—staring at Jimmy—his eyes wide. Jimmy froze for a split second. Long enough to catch Ryan's eyes dart over to his end table.

Jimmy pulled the trigger. Two quick shots in the chest.

POW! POW!

Ryan fell back.

Jimmy's ears rang, he heard dogs barking faintly. Muffled.

He took a few steps forward, fired once more, this time aiming for his head, but Ryan moved to dodge the bullet.

POW!

As he pulled the trigger he turned to the door. He heard something. He glanced at Ryan. Missed his head, but there was blood. Lots of blood.

Jimmy ran down the stairs and out the back door.

"No one disrespects Jimmy," he said under his breath. He grabbed his bag on the way out the backyard as he ran back to his truck.

He walked in his house with the bouquet of flowers he'd picked up on his way to Ryan's house. Robin sat at the kitchen table drinking coffee and staring out the window.

"Surprise," he said, holding the flowers out.

She jumped, spilling her coffee. Her hand covered her heart. The look on her face was priceless.

"Jimmy! What . . . what are you doing home?"

"Now is that any way to greet your husband?" he asked. "I bought you some flowers." He gave her a smile from ear to ear, set the flowers on the table, not bothering to give them to her.

"They're lovely. Thank you." Her hands trembled. He wasn't

sure if it was from all the coffee she had or from seeing him. Probably both.

"Let's go for a ride," he said.

"Wha . . ." she was speechless. Just like he wanted her.

"I thought I would get off early and we could take a ride. Just you and me. Like the old days."

"I . . . I wasn't expecting you home. I . . ."

"You what?" he asked, stone-faced. "Did you have plans?"

Her hand went to her mouth, instinctively gnawing her nails. The bitch didn't know what to say.

"No," she whimpered after a while.

"Then let's go babe," he exclaimed, smiling.

She looked around. "Let me get my purse and—"

"No, no. You don't need nothing. This is our time. Nothing to worry about. Let's go," he said.

This was getting fun. Watching her squirm. He could sense the wheels turning in that pea brain of hers. Like Isabel's little hamster running round and round his exercise wheel, with nowhere to go. He could smell the fear.

He stepped closer to her and she flinched, sucking in air. "What's got you all jumpy?" he asked.

"Nothing."

He grabbed her by the shoulder and squeezed. "You need to relax."

He led her out to the garage. She reached for the door handle to his truck. He jerked her back, "Oh no you don't," he said. "I told you. This is our day. I got your door." He pulled her to him and kissed her.

She didn't buy it any more than he did.

He opened her door, kissed her forehead and pulled the handkerchief off her head, stuffing it in her mouth.

Her eyes widened with fear. She tried to scream.

Dumb bitch. That's what the handkerchief was for. He pulled out his gun and pointed it at her head.

"Get in or I'll shoot you," he crooned.

She glanced toward the door from where they had just come.

"Get in or I'll shoot you—and then I'll go shoot your sister," he said in a much firmer tone. He knew exactly how to push her buttons. Susan had raised her after their mom was too ill. She never knew her dad. He'd left them when she was two.

She blinked, tears rolled down her face.

"Is that what you want? Susan dead? After everything she did for you, you want to be responsible for her death?"

She got into the truck. The plastic crunched as she sat on it. He grabbed the zip tie and secured her hands behind her back and then secured her ankles together. Her face, terror-stricken. He shoved her down to the floor of his truck.

"Don't move," he threatened, running back inside to grab her purse and phone. He took her battery out of her phone and tossed them both in a plastic bag with her purse.

He wasn't taking any chances.

Just a little longer and he'd reach Thompson Canyon Trail. He hoped he wouldn't see any hikers this late in the season. You never knew where they might pop out. He looked in his rearview mirror not seeing anything but dust. If anyone was out, he'd have to find another spot. He couldn't risk it.

It didn't take long to reach the fork in the road he wanted to take, the one that led to a four-wheel trail. Not many people took it unless they had a vehicle that could handle it. He highly doubted he'd see anyone out this way. Snow would come soon and they would close the road.

It was nice and rocky. He had to take it slow. He wanted to go further, but he needed to get back. He braked. *This will do.*

He glared at his worthless wife as he slid his hands into his gloves. He still had a high from today's activities. He shook his head thinking about what he'd done already. When he'd killed the Stucker family, he hadn't planned on killing again. But here he was.

"This is all your fault you know." The sight of her with a man old enough to be her dad crossed his mind. "Goddammit, you cheating whore. You just couldn't keep your fucking legs closed could you?"

She didn't respond. She couldn't. Her handkerchief was still shoved deep into her mouth. She looked at him, blinking the same long lashes she once used to seduce him with. Was she trying to send him Morse Code? He sniggered at the thought.

"I killed your boyfriend," he bragged.

She wiggled, not getting anywhere—her hands tied behind her back and ankles tied in front of her—good thing she was small or she wouldn't have fit scrunched down on the floorboard of his truck.

"You no-good bitch. I knew I couldn't trust you." He hit her with his gun on the side of the head. "Shit! Look what you made me do. Don't get your fucking blood all over my truck." He knew she wouldn't, he was too smart for that. He would dispose of the plastic later. He stepped out of the driver side, looked around, still alone. Walking over to the passenger side, he pulled her out of his truck to her feet. "Walk," he said, holding the gun to her head.

She couldn't move.

He pulled out his knife and cut the zip tie, throwing it back into his truck. He pushed her out, down off the side of the road. She stumbled like she'd never been hiking before. He stuck her with the barrel of his gun to get her moving. He wasn't a hiker, or a camper. Why would he? His good for nothing pops never did anything with him. He and his buddies did go four-wheeling on several occasions. The girls liked it. A quarter-mile in, he pulled her by the arm to move her around some rocks, down into a small gully.

Taking her handkerchief out of her mouth, he said, "You have anything to say before you die?"

There was a time he loved this woman. He'd thought he was incapable of love, then she gave him a daughter. He'd hoped for a son, he wanted to name him Will. He decided on Isabel, after Will's high school sweetheart. He missed his brother, but he learned to move on. He made peace with it.

"Please don't hurt our little girl," her voice cracked.

"Now why would I hurt *my* little girl? She ain't a stupid bitch like you."

The day Isabel came into this world, the moment he held his baby girl in his arms his world had a purpose. He was beside himself. Never in his wildest dreams would he have thought he, Jimmy, could be capable of such emotion. He'd gazed at her, his heart full and his life complete.

He glared at Robin.

Isabel had her eyes. It didn't bother him before but going forward he might find it hard not to think of the bitch before him, begging for her life.

Still, better Robin's than his own. He hated his dark eyes. *Dark like my soul,* he always said. Dark like his pops. And every day he looked in the mirror they reminded him of his past.

While he'd been thinking of the day Isabel had been born, his wife begged. "I didn't cheat on you. I only talked to him to convince him to drop the charges against you."

What the hell is she talking about? Jimmy scratched his head. Jamison! It was her. That's why he didn't have to do any time. And here he thought he was just a lucky S.O.B.

The thought of her talking to Jamison angered him more. And she was still lying to him. "I'm talking about your other boyfriend. I guess you have so many you can't keep them all straight."

"What are you talking about?" she demanded. No sooner did the words come out and her expression changed. "I . . . that—"

He'd heard enough. Before she could get the words out, he cocked his head to the side, raised his gun . . .

POW!

Her body fell back. Almost in slow motion—falling between some rocks. She moved to get up.

POW!

He shot her once more, this time in the head. He smiled.

"Not so pretty anymore, are you bitch!" he ridiculed.

A bird nearby cried, *caw, caw, caw.*

"That's right Mr. Crow. She deserved it." He looked at the gun in his hand. "I don't need this anymore," he said, tossing the gun next to her body. He'd stolen it in one of his burglaries, no way to link it back to him.

On his drive back, he considered what he would say to Isabel. He had to report her mom missing. He grumbled. The thought of asking his pops for help, annoyed him to no end. He still didn't think much of him, probably never would. Their relationship improved somewhat after Isabel was born. He stepped up, taking an active part in her life. He remained clean since Jimmy's mom died and he knew they could use the help. Especially after Robin stopped working.

First things first—cover his tracks, then deal with Isabel and his pops.

He acted on impulse, out of jealousy and spite. He didn't think about the consequences of his actions. Not the legal ramifications, but his daughter. Isabel. His little girl reminded him of her momma. She looked like him, poor kid, but she was her momma for sure. He didn't think what it would do to her. Frankly, he didn't think what it would do to him, being left raising Isabel by himself. What if he got caught? What if he went to prison? Isabel would be left with his pops—

The thought sent shivers up his spine. To think what his pops did to him. He wouldn't allow him to lay a finger on his daughter. Why didn't he think it through? Surely there were other ways to make her pay.

Isabel didn't understand. It took some convincing to get her to lie to the police and tell them he and her grandpa picked her up from school.

"Why? Mom told me never to lie. She wouldn't want me to."

"I've been out looking for her. I looked everywhere. I've been looking since this morning when she called me at work. I can't find her . . . and I have to call the police. She's been gone too long. They need to know."

"So why do I have to lie? It's good you've been looking for her."

"Isabel, stop. You're not listening to me. The police—they don't understand. That's not how they see it. They will think I did something to her."

"Why?"

"Stop. Please Stop. Just do as you're told. They always think the worst. It's their job. But if they think I was gone, they'll take me away. Do you want that?"

"No."

"Okay."

"I want my mom," she cried.

"I know you do, but I can't find her. She ain't nowhere I've looked so either she left us, or she'll be walking in that door any minute now."

"Did something bad happen to her?"

"I don't know, I hope not, but I need their help looking for her," Jimmy lied.

She ran to his pops, hugging his waist. "Grandpa, can we go look for her?"

"Not yet. Listen to your daddy now. We're going to call the police and let them handle it. Okay?"

"No!" she cried, running to her room.

"Shit, Pops, I don't know what to do. But I gotta call the cops. Go in there and make sure she doesn't tell them I left."

He gave Jimmy a look of disapproval. "You got yourself into this mess, you fix it."

"Do you really want her to have *no* family?"

"Fine," he said, stomping off.

Isabel cried. The crying wouldn't stop. Eventually, it slowed to more of a whimpering sound. What will she be like when she finds out her mom is never coming back?

"Just tell me one thing," his pops said after the police left.

Jimmy didn't answer.

"Why?"

Silence.

"Can you tell me that, at the very least. Why? What on earth did she do to deserve such a thing?"

Silence.

"If you expect me to keep on lying for you, you better tell me something."

"She cheated on me, okay. Is that what you wanted to hear? That my wife thought I wasn't good enough for her? I couldn't satisfy my wife enough, so she felt the need to go out there and be with another man." Jimmy's face turned red.

"No, son," he said looking down. "That's not what I want to hear. It just doesn't sound like—"

"You calling me a liar? I saw it with my own damn eyes, Pop." His voice getting louder.

"Did she admit to it?"

"Of course not. Why would she? I'm done talking about it. What's done is done." Jimmy stormed off leaving his pops alone in the kitchen.

He cracked the door. It was dark, quiet. Isabel's breathing could be heard from where he stood. He tiptoed in and kissed her on the head. He watched her sleep for a long time. Images of his daughter crying played out in his head.

"It's better this way," he whispered. He couldn't have a lying, cheating bitch raising his little girl. And he'd be damned if he'd let Isabel turn into an alcoholic whore like his wife.

He had planned the Stucker family killing for an entire year and it had paid off. He never got caught. This one snuck right up on him.

He needed time to think—sort things out. Get his head right.

Isabel flinched. Was she having a bad dream?

Jimmy ran his hands through his hair. He wanted to do right by her. Could he do it? Could he have his pops take her for a while?

Just till things calm down.

He hoped they'd never find Robin's body. If he only had more time to dump her body deeper in the woods. Time he didn't have.

Oh hell! he cursed. *Shoulda, coulda, woulda.* Maybe the goddamn animals will tear her fucking body to shreds and eat every last part of her. *That would be something,* he thought smiling.

Isabel moaned and her body quivered as if she could hear his thoughts. Jimmy closed his eyes. His attempt to hide from Isabel's pain didn't work. Her pain was ingrained in his mind.

He did that to her.

He watched her sleep and remembered holding her in his arms in the hospital. All seven pounds something. He had ran his rough finger along her cheek and she'd squirmed.

Starting with her forehead, down her nose, lips, chin, and back across her cheek; he stroked her silky-smooth skin with the back of his finger. When he got to her cheek, she had turned her small red face toward his hand.

"She's hungry," said a voice.

"Hmm," he'd responded.

"Give her to me babe. I need to feed our baby," Robin had said.

"Yes, she does," said the same voice again. "Did one of the nurses go over with you how to nurse?"

"Yes ma'am, she sure did," replied Robin.

"Well I'm right here if you need me," the voice said.

Jimmy couldn't get his eyes off his daughter, then and now. "My baby girl," he whispered choked up, swallowing hard.

"Oh Jimmy, I knew you weren't as tough as you let on. Our baby girl is melting her tough daddy's heart.

"Isn't that the way it should be?" asked the nurse, putting her hand on his arm. Jimmy hadn't even noticed her in the room.

He'd looked at her, her eyes were warm and sincere. Even so, he didn't want to let his baby go but knew she needed to eat to grow strong. He wouldn't let her be a scrawny kid, like he was.

After handing his baby to his wife, he watched her feed his baby girl. The whole routine made his heart heavy. *Amazing,* he'd whispered.

Robin smiled at him. "She sure is hungry," she'd said.

"You're doing great," he told his wife, fascinated. "How do you know what to do?"

"Miss Linda talked me through it. And I think she just knew the rest. Look at her. She knows what to do," Robin smiled, proud. Back then, he loved her, but he loved his baby more.

"Does it hurt?"

"No. Not yet anyway."

"Is she getting any milk?" he'd asked with interest. He couldn't tell.

Robin peered down. "I don't know, I can't tell."

The nurse had come over and said, "She's doing great. Right now, she's getting colostrum. The milk won't actually come in for about two to five days."

"What will she eat till then?" asked Jimmy, immediately nervous his baby would starve. He worried how she would get strong if she didn't eat. Did Robin know any of this? Why hadn't he thought about feeding his baby before. Robin planned on breastfeeding, but he didn't know she wouldn't have milk ready. He knew nothing about colostrum, or whatever it was.

"Colostrum is milk, it's what the mom produces before the *actual* milk comes in," the lady had said, "which takes anywhere from two to five days. The more baby feeds, the more milk mom produces." The lady had paused, looking at Jimmy's worried and confused face. "Don't worry Daddy.

She'll do just fine with what she's getting. Colostrum is actually very important for her at this age. It has antibacterial and immune-system-boosting substances that she needs."

He believed her, trusted her, and she'd turned out to be right.

Now, he took his daughter's momma from her.

He couldn't be around her, seeing the pain in her dark blue eyes. The sorrow and confusion, thinking her mom left—or something worse.

It's much worse.

SIXTEEN

MABEL WATCHED THE KIDS FILE INTO THE classroom and take their seats. She remained hopeful that Janet wouldn't bother to visit her class today.

She wondered how much longer she could maintain this front. She only became a teacher because her grandma suggested it after she graduated high school and still had no idea what she wanted to do with her life.

That's not true, she knew exactly what she wanted to do. She'd fantasized of saving people with Uncle Frankie since the day he started training her. As a child the dream was cute. As she got older and continued talking of protecting people like a super hero, her grandpa didn't find it so cute anymore. She even suggested joining the Army like him and Frankie. Grandpa said no way. She'd be found out.

So here she was—a teacher. Grandma had said, "You want to help kids, what better way to do it?" She was right, in a way. She loved the kids, but this wasn't exactly what she had in mind.

She set down her attendance book and looked out to the pool of faces staring back at her. Some excited, some sleepy, and some sad. The sad faces reminded her of herself at that age. She wondered if someone close to them had died. Or perhaps they got in a fight with their parents, sibling, guardian? Or worse?

She wanted to help and protect them. To take away the pain, the sense of loneliness, of feeling misunderstood. Give them an out. Then the same old question came back to her—is teaching the way to do it?

"Does anyone remember what's first on our schedule today?" she asked. They all worked on their projects last week preparing for their test on the forming of the government and the Constitution. By the not so happy faces looking back at her, they knew.

"Our social studies test," Anna blurted out. One of the smartest girls in class and the only one excited about it.

"Noooo!" Bennie cried out and everyone laughed. She wanted to laugh with them, but Bennie didn't need any more encouragement.

"You're ready," Mabel assured, scanning the worried faces. "You all are."

"Lucky you, Ms. Peters, not having to take it," Bennie grumbled and the class broke into laughter again.

"Yes, Bennie, I'm lucky. And you, sir, get to help me hand them out," Mabel teased winking at Bennie.

"Ms. Peters, I would be happy to," he chirped.

Our class clown, she thought. He preferred to socialize and make kids laugh over doing work and taking tests. He was smart as a whip, though, and didn't have to put much effort forth like most kids. Her challenge was keeping him focused long enough to not interrupt the rest of her students from learning.

Bennie finished passing the tests out. "Thank you for being a team player," Mabel said. Bennie screwed up his face and rolled his eyes. "I saw that," she added.

The class laughed.

Mabel rubbed her temples to get rid of the dull headache that plagued her head all day. She took a deep breath and reminded her students to keep it down. She glanced up at the clock. Ten minutes to go. "Class, let's start wrapping up. Finish up the problem that you're working on. If you don't finish, you'll need to do them for homework tonight. It's due Monday along with your reading. Clean up your desks and anything else you took out."

A few grumbled, but all in all it was a good day. The bell rang, signaling the end of the school day. It was Friday, and that meant no homework, unless you didn't finish work in class. For her it meant grading tests, assignments, and reviewing her plan for the following week. She loathed taking work home. Mabel peeked at her phone and saw she missed a call from her grandpa. Was he calling to cancel dinner?

"Bye, Ms. Peters," Anna said, as she walked out of class, always the last student to leave.

Mabel peered up from her phone. "Bye, Anna. Have a good weekend."

Looking back at her phone, she read her text, *Call me. Grandma and I are fine.* Relaxing, she touched the little orange icon from within the text and waited to hear his voice.

"Mabel—"

"Grandpa." She cut him off. "What's going on?"

"Ryan is in the hospital." He paused allowing her to digest the news. "He was shot earlier today in his home."

The news hit her like a ton of bricks. Nauseated, she dropped the phone and ran to the trash can. She wiped her mouth with the back of her hand, trying to clear her head. She couldn't think straight. She'd known Ryan forever. She couldn't lose him—not after everything he'd done for her and her family.

Lifting the phone back to her ear, she whispered, "Is he going to—"

"We don't know much yet. He was wearing his vest thank God. It stopped two of the bullets, but one hit his left shoulder. That's all I know so far."

She had trouble processing the news. She imagined his wife, Lillian, going crazy . . . and his son—their world coming apart—something she knew all too much about.

"Are you there?" he asked.

"I'm here," she said, slumped over her desk. "How?"

"I don't know. I'm headed to the hospital now."

"NO! What if someone recognizes you?" she asked, bewildered.

"I have to. Lillian needs me and so will Ryan. I've changed over the years."

Briefly Mabel thought of her own mom. Smiling, laughing one moment—then the news came about her dad, there had been an accident and her dad had died—her mom fell to the floor and didn't speak for what seemed like hours.

"That's crazy," Mabel replied. She would not allow her grandpa to put himself in danger. "It'll be swarming with reporters." The line quiet, Mabel thought she lost her connection. "Grandpa?"

"I'm here."

"I'll go," she added.

"What? No! Absolutely not."

They were at an impasse. "We both go."

"Fine," he reluctantly agreed. "We can offer support and sort through this . . . mess."

This time her mind drifted to her man in black. They never did find him. Her cold-hearted killer. The thought sent chills down her spine. What if he was at it again? For all she knew, he always had been.

"Do you think . . ." she went silent for a second. "What if—"

He knew exactly where her mind went. "Don't jump to conclusions. He's a detective. He puts his life on the line every day. I'll pick you up on the way. How does . . . ," she imagined him looking at the watch she bought him when he turned seventy, ". . . four sound?"

"I'll be ready. Love you."

"Me, too."

She shoved her work in her bag, deciding it would have to wait after all. She couldn't think about work, not with Ryan fighting for his life.

SEVENTEEN

THE MOMENT SHE GOT HOME, SHE DECIDED on a run. It would help clear her mind. Lacing up her orange Nikes, she headed out the door. It didn't take long for the man in black to occupy her thoughts like he always did. Six months back in Colorado, and no closer to finding him.

She wanted to find him so badly . . .

The weeks, the months, the years go on. Life goes on and yet he's out there—somewhere. Nothing changes. She can't move forward or side to side—like quicksand swallowing her up. She tries to free herself, but the more she fights the more it pulls her down.

Mabel picked up her pace, running harder and faster as the thoughts devoured her mind. As she neared her halfway point, off Riverfront Park Drive, she stopped at a gas station. She needed water and hated carrying it.

"My day just got a whole lot brighter," the tall, skinny, black man behind the counter exclaimed.

"Hi Andy," she said grinning. *My day just got brighter, too, my friend.* "Good to see your handsome face today." She was fond of Andy. He reminded her of an old childhood friend.

"Shoot, Ms. Peters, you always know how to make a man's day." His eyes lit up. "How are those kids treating you? Have you had to hand out any ass-whoopings yet?" he asked, laughing.

"Ha-ha. You know they're far too young for that. I only hand them out to people who know better. If you really want to know, they're good. Perfect little angels."

"I remember fifth grade and we were no angels—that's for damn sure."

"True statement. Some kids aren't. But I know you were—otherwise you wouldn't have turned out so charming," she said, winking at him. "How's your mom doing?"

"She has good days and bad days," he said, putting his head down. She immediately regretted asking. "My auntie wants to take her in, but I'm not sure if that'll work. I'll have to think about it. Momma's all I have."

"You can visit her, can't you?"

"Sure, but my auntie lives in Tennessee, so it ain't like an easy trip. She asked me to come too. I just don't know if I want to."

"What does your mom want to do?"

"She said it's up to me."

Andy worked hard to take care of his mom. Mabel would miss him if he left, but she knew from first-hand experience the importance of being around family.

"Weigh the pros and cons of moving. Try writing them down. It might help."

He smiled. "Look at you. I ain't your student, Mabel."

"Just humor me. I'll be in tomorrow."

"Whatever."

She narrowed her eyes at him.

"Okay, okay. I'll do it," he laughed.

She felt far better as she ran up her street than she did when she left it an hour earlier. Despite having to cut her run short, she needed the open air and time to think. Colorful leaves danced around with the help of a cool, October breeze. Gorgeous as they were, she hated to see them fall. Once a few had fallen, they all followed suit—leaving the once bushy trees bare and exposed. Exactly how she felt.

When she was twenty she'd decided to get her second tattoo. She'd considered a tree tattoo, one half of the tree with bright yellows to vibrant reds showing off the transforming leaves of autumn. The other half exposing bare branches. Aside from her general love of trees, it would represent her transformation over the years. The exposed bare branches representing how she feels without her family.

But it hadn't felt right. Not yet. She would get there in time.

For now, she had a dragon tattoo that flew high on the back of her neck. It represents honor, bravery, and courage. A reminder to use her skills for good.

You're a natural, don't take that for granted. Being a bully is easy, it's harder to remember your morals, Frankie told her time and time again.

She rubbed her wrist, thinking of her first tattoo. On her eighteenth birthday Frankie and Grandpa put the idea in her head. It had been seven years since she lost her family. A rough seven years, and she was proud of everything she'd accomplished.

She had been both excited and scared. Her grandpa reassured her it would hurt only a little. *Mind over matter,* he had said.

Frankie had told her she'd be fine, she was the toughest girl he knew, tougher than most men. Grandma hadn't agreed with her decision. She blamed the men for talking her into it.

She'd said, "Why you men think an eighteen-year-old girl needs a tattoo is beyond me. She has plenty of years ahead of her to ink her body up like the two of you."

They weren't making her do it. She wanted a tattoo. And she wanted to defend the men who gave her permission.

Grandma often got herself worked up when it came to Mabel. She loved her for it, but sometimes she went overboard. She overheard her grandma, on more than one occasion, tell her grandpa she didn't agree with Mabel's combat training. *She's too young,* she'd insist. She had just completed her training in various martial art styles and weapons training. She had become a mini Frankie.

Frankie took her to see Sam, the tattoo artist who'd applied more than half the ink on Frankie's own body. When they arrived, she thought he had lost his mind. They stood outside Black Widow Tattoo in Southeast Portland. She saw two issues right off the bat.

One—the name. Deadly bite came to mind. That couldn't be good. Two—the little shop was in an older part of Portland; some referred to it as the wrong side of the tracks. Mabel didn't like to judge things by the exterior, but the place scared her. Especially since it meant allowing someone to scar her for life.

All her excitement—gone. She could wait. Her grandma had been right all along.

"I'm not going in there," Mabel had exclaimed.

"Did you change your mind?" her grandpa asked.

"Yes . . . no. I just don't want to get one . . . in there." She shivered thinking about it.

"Why not?" Frankie looked offended.

"It doesn't look safe."

"You're being ridiculous. Would I take you anywhere that wasn't safe?"

"No." She knew he wouldn't, but she still had some doubts.

Frankie held the door open and she stepped in, quickly scanning the room. It looked bigger on the inside. One big open space with little booths set up for privacy. The wood floor caught her eye first—a beautiful dark cherry color, complemented by borders throughout the room—also cherry wood. She expected a dark gloomy space. Instead, it was lively, the walls a dark tan shade, the barriers between each cubical painted dark green, with ivory and brown checkered curtains for privacy. The shop was not what she'd imagined at all.

Her enthusiasm started creeping back, topped with the stupidity she felt for not trusting her uncle to begin with, and shame for judging the place before giving it a chance.

"Hey, Frankie!" yelled someone from the back. "Give me a minute."

"Take your time, Sam," Frankie hollered back.

The place had an energy to it. Every booth had a customer, and no one screamed out in pain. Surely that was a good sign.

One of the tattoo artists looked back at Frankie. "Hey, big guy. Where you been?" He wore a gray fedora and bow tie from what she could see.

"Hey, Zane! Staying busy and hanging with family. This here is one of my old military pals, John Peters and his granddaughter Mabel. She's getting her first tattoo today."

"No shit! And you brought her here?" he asked shaking his head.

Mabel gulped. Was he serious?

"Look at her face," he said laughing. "Just giving you shit kid. This is the best place in Oregon. Shit, the best place in the West."

Sam walked up. "Stop scaring my client, jackass. Mabel, you ready?" Sam asked in a smooth voice.

"Yes." She liked this Sam. He had tattoos covering both arms and coming out of his shirt, up to the middle of his neck.

He caught her staring. "Are you wondering if they hurt?"

Mabel nodded her head.

Sam went into detail on what to expect. Frankie and Grandpa had already explained it to her, but somehow hearing it from him—the person who did the work—put her at complete ease. He talked to her the entire time he worked. He said a few words to Frankie and Grandpa, but mainly focused on his work and making small talk with her. She only closed her eyes and gritted her teeth during the first minute. She concentrated on her breathing and his silvery smooth voice.

He finished before she knew it. She couldn't take her eyes off the small bear on her wrist. Her hand went to her chest feeling for the pendant she never took off. Finding it, she rubbed the little bear between her fingers. Her dad's voice faint, *Hey bear, hey bear.*

"Mabel!" said a gruff voice. "How are you, dear?"

She startled, not immediately recognizing the voice. She'd been deep in thought. "Ms. Benson, I'm good. How are you?" she asked walking toward her.

Her neighbor stood by her fence. Her appearance was off. She was wrapped in a long pink flowered robe and slippers, no makeup or heavy perfume. And today was a blue day. Ms. Benson wore blue every Friday. A flowered maxi dress—one for each day of the week—except Sunday. Sunday was God's day according to Ms. Benson. She alternated between three colorful appropriate Sunday dresses.

"Not well, dear. I've been fighting a cold. Don't get too close," she warned. "I was just getting my mail and saw you run up."

Ms. Benson's fist met her mouth just in time for an explosive coughing fit. She bent forward catching herself on the mailbox. *Ahem-Ahem,* she continued, trying to clear her throat.

Mabel eyed her with disgust written all over her face. "Have you been to a doctor?" she asked, taking a step back. An image of her last bed-ridden cold crossed her mind.

"As appealing as it is to have a young doctor touch this old lady, I know it's just a stupid old cold."

Mabel smiled. Her neighbor, the *dirty* old lady. Always flirting with Lucas and her grandpa. "Ms. Benson, a little old cold can turn into bronchitis or pneumonia if you're not careful."

"Bloody hell, Mabel! You act like I was born yesterday. Now stop fussing over me." Ms. Benson started another coughing fit, this time choking on her phlegm.

Mabel didn't know whether to run or call an ambulance, but the fit ended quickly enough.

"Are you sure you'll be alright? Anyone here to take care of you?" she asked, looking toward Ms. Benson's house.

"I'm fine," she protested, dragging her feet along the sidewalk as she waved Mabel off.

Mabel watched Ms. Benson disappear into her infected house. She couldn't help but worry about her neighbor. She lived all alone in that big house. All her kids, grown. Her son came by to check on her a few times during the week. Mabel hated being sick. She made a mental note to clean everything in her house this weekend.

Making her way into her kitchen, she told herself to check on her neighbor before she left. She wiped the sweat from her face. Her mouth still dry from her run, she poured a glass of water and gulped it down. It instantly quenched her thirst. She eyed an apple—later, she thought.

She put her hair up, started the shower, and stepped into the cool water. Invigorating. What a day she'd had. It was nearing four thirty and so much had already happened. Wishing she could crawl up in a ball, under the covers, and call it a day, she forced herself to hurry out of the shower. There was too much to do.

She dried herself off, tied her hair into a ponytail, and examined her thin face in the mirror. The dark circles were a tell-tale sign she wasn't sleeping well. Disappointed that her face would give her away, she put a few drops of makeup under her eyes and finished with a little powder. Giving up, she slid into jeans and a t-shirt.

She heard the front door open as her phone buzzed. Grandpa had arrived. Hurrying down the stairs, she halted halfway down. Lucas was home early.

"Hi babe, your grandpa just pulled up." He looked disappointed, just as she thought he would. It took her a second to notice the flowers in his hand. "He asked me to get you. You going somewhere?"

"Um . . . I was going to call you."

"Oh. These are for you," he said, presenting the flowers. "I got off a little early to make you dinner tonight. You're favorite—lasagna."

She buried her face in the flowers, sniffing their sweet scent in to hide her shame. "I'm sorry," she said, giving him a quick hug, thinking, *I'm such an ass.* "My grandpa needs me right now . . . ." She thought about telling him about Ryan but didn't want to get into it.

He looked like she'd just punched him in the gut. "I can't win with you. I . . ." He didn't finish, just shook his head in disgust.

"Really Lucas? You want to do this now? This isn't about you!" she shouted, stormed past him and slammed the door. She needed to get away from him. She knew she was being unreasonable but didn't want to discuss it. Not today. Save the fight for tomorrow.

Lucas opened the door and yelled out, "It never is—is it Mabel!"

She grunted and kept walking.

"Get in, Grandpa," she instructed.

Her grandpa got in, saying nothing. Instead of turning the ignition over he sat there. Mabel was too mad to speak. She looked out the window pulling a piece of her ponytail between her lips.

"Mabes," he finally broke the silence. "You know what you need to do."

"I know," she said in a whisper. "Can we go now? I don't want to discuss it right now."

"Sure thing," he said with a smug smile.

"Sorry you had to see that."

"Nothing to be sorry about."

Mabel knew what she needed to do alright. She couldn't keep putting it off. She owed it to Lucas. He was a good man. He didn't deserve this treatment, and even though she really did love him, she wasn't sure she loved him like he deserved. She'd managed to keep her real relationship with Ryan away from Lucas, but now . . . she knew it would cause problems.

As they pulled out of her driveway, Ms. Benson's son

pulled up to her house waving. Mabel felt some relief that her neighbor would not be alone. In her own turmoil, she'd forgotten to check on her.

EIGHTEEN

JUST AS SHE SUSPECTED, THE HOSPITAL WAS swarming with reporters. Grandpa drove around the outside of the parking area.

"It's disgusting," Mabel said. "No privacy. And the killer's still out there. Does it not occur to them that their reporting will only put Ryan in danger? Why advertise where he's being kept? Why advertise his name, his family, his doctor, everything? It makes me sick!"

"Save it Mabel. You're getting yourself worked up over something you have no control over."

"How are we going to get through that?" she asked, pointing to all the people and cars blocking the entrance.

"We'll go through one of the side doors. Doc's already inside. He said to meet him on the west end."

How could he be so calm? Mabel's stomach was in knots. She didn't worry about herself, but she worried about her grandpa. They were taking a risk, even though they were avoiding the cameras and the people who knew him.

As promised, Doc held the door waving them in. He worked at the hospital when needed. It made it easy for him to come and go as he pleased. No one questioned people tagging along with the good Doctor Melvin.

A news story on Ryan caught Mabel's eye as they walked by a waiting area. She stopped, staring at the screen.

"It's been on all day," Doc said.

A police detective was shot in his home earlier today in Colorado Springs, Colorado, around two p.m. Friday. A neighbor reported gunshots and a suspicious man dressed in black exiting the detective's home.

The injured detective was taken to a nearby hospital with three gunshot wounds, two in the chest and one in the shoulder. Reports state that he's currently in surgery. His bulletproof vest protected him from the chest shots, which may have saved his life. Police have not released his name.

The suspect is considered extremely dangerous and a clear threat to law enforcement officers and the public . . .

Her grandpa gently tugged at her arm, pulling her away from the screen. "Let's go," he said in a low voice.

They haven't released his name. Yet. Mabel sighed.

Not knowing what or why this happened gnawed at her insides. She followed Doc, taking in her surroundings. The faces, eyes, mannerisms, loners. Would the shooter show up at the hospital? Would he be that brazen? She caught a glimpse of a man wearing a ball cap, black jeans, black sneakers and an orange Bronco shirt. His eyes were hidden from his ball cap. Was he watching them? Or was it her imagination? He stared at her grandpa for a long time and then turned away when he noticed her watching him.

Another man wore a gray pullover, black sweats, and gray

running shoes. And another wore black slacks, with a black overcoat, and black dress shoes. He caught her looking and smiled at her with bright blue eyes. She noticed his peppered hair and rosy cheeks. She was being paranoid. Everyone was her man in black. Everyone shot Ryan. Everyone was coming back for her.

Her grandpa's step quickened, he pulled her closer and gave her shoulder a squeeze. Her tension and paranoia must have been radiating out of her. She offered him a slight curve of her lips, all she could muster.

Ryan was on the second floor. They took the long way around to the elevators and up to the surgery waiting area. An officer stood by the elevators checking IDs.

The moment she stepped into the waiting room she spotted Lillian surrounded by people Mabel didn't know, except for Jackson and Lillian's father, whose name she couldn't remember.

Lillian spotted them, tears rolling down her face. She ran to Mabel's grandpa, wrapping her arms around him, sobbing into his shoulder.

"Forgive me, John." She wiped his shirt. "Thank you for coming."

He grabbed her by the hand and pulled her to sit down. "I wouldn't want to be anywhere else."

Mabel gave her a hug, "I'm sorry, Lillian." She didn't know what to say. Her own mother flashed before her. Seeing Lillian always made Mabel think of her.

"Mabel," she managed a smile. "I'm so glad you're here. Ryan will be happy as well." Her dark brown eyes, bloodshot from crying.

"How is he doing?" her grandpa asked.

Lillian looked down. Mabel's eyes followed hers and noticed

her hands shaking in her lap. Mabel's eyes drifted back up to her pale face and extra rosy cheeks. Her lip quivered. Even on her worst day, she was stunning. When Mabel cried her eyes swelled up, face spotted, snot ran down her face—*what a God-awful sight,* thought Mabel. She wished she had half the beauty Lillian had.

"I don't know yet. They say the bullet barely missed his heart, but they're hopeful. I wish Doc was the one doing the surgery." She looked around expecting to see him.

"He's back there now. He'll make sure Ryan's well taken care of."

Lillian nodded. "How long are you staying, John?" she asked, with a more serious tone. "You two shouldn't be here."

"Don't worry about us. I hope it's not too soon to ask, but what do you know?"

Lillian glanced at the policemen standing by the door, then looked over her shoulder at the two officers getting coffee. "There was one shooter. Our neighbor, Scott, saw him coming out the back door. He called 9-1-1." She looked around again, speaking in a low tone and shaking her head in denial. "Ryan stopped by the house to shower before heading out to have lunch with a new contact, some woman—and he never made it."

"Are they connected? The shooter and the woman?"

"I don't know. We don't even know who she is. He doesn't give me the details of his clients. The police are waiting for him to come out of surgery."

"Do they have any leads on the shooter?"

"Nothing, besides that he wore a mask, gloves, and dressed all in black." She glanced at Mabel. "Scott assumed it was a man, from his build, but he only saw him from a distance."

"Lillian," he put his hand on hers, "if you need anything at all, just say it."

"Mrs. Cross?" called out a man, walking toward Lillian. He must have been the surgeon or one of the doctors in the room.

"Yes?" she replied, her voice unsteady.

She met him halfway. He spoke to her in a hushed tone.

Doc came out at that time, his face apprehensive. He motioned for Mabel and her grandpa to meet him in another room and shut the door. Away from eyes and ears of the police? Or Lillian too?

"What's going on Doc?" asked Grandpa.

"They did what they could for him. Time will tell. They're moving him to intensive care."

"Is he awake?"

"He came to, but they're only letting Lillian in to see him for a short visit."

"Damnit Doc. Can you get us in there?"

"Sorry, John. It's too soon. Maybe tomorrow. I'll stick around and try to do what I can, but you and Mabel need to get going. I'll call you as soon as I hear anything."

Her grandpa started pacing, his face red. He looked out the small window on the door. "Fine. Call me. Find out what you can from the police too."

"I will."

Mabel opened the door and found Lillian gone. Doc followed them back out the door they came in through. It was dark outside now, a chill in the air. As they drove around the hospital, the news vans were still parked out front.

Neither one of them said a word for twenty minutes. Both in their own thoughts. She thought of Ryan and what lengths he went through to help keep her safe sixteen years ago. She couldn't lose him too.

She sat upright in her chair with her hands out on the table. In spite of her attempt to look poised, she failed miserably. In all John Peters's past observations of his granddaughter, the more proper she acted, the more troubled she was.

"Grandpa, I'm fine," Mabel groaned. "And don't think I haven't noticed the fact that you haven't taken your eyes off me since we left the hospital."

"First off—how did I get us to this restaurant in one piece?—If I had my eyes on you the whole time?"

She gave him a slight smile

"Second," he said, with a scowl on his face, "you sound like me." Her smile grew. He loved her smile. "And you're not a good liar—just like me." Exhaling, he grabbed her hands as her smile disappeared. "What are you doing? You never keep anything from me."

The waiter interrupted the moment and took their order. For being hungry, they both ordered light. Neither of them had eaten since breakfast. He insisted on feeding their bellies. Mabel argued, but he won. Honestly, he wanted more time alone with his granddaughter.

Fear crossed her face. "I waited for the moment to face him for so long. I imagined what it would be like. What I would do. But I never imagined Ryan or anyone else getting hurt."

John wanted to hug her, wipe the tear forming in her right eye. But he held back and let her talk.

"I know it's him. It's me he wants. Everyone put themselves out there to protect me. And what have I done?" Her expression hardened.

Hard on herself like usual, he thought. He fought the urge to shake his head no. It was hard to watch, but he let her continue.

"I lied to you about moving back to Colorado. I moved here to find him, but I didn't want anyone to get hurt . . . ." She shook her head.

"Oh, Mabes, don't be so hard on yourself. I know you. Sometimes, I think, better than you know yourself. The thought of that bag of shit—"

The waiter showed up with their food, the look of disapproval on his face. It was not John's fault he had bad timing.

They ate half their meals in silence, both in deep thought. Mabel was born with a strong heart. That's how she lived through a killer shooting her. That strong heart saved her life. Now that same strong heart would get her through this. How could he help her see that?

She moved her food around her plate.

"What *exactly* are you beating yourself up for?" He reached out for her hand.

She considered his question. "I shouldn't have waited. I should have—"

"Stop!" John said putting his hand up, with his fork. "Stop doing this to yourself. *You* are an incredible person who is capable of more than anyone I know." He squeezed her hand. "But the one thing you suck at is honoring and respecting yourself."

She pulled her hand away from him and reached for her napkin, twisting it. He'd hit a sore spot. He loved the humble side of Mabel, but that wouldn't serve her well when dealing with killers. He knew she was done eating when she continued moving her food around her plate. He motioned the waiter to pick up their plates.

"You're my grandpa, you're supposed to say things like that," she said.

He laughed. "You're damn right I'm your grandpa, but I don't have to tell you anything I don't want to. Look at me."

She looked up from her plate.

"You should have been honest with me. No matter what you thought I might say. We're in this together. Going after a killer, a bad man, takes practice. *Real* life practice. We may have prepared you to fight, but we didn't prepare you in real life scenarios. That's on us—not you."

"What are you saying?"

"I know I've been shielding you, afraid of you getting hurt. That's on me."

"It's not your fault, Grandpa."

"No, it is. I'm a grown-ass man, I can take it."

The waiter looked at John, overhearing his comment—*again*. He's what John would have considered tall, dark, and handsome. But Mabel didn't seem to notice. He was about her age too. The chap was as jolly as Santa Claus, but John guessed he scared the dickens out of him. The waiter cleared their plates and refilled their glasses.

After he left, John continued, "Do you know what Frankie does for a living?

"He's retired. Does side jobs saving people."

"Sort of. He's been asking me for years for you to come work with him."

Her eyes grew with excitement and a small smile made it across her face.

"I told him no all these years." He looked away, ashamed to hear the words come out of his mouth. "If you can find it in yourself to forgive me—" He looked at her. "I only wanted to protect you. But now . . . now I see that I've only been hindering you."

"What does he do?"

"He's the man to call when you want a job done. He mostly works with kidnappings and abductions, but he has taken other jobs too."

"What kinds of jobs?" She raised an eyebrow.

"He's not a contract killer if that's what you're thinking."

The waiter handed John the check. More like tossed it. He had impeccable timing and big ears.

John shook his head. "He's more of a humanitarian. Although, he does have to make a living, so he gets paid to do it. With that said, he doesn't do it for the money. He's helped plenty of people that didn't have money."

"She paused, thinking. "Does he work with the center for missing children?"

"No. Although they have the same mission. Frankie is the one who does the leg work. He finds the missing person and extracts them. His priority is children, but he takes adult cases too."

"So it's dangerous."

"Extremely."

"He's killed . . . bad guys?"

"Yes, more than he'd like. There are too many out there who don't give up willingly."

"He's a hero . . ." she smiled.

"He likes the term 'guardian,'" John said, smiling. "You know the big man and his big ego. But truly, he deserves every bit of it. For every life he saves, he is a goddamn hero." He waited for her to say something. She didn't.

He could see her mind working.

"Did you know there are over four hundred thousand missing children reported every year?"

Her eyes grew. "No. I figured it was high . . ." She paused.

"Why does he do it?"

"That, my dear, is a conversation for you and the big man to have. I'm sure he'd love to have it with you."

"And he wants me to help him?"

"Why wouldn't he?"

"You think I'm capable of doing something . . ." she couldn't find the words, "something that big?"

"In all honesty, I don't want you out there putting yourself in danger. But darling, you are very capable. I've seen what you can do."

"But I doubt myself, you said it yourself. Those children, their lives in my hands . . ."

"Sweetheart, you don't have to decide right this moment, today, or tomorrow. I just thought you needed to hear it from me that I believe in you. I'm ready to let you flourish. Conquer your dreams and overcome your nightmares. Fly if you will. I've held you back long enough. I know you don't like being a teacher. You never have. I made you do that."

"Wow." Her eyebrows rose as she said it. "This is all coming at me so fast. Now you're admitting that I never wanted to be a teacher? And blaming yourself?"

"I guess I am. Do you deny you don't want to be a teacher?" he asked.

"No," she smirked. "But my favorite part of my job is the kids. Not the everyday part of going into a school and teaching."

"That's what I thought. I've known it for some time and allowed you to be miserable."

"I'm not miserable," she defended.

John gave her a look. "Okay. Maybe not miserable, but do what you want to do. If it's with Frankie, great. If not, that's fine too. You want to be an astronaut, go for it. Just be you."

A smile crossed her face. She didn't say anything, just remained focused on his eyes.

"What?" he asked, curious what she was thinking.

"Does that include being Melodi? Melodi Stucker?"

He thought about it for a moment.

Why *wouldn't* she want her identity back? She lived longer as Mabel than she did as Melodi. But being Mabel caused her heartache, held her back. Melodi would set her free. "If that's what you want." He smiled, cupping her cheek in his hand.

Lucas was in bed reading when she got home. "Sorry," he said as soon as she walked into their bedroom. "I shouldn't have pushed you," he continued. She started to speak, but he interrupted her. "Wait, I have to say this." He sat up and motioned her to sit next to him. "Today was a difficult day for you, and I made it about me. If you can, forgive me." He put a loose strand of hair behind her ear. "We can talk more about us . . . later this week."

She opened her mouth to talk. He put a finger gently over her lips to stop her words from coming out. "I know you're struggling with us living together—"

She moved his hand. "Lucas—"

"Not tonight Mabel. It's okay. Later. Tell me—how's Ryan? Your grandma called me and I saw the news."

Her lip quivered, trying to find the words.

Lucas sensed her difficulty, put his hand over hers and squeezed. He didn't speak, giving her time to collect herself. She'd trained him over the years not to push her. That was his reason for apologizing. She didn't deserve him, she knew it. She trained him—how ridiculous was that. Why did he put up with her?

She loved him for it. He told her once she was like preparing a perfect cup of coffee. If he rushed her, she was bitter or bland. If he took his time with her, put a little effort in—she was heavenly, perfect, just right. He couldn't ask for more.

She would have taken offense if it hadn't been true.

"Too soon to say," Mabel said, without looking at him. "He came out of surgery just before we left, but we didn't get to see him."

"Sorry, Mabel. How about Lillian?"

"She's trying to hold it together." She wondered if he thought it weird that she didn't invite him to go with her. For not knowing her past, he knew the few people close to her meant the world to her. She'd do anything for them. Shouldn't that include him?

It should. But he didn't know all her deep dark secrets.

"What are you doing tomorrow?" she asked.

"Uh . . . I'm not sure. I didn't have any plans. You?"

"I'm going to Cheyenne in the morning. Want to go with me?"

"Are you sure you want me there?"

She looked at his face, his eyes—he was serious. "Yes. I do." She did. Part of her did. Part of her wasn't so sure.

"Okay. I'll come then. How about I take my car. That way if you want to stay longer, you can."

She smiled and exhaled. She kissed his lips, holding the kiss for a few seconds.

"I'm exhausted," she admitted, getting up.

Relieved they'd talked, she brushed her teeth, washed her face, and got undressed. Crawling into bed next to him, she curled up against his warm body. She didn't want to be alone.

The night wasn't over, and she knew she'd have nightmares. He kissed her forehead, turned her around and wrapped his arms around her. His body wrapped perfectly around hers. She half expected him to make love to her, but before she knew it, he was snoring in her ear.

She laid that way for what seemed like hours, finally falling asleep in his arms. She was safe.

NINETEEN

DISTURBED BLARED OUT OF HER CLOCK RADIO. Lucas groaned. She rolled over, hit the off button and her head screamed at her, pulsing in pain. Another sleepless night, with a headache on the side—like one too many screwed up to-go orders where they always got the side wrong. You never want to drive all the way back. Calling doesn't do you any good, because the next time you go to get your free order, they screw it up again. A never-ending cycle of pain.

Mabel reached into her nightstand and took two pills, washing them down with leftover water from the night before.

"Another headache?" Lucas moaned.

"Yep," she croaked, heading for the shower.

Would today be the day she relieved him of her complex life?

Lucas made her life easy in many ways and difficult in others. Difficult would be following her to Colorado six months ago. That's when their relationship took a turn for the worse. He didn't know her truth. She never told him. He only knew her lies that her mom and brother died in a car crash when she was young, with her dad. He didn't know her real name, he didn't know anything.

Lucas and Mabel. It doesn't roll off her tongue as fluid as it used to. She'd changed in the past six months and her nightmares came back with a vengeance.

Would her man in black do the same? Or would she get to him first?

The lying—she didn't regret it for years. She understood it. She accepted it. Now it was eating at her sanity.

Mabel threw her yogurt cup in the recycle bin as Lucas entered the kitchen. Her heart skipped a beat at the sight of him. She gave him a peck on the lips. Before she could get away, he pulled her into his arms and kissed her. His mouth warm against her cool lips. Her heart beat frantically. She gave in, kissing him back because she could not deny she wanted him. All of him. She wanted their relationship to work. But as usual, doubts took hold of her. She let go.

"Ready?" he asked, breathing heavily, holding her close, giving her the look that melted her heart long ago. The look that told her she was the only person in his world that mattered. The same look that her dad had given her mom. The same look that had made her fall for Lucas, long ago on that spring day. The look that scared the shit out of her.

"As ever," she said, freeing herself. She couldn't keep doing this to him.

His eyes glazed over. He knew. How could he not? She hated herself for hurting him. He deserved all of her, something she was incapable of. Not now. Maybe never.

Cheyenne, part of the High Plains, was relatively dry and flat. Grandpa's property laid on the southern end, not far from the Colorado border. He bought it off a rancher who'd moved his family to Texas. Grandpa was no rancher, but he fell in love with the stunning landscape and cedar house nestled in the middle. There weren't many spots in Wyoming you would consider stunning, but near the river, you found the greenery. That was the land Grandpa bought. He talked about raising horses, which she would have laughed at a year earlier, but now she could see him doing just that. The peaceful life suited him down to his new cowboy boots and felt hat. She admired that about him. He always found a way to make things work and be happy. He didn't choose to move again, but he made it work for him and Grandma. They were happy here, just like they found happiness together in Portland.

It made Mabel think of what he had told her long ago when she was struggling with her past. *Be true to yourself, Mabel. Be proud of who you are and where you came from. Even the bad times. It may hurt to think about them, but they make you stronger.*

All she could think about was how could she be true to herself if she changed everything about who she was? She lost everything and part of that was her fault.

He read her mind . . . like he usually did and said, *You're alive. Whether I call you Melodi or Mabel—you're alive. Whether you live in Colorado or Oregon—You. Are. Alive. You decide what will and will not impact you—and whether it will impact you positively or negatively.*

They were harsh words for a thirteen-year-old who thought she'd lost everything. But she needed to hear them. She let him in for the first time since her dad died, accepted him for the great man he was. She loved him more than she ever thought possible. He understood her.

Mabel followed him out to the gazebo, where the two of them spent most of their time, simply relaxing and enjoying each other's company. Grandma joined them occasionally, but she spent most of her time painting. Grandma was creative and artistic, unlike Mabel. She'd picked out the most beautiful ivory sectional furniture that lined half of the gazebo around the fire pit. Sitting in it, you had a spectacular view of nothing but trees, grasses, and shrubbery. It felt like a sanctuary.

"Now that I have you alone—tell me about you two. What's going on?" Grandpa asked.

Lucas was in the house talking with her grandma about his family. She knew his aunt and wanted to know how she was doing.

Did her grandpa pull Mabel away for this? She should have known. She looked the other way, avoiding his questions.

"Mabel. It's good to talk. Stop burying your feelings. If you can't talk to Lucas, who else are you going to talk to? Is there some other man I don't know about?"

"No!" Her voice came out higher than expected. "Seriously, Grandpa?"

"Then talk," he said, her reaction not phasing him one bit.

"I'm tired of lying to him. I can't do it anymore."

"What are you saying?"

"I'm saying, if I can't tell him everything, then I can't be with him."

Silence.

"Do you plan on marrying this man?" he asked in a low voice.

"I don't know. Lucas hasn't proposed, but he has brought up the idea of marriage a few times."

"And?" he probed.

"And I avoided the subject like the plague. He hasn't brought it up since we moved."

"So you don't see yourself being with Lucas forever?"

"I don't know."

Why's he pushing?

"What do *you* want, Mabel?" he continued.

"That's just it. I don't know. I don't know if I'll ever know." She paused hoping he'd change the subject.

He didn't. He waited for her to continue.

"There's a hole in me that I've tried to ignore over the years, but it's there. I need to deal with it. A hole that Lucas can't fill or anyone else for that matter. The part of me that was stolen when my family was taken from me" she swallowed hard. "I can't get past it. It's . . ."

"It's what?" he asked.

She took her time. Trying to articulate what she wanted to say was difficult. Their talk last night helped, but she hadn't told him everything. "It's all coming back, Grandpa." She avoided his eyes. He knew she had nightmares, but he didn't know how bad they had become. "I never told you this because I thought you would be mad at me . . ." It was coming out all wrong. ". . . It all points back to my man in black. He's still out there, and my nightmares are worse." She met his eyes, afraid of his reaction.

Grandpa wasn't looking at her. His eyes fixed, looking off into the house somewhere. He finally said, "I'm sorry, Mabel. I didn't know."

"How could you? You can't always protect me. I need to find him."

"What? What do you mean—*you* need to find him?"

"I'm done. I'm done being a coward. I'm done doing nothing. I'm done—"

"Mabel," He put his hand on her arm to stop her. "Have

you thought this through?"

"No. Not really. I've been too busy hiding, keeping it from you, and keeping everything from Lucas, and having nightmares, and falling apart," she said, rambling. "Don't you see? I can't go on living this way. I just can't."

And there they came—as hard as she tried to fight them back—the tears sprung to her eyes nonetheless.

"We do this together."

"I appreciate the offer, but this is something I need to do on my own. I need to face him."

"You're pushing it."

God, that's where she got it from. Heaven forbid she go too far.

"I'd never forgive myself if anything ever happened to you or Grandma."

"And you think I would be able to forgive myself if anything ever happened to you and I did nothing?"

He's right. Like always. "Fine. You're the brains. Let's solve this—together."

"But first, can we focus on Ryan?"

"They're connected."

"What would make you say that?" he asked.

"It's a feeling I get. Not to mention, dressed all in black, attempted murder of the detective that investigated the case of the man in black sixteen years ago. *That* doesn't make you think it might be connected?"

"Well, it's a coincidence, but no, I don't think it's the same man.

"How can you not?"

"How can you? It's been sixteen years. What makes you think the same man came back for Ryan?" Before she could answer he continued, "Because if he went after Ryan, then he must know who you are. If that were the case, then why didn't he come for you instead?"

"You saw Lillian's face. She thought the same thing."

"She thought of a memory, a bad memory. Just like you. That doesn't make the two men one and the same."

She couldn't argue with his logic, but that didn't change her mind. "Fine. Either way, I'm finding him."

"I know you will. I'll do some digging. But right now, what are you going to do about Lucas?" he asked, never leaving a stone unturned.

She sighed, wishing he wouldn't probe. "I can't think about a future with Lucas until I've dealt with my past."

He dropped it.

She checked on Lucas before meeting her grandpa in the barn. Grandma had him all to herself and enjoyed every minute of it. Mabel couldn't avoid Lucas and either they moved forward together, or apart.

Mabel and Grandpa spent the rest of the morning sparring in the barn. She noticed Lucas watching in awe. She heard him sneak in and take a seat. He knew she could fight, he just didn't know how well.

"Lunch is ready," he said, after five minutes passed.

"We'll. Be. Right. There." Mabel said in-between punches and kicks.

"Lucas, you're next," announced Grandpa. "I need a break."

"Uh, I don't think so. I need my bones, thank you."

He laughed. "Oh, come on. You mean to tell me you two have been together for . . . what, like six or seven years and you still haven't gotten into the ring with her?"

"No, Sir. She kicks my butt running too, so I like to work out with my weak friends to boost my ego."

"Hahaha," Grandpa laughed louder. "Sometimes I do the same," he admitted.

As she entered the gas station, a blonde clerk smacking her gum behind the counter greeted her. *Where's Andy?*

"Good for you out running," the blonde clerk called out. "Wish I could get off my fat ass . . . oh, excuse my language," she said looking around, "get off my rear and go run. Of course, I'd barely make it to the corner before falling over and passing out." She laughed at herself.

Mabel handed her a bottle of water. "Where's Andy?"

"You know Andy?" she squealed. "A pretty lady like you?"

"Well he's not my boyfriend if that's what you're getting at," she replied, annoyed that her friend Andy wasn't working. She looked forward to seeing his smiling face.

"Oh, I meant no offense sweetie. It's just that Andy, you know . . . you just don't seem the usual girl . . . friend that comes in looking for him. That's all," she said, looking Mabel up and down. "That will be one-o-seven, hon."

"Not your sweetie or your hon," Mabel said as she handed the babbling clerk her money. By the look on her face, not many people stood up to her. "Not a big deal, he's usually the one here when I come in. I can't remember the last time he wasn't."

Mabel had met Andy on her first run, six months ago. He never let her forget the *ass-whoopin'*, as he put it, she laid out that day. A couple of white, punk, asshole boys—she guessed eighteen or nineteen—came in making snide comments about the black boy behind the counter.

Andy was no coward, but he had been in trouble before and didn't want any part of going back. The new Andy bowed his head and hoped trouble would go the other way.

Andy asked them nicely to leave. One of the assholes looked at Mabel and winked. She told them, *the gentleman asked you to leave—now pay for what's in your hands and get out.*

That made them angry. In a way, she'd hoped it would. One of them reached out to grab her arm and found himself on his back so fast he didn't know what happened. The other asshole gawked in disbelief, as his friend asshole lay on the ground holding his balls. They would hurt for some time.

He helped his asshole friend with the hurt balls up and they left.

Andy jumped up and down, one hand pointing at the assholes—mocking, the other covered his mouth, *Wahahahahahaha! Woooooohahahahahaha!*

They've been friends ever since.

"Oh. Didn't you hear? Someone robbed us last night, and poor Andy was the one working," the babbling clerk said, her gum smacking returning when she stopped talking.

And here she thought her day was crappy enough. She'd been wrong. She tried to be optimistic, but that never seemed to work in her favor.

"No, I didn't know. Sorry to hear that. Is he hurt?"

"He's shook up. Can't say I blame him. He's got a big knot in the back of his head where they hit him with the butt of the gun. He'll be okay though. He's taking some time off. It was one guy, wore a mask, but don't they always?" she asked as she babbled on and on.

"What color?"

"What?"

"What color was the mask? What color was he wearing?" Mabel asked, fully aware she was being paranoid.

"I don't know," she said, giving Mabel a worried look.

"Do you know when he's coming back to work? I'd like to check on him."

"I think he'll be back in a few days. I told him to take more time, but Andy needs the money."

She regretted asking. Babbling clerk talks too much.

"He really can't afford to take any time off and stupid worker's comp ain't worth fighting with," she continued. "I don't know how it all works, but he said he don't want to deal with it."

Mabel grabbed a receipt nearby, wrote her number on the back and handed it to the babbling clerk. "Tell him to call me. He'll know who I am."

The babbling clerk looked at the number, mouth open and speechless for the first time since she entered.

Mabel rushed out the door, gulping half her water down before she reached the parking lot. Cutting across the lot, her mind spinning, she bumped into a family coming out of a Tom's Pizzeria. A little boy, about six or seven with sandy hair, was speaking a million miles an hour. The dad held the mom's hand as they walked, the boy led.

"Excuse me," said the mom and dad at the same time. They looked into each other's eyes and smiled.

"I'm sorry," the mom said. "We were both focused on our boy here and weren't watching where we were going."

"No, no. It's my fault," Mabel confessed, choked up. "Have a good day," she added, running off before she began to cry in front of them.

She felt anger and hate swell up inside her. She tossed her half empty-bottle in the trash and continued her run. She cursed herself for not teaching Andy any self-defense moves. It may have helped him last night.

Thoughts of her friend were replaced by Ryan Cross. She

had just seen Ryan a couple of weeks ago at her grandpa's. He made it a point to mention something good about her dad every time she saw him. She liked hearing stories about her dad from someone who cared about him. Best buds from diapers through college, he would say.

Everything else was a blur as she ran past the line of houses and made her way to the river trail. She ran past bikers, runners, and dogs walking their people.

Why don't I have a dog? she thought. Dogs she could do.

Her grandpa picked her up again on Sunday to visit Ryan. Doc somehow had Ryan moved into his private infirmary. Since there was a cop killer on the loose, no one argued. She guessed he wasn't taking any chances.

"How's Ryan?" Mabel asked as they merged onto I-25 Southbound.

"Recovering. He's going to be fine."

Mabel watched him as he spoke, half hearing what he was saying. She hadn't noticed before, but her grandpa was getting old. Sure, she knew he was getting up there—he turned seventy-three this year—but he was one of the fittest people she'd known. He still is to an extent, but she could see the years finally catching up with him. She didn't know what she would ever do without him and didn't want to think about it—ever.

Doc stood at the door looking down either side of the street. *He's just as paranoid as me, she thought.* She wondered if he'd noticed the green Volkswagen parked two houses down with a man sitting behind the wheel. Or the two ladies walking their two dogs, a white standard poodle and light brown terrier. Or the blue van with tinted windows and California plates.

Doc hugged her and led them to Ryan's room.

The first thing Mabel noticed was the smell. The impact blasted her all at once. The odor of cleaning supplies and medical equipment—suddenly she was eleven again—laying in the exact bed Ryan lay in. She froze. Her mind swirling with memories. She hadn't anticipated it all coming back this way. She had visited Doc's house a couple of times since she'd been back but always stuck to the living area.

"Mabel," croaked Ryan. "John?" he questioned, seeing the look on Mabel's face.

Doc led Mabel out of the room to the kitchen. "Sorry, Mabel. I didn't think. You alright?" He offered her a tall glass of water. "Here. Drink this."

She sat on the ivory leather stool, watching Doc, as he moved around the kitchen.

Her mouth dry, she gulped it too fast. "I don't know what came over me," she said, looking at his worried face. "That room . . . I was taken back. Is that weird?"

"Not at all. I should have taken you in there sooner. Not waited till Ryan lay . . ." He shook his head. "It was stupid of me."

"I'm fine now. I want to see Ryan," she said standing up. "He probably thinks I've lost my mind."

He watched her carefully. "If anything, he's worried and wants to know you're feeling alright. Sit," he demanded. "How are you doing Mabel?"

"I told you, I'm fine."

"No, I mean . . . we haven't talked about how you're coping, and with the current events . . . Ryan I mean. I would imagine it may bring up some old feelings."

She sat back down. Did it show, or did Grandpa say something to him? It didn't matter, either way, it felt good to finally talk about it with people who knew the real Mabel. After asking her a million questions, he finally asked the one she dreaded—had she been seeing Jill, her therapist since she'd been back. She had but canceled her upcoming appointments. They weren't helping. He didn't judge her like she thought he would. She told him about her plans to find her man in black—again, no judgment.

"I'm here for you," he replied, his eyes telling her what she needed to know. He would do the same thing. He didn't expect anything less.

Grandpa interrupted their conversation, taking a moment to look her over. "You ready to see Ryan? He's asking for you."

She smiled, "I am," she said standing. "You coming?" she asked when he didn't follow her.

"No," he shook his head. "You two catch up." He paused. "Oh, and Mabel?"

"Yes?" she replied.

"Try not to grill him about what happened. I'll fill you in later."

"Okay."

Mabel took a deep breath and slowly turned the doorknob. Her stomach turned as she entered the room. She forced a smile on her face—for Ryan.

"Hi," she said, giving him a kiss on the cheek.

He grinned, his eyes looking tired. "Mabel. It's so good to see you. I heard you and John came to visit me a couple of days ago. Sorry I missed you."

"Well, you were kind of busy. We forgive you."

She sat on the chair beside his bed, terrified. Her heart aching for the man who put his life on the line daily. He took all the necessary precautions to keep himself safe, to come home to his family at the end of the day. Ryan was a smart man. A man who wore his bulletproof vest to every meeting, every mission, every time he was out in the field. He should have been safe in his home.

"Are you hearing me? Mabel?"

"What?"

"Did you hear what I said?"

"I'm sorry Ryan. I—"

"Be careful Mabel. You hear me? Watch yourself."

"What are you talking about?"

"Your grandpa told me what you're planning."

Her first instinct was anger at her grandpa. She then realized he was being protective—as always—planning and getting everyone involved. Why tell Ryan though? It's not like he can help in his state. She'd have to find out what her grandpa hoped to accomplish by adding to Ryan's stress.

She didn't know how to reply to the man who had investigated the murders. How do you tell the man who *didn't* solve the crimes against you, that you couldn't go on living and you would do what he couldn't?

"I'm older now," she said.

"Every part of me wants to tell you to leave it up to the police, the . . . detectives . . . but you did that, and look where it got you."

"Ryan please. I don't blame you."

"I know. What I'm trying to say—is I would do the same thing. If I could be out there right now—hunting the man who did this to me—I would. Believe me, I would. I don't blame you—one bit." He reached for her hand. "Please don't go at this alone. Let your grandpa help. Call Frankie."

"I will," she promised.

"I'll give your grandpa whatever he needs to help you."

He'd put his career on the line for her once before and he

was doing it again. She walked out of the room knowing if she found her man in black, she would find Ryan's shooter as well. This would be for him too.

"Where's Donna?" asked Mabel, joining Grandpa and Doc in the large living area.

"She's with her sister who got into another argument with her husband. Donna's supporting her," he said, rolling his eyes. "She'll be home later."

"It's hard to find great men like you and Grandpa."

"Thanks, Mabel," he said smiling.

Grandpa got right to it. "Bottom line is, Ryan wasn't able to give me or the police much information," he started. "Ryan got a call from a woman a few weeks ago. She claimed to have information for him about a previous case he worked. She refused to give him any details over the phone, including her name. He said she seemed superficial—his word, not mine. He believed she was crazy, but he wasn't about to pass up a tip, no matter how bad it sounded."

"Did he ever meet with her?" Mabel asked.

"No. They set up several meetings and she never showed. Friday, the day he got shot, was their next scheduled meeting. He told her to stop playing games with him. If she didn't show up that day, she could go down to the station and make her report. She insisted she had to talk to him."

"Then she had something to do with this. Did she set him up?"

"Could be. The police are investigating. Ryan already traced the first call. It was made from a payphone. If the rest came from a payphone, they may never find out who she is."

"Cameras?"

"They're checking. Hopefully something comes up," Grandpa said not taking his eyes off Mabel. He settled into the sofa next to her. "The description he gave of the man that shot him, it matches."

Doc took a deep breath, as his eyes drifted to Mabel and back to her grandpa. He straightened his posture in the chair, visibly uncomfortable by the silence.

It shouldn't have surprised her to hear the words, yet she was speechless. "Come on," she said after a minute, breaking the silence. "We're closer," she said, convincing herself, ignoring the unease and anxiousness she felt running through her body.

Her grandpa ran his hand through his hair and started rubbing his hands together. Mabel could feel his frustration. He finally looked at Mabel, put his hand over hers and squeezed.

She couldn't be there anymore. She tried to keep her composure, change her thoughts, but what she needed was a change of scenery.

TWENTY

HER GRANDPA AND GRANDMA WERE IN THE kitchen making breakfast. They shouldn't have. She'd have told them so, but it would have hurt their feelings. They liked taking care of her. Grandpa never slept past five-thirty. Mabel never woke before six.

She opened the cupboard and found the ibuprofen, taking two and washing them back with a glass of milk. She only drank milk at their house. Weird, now that she thought of it. For some reason, it tasted good in their house. She had even bought the same brand for her home, but it wasn't the same.

She had thirty minutes to eat, finish getting ready, and get out the door. She caught her grandpa staring at her. She smiled with one cheek full and said, "What?"

"Nothing. It's good to see you eat like you used to. You need some meat on your bones."

"This is the way food should taste," she said. "You know I'm not a very good cook."

"If you would've sat still for a minute dear, you might have learned something," Grandma said.

"Grandma! I'm offended."

"Sure, you are," Grandpa said. "Now eat up and get your butt on the road. We don't need you driving like a nut out there."

Mabel gasped, embellishing the moment.

"I've seen you drive," he said.

"What is this?" asked Mabel, laughing. "I spend time with my two-favorite people in the whole world and they bust my chops. Fine," she said, stuffing the last bite in her mouth. "Promise you'll call me the moment you hear anything about Ryan."

"You know I will."

Maria Wilde, the school administrator, called out to Mabel as she walked into the school. "Good morning Mabel. Ms. Strom asked me to get you. She wants to see you this morning, first thing."

Not again!

"Uh, okay," she muttered. "Thanks for the message."

Finding the door open, she tapped the door frame with her knuckle. "You wanted to see me?" she asked.

Janet looked up from her computer wearing glasses. Mabel seldom saw her in them. She took them off before speaking. "Ah yes. Mabel, good morning. Sorry to stop you once again in the morning, but I wanted to make sure you received my message about a new student, Isabel, she starts today in your class."

"Oh. I didn't realize," she said, looking at her phone.

"We didn't receive notice until late yesterday. I probably should have called you. Anyhow, she starts today. We don't have a lot of information on her. From what I know, she moved here on short notice and is now living with her grandpa. We're waiting on her school records. Sorry to spring this one on you, but I think adding another girl will work best for your class. Once we get her records and learn a bit more about her, we can make an informed decision about whether we need to move her, but I'd prefer not to do so once we place her. I tried to get her grandpa to hold off for a couple of days, but he wouldn't have it. You okay with that?"

"Absolutely. Thanks for stopping me this morning. I better get to class and get a seat ready for her."

Janet considered Mabel, "I'll pop in later today to see how things are going."

Mabel hurried to class to prepare. A new girl would help ease her mind. Unexpectedly, she felt shame for looking forward to a new student to help ease her own pain.

This girl's distress and anxiety of moving in with her grandpa, moving to a new town, new school, everything rushed—Mabel knew all too well what that felt like—it wasn't a good situation.

Today was about Isabel, not Mabel. She'd do what she could to make it a trouble-free, easy day for her.

The bell rang for class to start and the new girl had not yet arrived. Mabel called out the first name on her list when the door opened. Every head turned, including Mabel's, to gawk at the commotion. Principal Strom walked in, followed by a girl wearing a frayed blue dress, her short blonde hair in disarray. She moved a piece of her hair from her lips as she looked at Mabel, revealing deep blue eyes—eyes that would have been absolutely striking if it weren't for the redness and dark circles taking them over.

She'd been crying.

Mabel's heart sank, remembering how many times she cried. She'd been thankful her grandparents homeschooled her. What on earth could this girl be going through?

Principal Strom moved to the front of the class, resting one hand on Mabel's forearm.

Mabel glanced at Janet's hand, realizing she'd been absently rubbing the little bear tattoo on her wrist. The tattoo she got when she turned eighteen.

Her eyes darted up to meet Janet's as she quickly dropped her hands.

"Isabel, this is your teacher Ms. Peters." She gave Mabel a look that asked if she was okay.

Mabel nodded yes. She felt her face blushing.

"Ms. Peters, meet Isabel, your new student," she added, putting her free hand on Isabel's shoulder.

"Hello, Isabel, welcome to our class, we've been expecting you," Mabel said, forcing a smile. She could not let this girl see how she was affecting her.

"Hi," she said, peeking a glance at Mabel. "Sorry I'm late," she added, lowering her gaze.

"Class—this is Isabel, please welcome her to our classroom," Mabel said with too much gusto.

"Hi, Isabel," the students shouted in unison.

"Isabel, why don't you sit in that row, there—behind Anna." She pointed toward the empty seat. Anna waved, smiled, and patted the desk behind her.

Isabel smiled back at Anna.

"I'll come chat with you in a while," Mabel said, as Isabel walked to her seat. "Principal Strom, will you be joining our class?" she asked, directing her attention toward Janet.

"Not today," she replied. "I just wanted to personally walk our newest student to her first day of class." She turned to the class "Bye, class, see you for lunch."

"Bye, Principal Strom," the class shouted back, as she walked out the door.

Once the class settled in, reading their chosen books, Mabel asked Isabel to join her at the round table near the back of the class. The girl pulled a chair out, careful not to drag the legs on the ground. She was taught politeness, a good quality.

"Isabel, I'm glad to have you in our class," Mabel said in a quiet tone, making sure to not disrupt the class.

"Um, thanks." Isabel busied her hands, not sure what to do with them.

"I'll tell you a little about myself first and then I'll give you a chance to tell me about you. How does that sound?"

She nodded.

"Well, this is my third-year teaching fifth grade and my first year here at Northridge Elementary. I moved here from . . . ," Mabel stopped herself, not sure she should go on. She had always hated talking about herself. When she did, she sold her lies well, but it still left her feeling uncomfortable. She learned to stay guarded. But Isabel was just a kid and she needed her to feel comfortable around her. "I moved here from Oregon, where I grew up. I always wanted to live in Colorado, so here I am." She felt a knot in her stomach.

"Do you have any kids?" she asked, interested.

"No, I don't. Not yet."

Isabel looked away, she was losing her. "I . . . I moved here to live with my grandpa," she said, still looking away. Tears formed in her blue eyes.

Mabel felt an instant connection. A connection she couldn't explain. She wondered if other teachers had similar connections with their students, this quickly. She fought the urge to take Isabel and hold her. Tell her everything would be okay.

"I used to live with my grandparents," Mabel said.

"You did?" Isabel gulped, eyes wide, her attention back on Mabel.

"Yes." Mabel glanced at her wrist. "When I was young . . . like you. They raised me." Mabel had to change the conversation, this was too much. She needed Isabel to do the talking. "How about you?"

"Um, I . . . didn't always live with my grandpa." She looked away with tears in her eyes. "Before . . ."

Before what?

Something happened she didn't want to talk about. Whatever it was, it was clear she wasn't ready to talk about it. "You don't have to talk about yourself if you don't want to. Just know that I'm interested in getting to know you better. If I can help you in any way, I'm here for you."

"Grandpa didn't even come meet you."

"Would it be possible for me to meet him? I think it would be good if he knew who your new teacher was. I want him to know I'm here for you."

"Sure," she said with a half-smile.

"What's your favorite subject in school?"

"I like to read." She lit up, life coming back. "And draw," she added, "so I guess art."

"What's your favorite book?"

"I like anything, really, but I'm reading *Moon Over Manifest* now and I really like it. I want to read the *Twilight* series, but my dad says I'm too young—which is just silly—I already saw a couple of the movies at my grandpa's and they weren't scary."

She has a dad. Now to find out if he is around and where her mom was.

"Our library day is on Friday. Although, we have plenty of books over there to get you started." Mabel pointed at the books across the room, relieved to get the girl's mind on something else. "Why don't you go pick out a couple while I check in on everyone."

"I can really take some home with me today?"

Mabel couldn't help but smile. "Sure, just write your name down for whatever books you take. Then on Friday, you can check out three books in the Library."

"Wow, thanks Ms. Peters."

"You're very welcome. After you pick out your book, take a seat and read quietly for the rest of reading time."

She was already on her way to the books before Mabel could finish. She watched her with mixed feelings. Would she be alright? It was hard to tell with kids.

Mabel had lost so much. She couldn't compare herself to Isabel. She would take it day by day. Perhaps she would get a better feel when she met Isabel's grandpa.

Mabel had no idea what to expect from Isabel, but she was getting along fine for her first day in class. Turns out Isabel is friendly, drawing kids to her with little effort. Mabel suspected Bennie had a crush on the new girl.

Walking over to her desk she asked, "Isabel, are you riding the bus or is someone picking you up?"

"My grandpa is picking me up."

"Good, I'd still like to meet him. Is that alright with you?"

"Okay," her face lit up. As the day went on, she warmed up to Mabel. Not the same closed-off kid she showed up as this morning.

"Ms. Peters . . . Ms. Peters . . ."

Looking through the hodgepodge of parents, grandparents, and kids, she spotted Isabel.

She approached with an older man, pulling him by the hand, weaving through the maze of kids and parents. "Ms. Peters, this is Grandpa Will," she called out from across the lawn.

Pleased that Isabel remembered, she watched him bump into people as Isabel pulled him through the crowd. In a crude way, she found it hilarious. Kids don't care—they only have their end result in mind. Her grandpa apologized to those around him, as Isabel moved in and out, somehow, not bumping into a single person.

When they reached Mabel by the flagpole, Isabel's grandpa was looking down at his shirt, tucking it in.

"Hi, I'm Mabel Peters, Isabel's teacher. It's very nice to meet you," she said, reaching out to shake his hand.

"Good day Ms. Peters," he said, half-heartedly. "My name is Wilbur, Isabel's grandfather . . . or as she calls me—Grandpa Will." He smiled, looking at his granddaughter.

She paused momentarily, taking note of his dark eyes. She could see on this bright sunny day, that his eyes definitely had a hint of dark brown in them. They looked so familiar, yet kind.

Isabel touched her hand, bringing Mabel out of her rudeness. She smiled. "Wilbur, sir, I'm glad I got a chance to meet you, thank you for taking a moment out of your day."

He raised one eyebrow. "Well Isabel here didn't give me much of an option, did she?" he said rubbing her head.

"No, I guess she didn't," Mabel agreed. "If you want information about the school, our class, a tour—anything at all—let me know." When he didn't respond, she continued, "We also have student conferences coming up in a few weeks. Hopefully, you can make it." She tried to sound excited, but he made it hard. "Isabel is adapting well in class and already made friends. I can see she is a bright kid with a great personality. Her friendliness draws all the kids to her." She said breathlessly. She was rambling. "She's a natural leader."

"Yes, she is. Always has been," he said proudly. "It's good to meet you, Ms. Peters." He nodded, grabbing Isabel's arm, pulling her away.

He was clearly done with their conversation. *He doesn't like me,* thought Mabel, feeling defeated.

"Bye, Ms. Peters, thanks for the books," Isabel called out. "See you tomorrow!"

"Bye, Isabel, see you tomorrow."

Well that didn't go as well as she hoped. Maybe if she didn't act like a freak every time she met a man with black eyes.

She let out a heavy sigh as she walked back to her classroom.

On her daily run, she thought about the night she lost her family. The plan was to have dinner at her grandpa's that night, but they didn't because of her stupid fight with her mom. She had given the killer exactly what he wanted. Knowing that haunted her every day.

Thing is, the man in black wouldn't have known they had plans. He expected them to be home that night. He was watching them.

No matter how many times her therapist, the doctors, the police, her grandparents—everyone—claimed she was not to blame, she knew better. If her family would not have been home, her mom and Pete would not have died that night.

Would the killer have waited for them to get home? Maybe.

Would he have come back the next night? Maybe.

Truth is, there are too many unknowns to predict what would have happened if he found the Stucker house empty that night.

"Ow!" Mabel yelped. *What the fu—*

"Ma'am, I'm so sorry. Are you okay?" asked a man towering over her crumpled body.

Ma'am? She scrunched up her face in pain. One minute she's running and then *bam*, she's on the ground.

"I . . . I think so," she stuttered, looking at her skinned and bleeding hands. Her mind drifted to that night when she fell and skinned her hands. She began to cry, uncontrollable tears flowing down her face. Her hands instinctively found her eyes, attempting to wipe away the tears—but in the process, she smeared blood on her face. She lost control, her thoughts taking over, buckets of tears streaming down her face. She hadn't cried this much in—she couldn't remember how long.

"I don't think you are," his smooth voice said. "Let me help you up. I'm parked around the corner at the park—over there," he said, pointing. "Just around the pond. My name is Mike. I'm sorry I knocked you down. I didn't see you coming around the fork. Those damn bushes. I'll write to the city to get them trimmed."

Was he serious?

Normally, Mabel wouldn't allow someone to take care of her, aside from her grandparents, but there was something different about this man. She made no attempt to shake him off when he helped her to her feet and didn't pull away when he hung onto her wrist longer than needed.

Ouch—her butt, sore and probably bruised. Her hand instinctively rubbed her left cheek. She most likely looked like crap, but she didn't care. She looked up at his worried face, his attractive, sweaty, but still gorgeous face. His eyes, tender and caring. He smiled. Stunning.

Stop! This wasn't like her.

"I'm Mabel. And it's not your fault. I've had a bad day and wasn't watching where I was going."

"Mabel, it's nice to meet you. Although, I wish it were under better circumstances," he said, flashing his straight white teeth. "I have some wipes in my truck for your face. You have some blood on it and I have band-aids." He blushed. "If you haven't guessed already—I'm a dad, so I'm always ready for a booboo," he added with a serious face, and broke into his gorgeous smile again.

Mabel grinned, "Well, Mike, your preparedness worked out in my favor today."

Dad?

When they got to his truck, she cleaned herself up letting him bandage her hand. She told him she would do it, but he insisted, and she didn't argue. She could tell he was a good dad.

"I feel terrible. There's a little café on Main Street that has a variety of healthy drinks. Care to join me?"

Her eyes glanced at his left hand. No ring. He could have taken it off to run. If she didn't have Lucas and she wasn't meeting her grandpa—maybe. Although, it didn't sound like a good idea.

"I'm fine. Really. You've already been a huge help. I need to get going. Thank you . . . for the invite."

"It was nice meeting you, Mabel. Hopefully, we'll run into each other soon."

She watched him get into his truck and drive off. As she started running again, making her way back home, she thought about how he miraculously changed her mood. Was it his deep voice, gorgeous face, or how he was a gentleman?

Oh, God. She probably gave him the wrong impression.

TWENTY-ONE

MABEL PRAYED THERE WERE NO POLICE waiting for speedsters. If there were, she'd be a sitting duck, be pulled over, given a ticket, and be late. Grandpa wouldn't judge. He would just give the look that said he didn't like her putting her life at risk. He'd left her a message saying to meet at his place at five.

Mabel did some of her best thinking on her hour drive to her grandparent's. Avoiding the Interstate, she took the less traveled road, US-85 S. Some weeks she spent more time at her grandparent's than she did at her own home. It was one of the few places she could be her true self. She'd spend hours fine-tuning her combative skills.

An hour later Mabel passed the wooden gates that led into his land. As she drew closer to the cedar house, her heart quickened. She couldn't get there fast enough. He didn't say he had any news, but she was hopeful. Throwing her car in park, she jumped out and ran up the wooden stairs letting herself in.

As she entered the foyer, she threw her bag and keys on the table and yelled out, "Grandpa, I'm here."

"Mabel! Look at you, girl," cheered Frankie, coming from the kitchen.

"Uncle Frankie!" Mabel screamed. "When did you get here?" she asked, jumping into his arms.

He gave her a big bear hug as he twirled her around. "Your grandpa called me Friday. I came as soon as I could."

"He didn't say anything."

"I wanted to surprise you," A wide grin spread out across his face. "Girl—you are looking good . . . well, except you need some meat on your bones. Your grandpa was right about that."

"Not you, too," she scolded. "It's good to see you," she said, hugging him again. She hadn't seen him since she'd left Oregon six months prior. Her face hurt from smiling. This man had a way of relieving her stress. "I've missed you."

"Me too. When are you moving back?"

Her face went flat. She wished. Living here stressed her out. But he was here now, and that was what she needed. The two of them—together. Thoughts ran through her head.

"If you two are done, I need to fill Mabel in," Grandpa said, peeking his head into the living room.

Mabel looked at her grandpa and back at Frankie. "Geez, no time for catching up I guess."

"Nope." Frankie had one arm around Mabel as he led her out to the gazebo where her grandpa and Doc were talking.

Just like her grandpa to meet outside in his gazebo as opposed to his office. He hated offices, loved the outdoors, and, frankly, so did she.

"Mabel, stop daydreaming and have a seat," he said, patting the cushion next to him.

The sun was out, but there was a chill in the air. The gazebo blocked the sun. Perfect for summer, not so much when it was cold out.

She sat next to her grandpa and Frankie sat next to Doc who sat across from them.

"This mystery woman called Ryan three times," Grandpa said. "All three calls came from the same payphone, a hotel in Old Colorado City."

"That's near Manitou Springs." Mabel interjected. Manitou Springs was the home of her dark secrets, where she lived until she was eleven. Where she lost her family.

Grandpa nodded. He didn't look surprised

"Do they have cameras?"

"Not on the outside where the payphone is. It's a small hotel. Family owned. No witnesses either." He saw the look on Mabel's face. "Don't worry, they have intelligent people on it. They're talking to everyone who stayed there during the calls and to all businesses in the area. They're even going back through all of Ryan's cases."

Mabel gulped.

"I already asked," Grandpa said. "He had two separate files for your case. One where your body was never found and one where you lived . . . you know the rest."

"What if—"

"They're not going to find it. It's all on here," he exposed a hard drive. "Ryan kept this one in his safe. Lillian took it Friday, before anyone even knew they had a safe."

Relief didn't come. Everyone took a huge risk protecting her. Now Lillian was hiding evidence. It made her sick to her stomach. She hated herself for allowing this to go on.

"Hey, Mabel," Frankie interrupted her thoughts. "You and

me," he signaled with his finger and thumb, "outside—now." His eyebrows rose up and down playfully.

She hesitated, looking at her grandpa. She could use a workout with Frankie.

"Go," he encouraged, smiling.

She didn't need any convincing.

After their workout, she wiped the sweat from her forehead and made her way back to the house. Frankie had kicked her butt. She needed it. She missed working out with him.

In the kitchen she found her grandparents cooking up a storm. "Look at you two. How cute," she said, kissing her grandma on the cheek.

"Oh dear, go shower. You're sweating all over dinner," her grandma laughed.

"Thanks, Grandma," she pouted. "Where's Doc?"

"He had to go home, Donna's not feeling well."

"Grandma working you too hard?" she asked the old man sweating profusely. "You're looking a little flushed, Grandpa."

"Doesn't she always? Open the door would you, I'm dying in here," he said.

"Will do. But first Grandma needs a hug," she said, wrapping her sweaty arms around her grandma.

"Mabel, I'm going to beat you," she said, chasing her out of the kitchen. Mabel squealed like a kid again.

The hard drive Grandpa mentioned intrigued her. She'd never seen Ryan's case notes. Never talked to him in detail about what happened that night.

Should she take a peek?

What would she find?

By the time she'd finished with her shower, she was fired up thinking about it. All she had to do was find out where her grandpa put it. She recalled him taking it out of his shirt pocket. She pulled her wet hair back, tied it in a ponytail, and got dressed. As she hurried down the stairs, the smell of homemade marinara lingered in the air.

"Just in time," Grandma beamed. "Take a seat."

The chicken parmigiana and spaghetti tasted just as good as it looked. They were all a bunch of pasta-loving fools. Everyone helped clean up because Grandma would have their hide if they didn't.

Mabel noticed the hard drive in her grandpa's shirt pocket. "Grandpa?" she asked when she had him alone.

"Hmm," he responded.

"Have you looked at the hard drive?"

He looked at her suspiciously. "Yes."

"Do you think I can?"

An odd look crossed his face. "I knew it was only a matter of time. I'd prefer you not. Nothing good will come of it."

"I need to know."

"You do know."

"I don't know everything."

He let out a heavy defeated sigh. "I will tell you everything I know. Everything I saw," he frowned, "if you promise me, to never look at this hard drive."

"Why?"

"Mabel," he shook his head, "there's only heartache in here. The pictures will haunt you forever. You already have enough to deal with. Please . . ."

"Okay. I won't look. I'm sorry. I . . . didn't think about that." *Why did she keep making everything about her?* "Only tell me what you know I need to hear."

She couldn't bear to have him relive it. But if there was

something—anything that would help her recall—she had to hear his story.

TWENTY-TWO

TO HEAR THE STORY IN GRANDPA'S WORDS WAS both heartbreaking and rewarding. Mabel had a lump in her throat when he spoke of finding her mother and brother. It hurt to swallow, her heart ached. She was eleven when she stood at the door of her mother's room. At the time, she didn't know her mother and brother were dead. From her point of view, they were sleeping. Too young at the time to know any better.

As for the killer's eyes, she'd never forget. That's what she remembered sixteen years later. His dark evil eyes.

She was thankful she didn't see the pictures in Ryan's files. To think her grandpa found them. Even him speaking of it gave her a visual she wished she didn't have. But now she knew. She'd known he shot them, but now she knew exactly what kind of monster he really was.

Knowing someone like her grandfather could go through so much heartache, so much stress, and come out strong made her believe that she could, too. Everyone has their own way of healing. Her grandpa was taking care of her, keeping her safe.

Hers was finding the man who'd ripped her world apart.

It all started with a black-eyed demon. He caused all the problems.

She pulled into her garage at eleven-thirty that night. As she tossed her keys on the table, she felt drained, body and mind. She wanted to go to bed and close her eyes.

But Lucas was waiting up for her. She found him in the living room, with only the light of the lamp on next to him. He told her they needed to talk. She didn't ask what about. She knew.

As she got closer she saw him holding the picture he took of her on their first date. He stared at it, intensely. She didn't recognize that version of herself. The girl in that picture was giddy, blushing, eyes sparkled. He loved that picture. He said it was the moment she fell in love with him. He said he fell in love with her the first time he laid eyes on her. She didn't think it worked that way.

She settled in on the sofa, closest to where he sat, hands trembling in her lap.

"This isn't an easy decision I've come to." His eyes didn't leave the picture.

Her heart pounded. She braced herself for the worst.

He spoke to the picture in his hands. "I thought of simply getting on a plane and making it easier on the both of us."

Her heart sank. Tears filled her eyes.

"This was a bad idea, right? Me moving here with you." He glanced up and met her gaze.

Mabel closed her eyes without responding.

"I'll take your silence as agreement."

She let out a *humph.*

He paused. "Don't go blaming yourself. I take sole responsibility for this one. My first clue should've been when you decided to move here and didn't ask me to come with you. After all, I stubbornly forced myself into your life." He chuckled. She still had her eyes closed. "Come on Mabel. The writing was on the wall and I ignored it."

She couldn't speak. The lump in her throat choked her. She fought with all her might to hold back the tears. She didn't deserve to weep for someone as strong as Lucas. Someone who put up with her nonsense and still took all the blame.

"This was a long time coming. I'm sorry for making you do something you weren't ready for." He hesitated. "I don't regret our time together," he said softly. "I love you, with all of me."

She hated herself at that moment. Don't feel sorry for yourself now, she told herself. You never deserved him. Lucas, a business intelligence financial analyst, gave up a once in a lifetime opportunity in Portland when he moved to Colorado with her. He took a lesser paying job just to be with her. She bit down on her bottom lip, thinking of everything he'd done for her over the years. Seven years. You don't spend seven years with someone you don't love.

Why does she continue to push people out of her life?

"Mabel?"

"Stop," she muttered. "Stop blaming yourself Lucas. This is on me. All me," she said opening her eyes. He got up and took a seat next to her. "Listen," she exhaled, "you're right about moving here. It was a bad idea . . . for you I mean. But only because I wasn't honest with you." She watched his interest peak. God, she wanted to tell him everything. "There's so much about myself I want to tell you, but I can't. Not yet . . . maybe never. And that's not fair to you. That's what I've struggled with Lucas."

"What are you saying?"

She'd already said too much. She rubbed the bear on her wrist, thinking of her family. "I'm saying I moved here to take care of some things. Things from my past. And until I do, I can't move forward."

"Stop." He took her hands in his. "Mabel. Why didn't you mention this before? I'll help you."

"No. You can't. I promise you . . . you can't."

"What is it? Tell me."

"Please don't ask me. I can't. I love you. But you're right, I can't be with you."

"I'll wait for you then."

Not what she had in mind. "What was your plan? Tonight?" she asked. She needed to get him back to his original intention. "Were you going to leave? Move back to Portland?"

"Is that what you want?"

She looked away, wiped her eyes as the man in black infiltrated her thoughts. "Yes." It was a whisper, but she might as well have shouted it.

"My flight leaves in the morning," he said.

TWENTY-THREE

WILBUR DUMEL WATCHED HIS GRANDdaughter as she slept. Her eyes twitched—was she dreaming? He hoped it was a good one. He felt miserable, even shameful after sending her to school in tears. He hated doing it, but her good-for-nothing dad left him no choice.

Isabel's enthusiasm when he picked her up from school came to mind. A complete one-eighty from when he dropped her off. Her whole face lit up when she saw her new teacher. She seemed nice enough, a bit young, but as long as Isabel liked her, he liked her.

Isabel was nothing like Jimmy. She may have his nose, cheeks, and chin—but other than that—she got all her good from her momma. Thank the Lord for that. Her momma was the best thing that ever happened to Jimmy, and he'd gone and thrown it all away.

Wilbur moved the hair from Isabel's face.

Jimmy always found a way to get himself into a mess. The

first time, Wilbur thought for sure he'd go away for life. What he did was unforgivable.

It's in my blood, he thought. *It's tainted.* And it runs through his boy.

I'm as guilty as you are son. I've been condemned to a life of hell—the hell I brought you into.

He drank to get away from it. And he quit for what?

To be forgiven? To face it straight on? Wilbur blamed himself for what his boy did that night. Maybe if Wilbur had been a better father.

Gently lifting her hand off the book she'd been reading, he slid it free, looking at the cover—*Because of Winn-Dixie.* Not the same book she had yesterday. She must have finished her other one. He set the book on the end table, flicked off the light on his way out, and quietly shut the door.

His boy may be a screw-up, but Jimmy loves Isabel and would do anything for her. Even so, she would be better off without him. As much as he deserved to go to prison for his crimes, Wilbur couldn't find it in himself to let that happen.

He was halfway to his bedroom when his phone rang. He knew who it was without looking. Head bowed, he sighed putting his phone to his ear, "What do want?" he asked.

"Nice to talk to you, too, Pops."

"Why are you calling? You shouldn't be calling this late. Just . . . just let her be."

"Listen old man, you need to watch your tone. That's my daughter you have there. You better not be filling her head with any of your shit."

"What do you want, Jimmy?" Wilbur moved the phone to his other ear.

"I want to talk to Isabel."

"She's asleep, she's had a long day. Just let her sleep."

Silence.

"Jimmy?" He raised his voice.

"Fine."

"Where are you?"

Silence.

"Where are you? What have the police said?"

"I gotta go," Jimmy said. Click.

"Love you, son," he mumbled under his breath. Jimmy made it hard to say the words out loud. He did love him. They never had a good relationship, even after he stopped drinking. Could he blame his son? All those days and nights Wilbur spent in a drunken stupor. He was never there for his boy, and when he was there he was either yelling at him or beating him.

He wasn't proud of it.

It was weird with Jimmy. The moment he laid eyes on the boy, the moment he came out of his momma, he had a feeling—a feeling that he was his bad seed. His punishment. He was drunk off his ass that day too. Like every day back then.

William, he didn't deserve. William was a gift and then taken away. A reminder that he didn't deserve anything good.

Take the good one, leave the bad one . . .

TWENTY-FOUR

She rolled over at the sight of a half-empty bed and balked at the sunlight peeking through the blinds. *Here's to a good day*, she thought. If she wished it, maybe it would happen. Climbing out of bed she focused on her day ahead. What would she say to Lucas? He'd left early for work and planned to take the first flight out today.

Eat first, then Lucas.

Mabel needed meat on her bones as everyone kept pointing out. She sat in the kitchen playing with the berries in her yogurt. She barely touched her bagel. She couldn't eat.

Should she call him? What would she say?

Nothing, that's what. She threw her yogurt cup and barely-touched bagel away as she lectured herself—*Get to work. Focus on your day.*

She poured a cup of coffee and headed for the door.

The next two days flew by. She went through the motions, but barely played a part in her life. Lucas went back to Portland, his absence leaving a huge void. She had hardly spent time at home the last couple of weeks and now she didn't want to be there at all. She found her house too big, empty, and deserted.

Work was a little better. It kept her mind off her personal issues. Isabel, the new girl, appeared to have underlying troubles. Mabel tried to get her to open up. It would take some time.

Today, Isabel walked into class wearing a blue and white striped shirt with old faded blue jeans. She looked good, content—much better than the last few days. Their eyes met, and Isabel offered a lopsided grin. Mabel returned a smile with a wink. As the day went on, Mabel tried to work up the courage to ask Isabel about her parents. She still didn't know what part, if any, they played in her life.

She remembered how hard it had been on her. She'd hated talking about it. Still did.

Before she knew it, the day ended and she'd lost her chance.

Thursday rolled around, and Isabel came in with red eyes and a forced smile. Mabel pulled her aside only to get a tight-lipped response. Isabel wouldn't say a word. She clearly didn't want to talk about whatever was bothering her. She kept her head down all day. After watching Isabel get into her grandpa's car, Mabel decided she would tell Isabel about losing her parents when she was young. She didn't have to give details. She just wanted her to know that kids go through rough times and they can make it through.

That afternoon, Mabel pulled into the gas station where Andy worked. He'd left her a message saying he would be working the second shift. A modified blue and white Honda Civic pulled up to the pump. A kid looking far too young to drive stepped out, his music blaring. She'd heard it before.

He looked at Mabel and threw her a head nod. Using one hand, he half attempted to pull up his pants that hung down his butt. *No judgment here*, thought Mabel. Kids have a hard-enough time just making it through their teenage years.

She took note of the two cars parked on the side of the building. She recognized one as Andy's. The Ford Focus, here on Monday, must belong to the blonde babbling clerk.

"Mabel, my lady. How are you today?" asked Andy.

"Hey you. I think I should ask you that."

"Hi, hon . . . my bad. I'm sorry. It's a bad habit of mine," said the babbling clerk. "Blame my momma. She calls everyone hon."

"Oh shoot, don't go disrespecting Mabel—she'll bring the heat!" Andy exclaimed, jumping up and down.

Mabel gave him a look that said *shut up.* He did.

"Hi, I never did get your name. I'm Mabel. You are?"

"I'm JoAnne. JoAnne Jankins—with an *a*, not an *e*—Jankins," she said stressing the *a*.

"Got it. Nice to meet you . . . officially. Since you're both here, do you have an office that we can talk in, Andy?"

"We sure do. JoAnne, you mind watching the store?"

"Not at all. Take your time," she said, smiling as she winked at Andy.

Mabel rolled her eyes, following Andy to the office. She watched Andy as he walked. He kept his hair short in the back. She could make out a bump and a red line.

The bastard, she thought. *Poor Andy.*

Andy made himself comfortable on the desk and motioned

for her to take the chair. She looked at it, wrinkled her nose, pursed her lips and shook her head no. You could catch something sitting on that thing.

"Andy, I know I'm not your boss, but this room is nasty. Dude, you should clean it up . . . or have JoAnne Jankins do it." She stressed the a when she said her name.

"I think I might just love having a boss like you," he said smiling. "I hear you wanted to talk to me. JoAnne said you didn't look happy about the robbery. You know, she thinks you and I are a thing."

"I know," she smiled. "I'd be so lucky," she flirted.

His face reddened. "You know I got a girlfriend. I'd dump her though, just for you."

"Is she good to you?"

"Yeah, she is. Going on four months next week. My momma likes her, too, and Momma don't like no one."

"Good, as long as she's good to you and knows what she has," Mabel said, thinking of Lucas and how badly she'd treated him. "I'm sorry about the robbery. How are you?"

He looked away, his expression hardened. "I'm doing okay." He went silent for a moment, reliving the event in his head. "I don't get why he had to hit me. He had everything he wanted. And it's not like I could identify him. He wore black, head to toe. And I did everything he said. The doctor said I have a mild concussion. It hurt bad too. I just wanted him to leave. I thought . . . I thought . . ." he fell silent, head hung low, eyes closed.

"Andy," she said, lifting his head to meet his eyes. He was fighting back tears. "He's a bastard. And you're alive. Do you trust me?"

"Yes . . ." he replied, confused by her question.

"Good. Now, JoAnne said something that got me thinking.

Where are the police on finding this bastard?"

"Nowhere," he said, rolling his eyes. "Like I said, he wore all black, including black gloves. No fingerprints."

She looked at the monitor set up on a filing cabinet. "Does this surveillance system actually work?"

"Yeah, but you can't see much of anything. It's black and white and he's dressed in black."

"Right." *Damn.* "But you could see his eyes, right? What color were they?"

"Brown, light brown. I told the cops that too. I didn't want to make eye contact because our training said not to stare robbers in the eyes. I guess they're like bears, makes them angry." He shrugged. "But I looked anyway. Real quick like."

Damn. Not her guy. Why did she feel disappointed? It was like she wanted it to be him.

"Why do ask?"

"I had a hunch," she said, watching him. "Can I get a copy of the recording?"

"You some kind of detective?" he asked smiling. "I could definitely see you as some kind of kick-ass assassin. Yeah, that's it. Mabel, the assassin."

"I'm not an assassin," she said, punching him in the arm. "Can I have the recording or not?"

He grabbed a disk from the safe and handed it to her. "Here, take this one. It was the one I recorded for my loss prevention manager, but I can record another."

"Perfect," she said. "I gotta run. Have you seen anyone yet, like a therapist or counselor?"

"They gave me a number, but I haven't called yet."

"Call. Take it from me, even though you think you don't need to talk about it—you do. And talk to your girlfriend, too, don't shut her out."

"Thanks Mabel," he said, hugging her before she walked out.

TWENTY-FIVE

MABEL HAD A SUDDEN RUSH OF HOPE THE moment Isabel walked through the door and smiled. She wore a dark yellow princess dress with a big white bow tied around her waist, a tiara, and sparkly slippers. The call Mabel made to Wilbur paid off.

Mabel watched the kids scrambling in, most of them wearing costumes—chattering and laughing. Anna was sitting on the end, dressed as Admiral Michelle Howard—the first woman to become a four-star admiral and the first black woman to achieve two-star admiral rank, as well as the first female graduate of the U.S. Naval Academy promoted to flag officer. Anna's father is in the Navy. She must make him proud. She was staring straight at Mabel, patiently waiting for roll call.

Bennie was dressed as Drax from *Guardians of the Galaxy*—of course he'd pick the funny one—while his best friend was dressed as Peter Quill. They were both goofing off, making their posse of boys laugh, while Bennie stole a glance at Isabel hoping she would hear him.

When recess rolled around, her head ached—reminding her that even though she wanted to talk to Isabel—she dreaded it. She had to get the conversation over.

Sitting upright in Mabel's chair, Isabel said, "I want to be a teacher."

"You do?" she asked smiling.

"Yep. Then I can boss all the other kids around." She laughed.

"You think that's what I do? Boss kids around all day?" Mabel asked with a smirk.

"No . . . well, sometimes. But you're a nice teacher. The best."

"Thank you, Isabel. That's very nice of you to say. I'm sorry I asked you to miss recess today. I just wanted us to talk, without distractions . . . and get to know each other a little better. It's hard sometimes during class when we're so busy."

"It's okay, I don't mind."

"You almost completed your first week. How do you like Northridge?"

"I like it," she said, shrugging. "But I miss my old friends. Jennie and Anna are nice though. They all are."

"It's good you're making new friends." Here goes. "I had to move, too, when I was young, your age, actually. So I know how hard it is to leave your old friends behind and make new ones."

"You did?" she asked, looking concerned.

Mabel nodded. "Remember when I told you I moved to Colorado?"

"Uh-huh."

"I actually moved back to Colorado. I left when I was eleven, like you."

"Oh, that must have been hard. I bet your friends are happy you're back," she said, smiling.

If you only knew, she thought. She left her friends behind to never talk to them again. She died, only she didn't die.

"There's more I wanted to talk to you about."

"What is it Ms. Peters?" she asked, studying Mabel's face.

"I've been watching you this week." She sounded like Principal Strom. She could have killed herself right then. "Well, I watch all my students, of course. But you're new, so I want to make sure you're adjusting to your new school and class. I've noticed that you've had some ups and downs. Everyone does, but at times you seem sad. Do you know what I'm talking about?"

The color drained out of her face. "Uh-huh."

"I know some of what you're going through, having to move and change schools. And for me, well that's what I wanted to tell you." She paused, finding the words. "I lost my parents when I was young. Both my mom and my dad. That's why I had to move."

Isabel gasped. Tears welled up in her eyes and poured down her cheeks. She wrapped her arms around Mabel's neck. Right or wrong, having Isabel in her arms felt right. It surprised her that she didn't cry herself. She was certain she would.

Mabel grabbed a few tissues off her desk and wiped Isabel's eyes. "I just want you to know, I'm here for you. I may be your teacher, but I'm also someone who went through a tough time at your age. When you need someone to talk to—and you will—I'm here for you." She offered her a reassuring wink and a smile. "You remind me a lot of myself." She breathed deeply. "I've never told anyone about my parents. You're the first person."

"I am?" she asked.

She nodded, "I would never ask you to keep a secret from your grandpa, but please don't talk about it in class, okay?"

"Oh, I won't."

"I know. Do you want to talk some more, or do you want to catch the last ten minutes of recess?"

"Uh . . ." she looked out the door and back at Mabel, "can we talk about something else?"

"Sure, what do you want to talk about?"

She watched Isabel as she struggled what to say next. She could see it in her eyes. Isabel wanted to say more. Instead, she opted to talk about the books she was reading. She left school with a smile on her face.

How could she expect more?

TWENTY-SIX

FRANKLIN DOWDY THREW HIS EXTRA-LARGE, heavy-duty duffel bag over his shoulder as he made his way to the wimpy white car he rented. He preferred his Ram—powerful and practical. Too bad he left it in Oregon. He loved his baby, just not for his hunting missions—it would draw too much unwanted attention.

The rental company was all out of SUVs *and* full-sized cars. At the time he thought the last thing he wanted to do was rent a van. Now he was wishing he had.

He popped the trunk and threw his bag in. *Goddamned crackerjack car!* he cursed, as he hit his head getting in. He was a big man, trying to squeeze into a stupid Hyundai Elantra. He cursed the rental company again. Can you really call yourself a rental company if you're all out of what your customer needs? He thought not. What was he thinking? He planned to *not* draw attention, and a big black man in a small-ass car drew attention.

He sat back, cramped, trying to relax. It was a clear blue October day. F*ocus on that,* he told himself. He could get used to seeing the bright blue sky every day. A perfect seventy-three degrees, fresh air—a bit dry for his taste—but nothing was perfect.

As he drove through Denver he found himself glancing over to his right, taking in the view of the Rockies. He could get used to this. What a drive . . .

He slammed on his brakes. His car skidding to a stop, nearly crashing into the car in front of him. He took it back. Traffic sucked here. He could do without it.

People don't know how to drive here! Much too aggressive!

Loosen up people. What's the hurry? He didn't see a fire. He sighed, accelerating once more. Maybe he missed the memo.

His motto was, 'slow down enough to enjoy life.' That's what he liked about Portland. Everyone was laid back. No rush. No hurry. Just breathe. Take in the fresh air.

Oh, damn. That's it! No oxygen up here in the mile-high city. He laughed at the thought.

Frankie visited Ryan for the first time since he'd been in Colorado. He still hadn't gotten over the fact that Ryan never solved the crimes against Mabel and her family. He tried getting involved. His first mistake was telling John. His second mistake was listening to him.

Frankie had a way of getting things done. That's why he worked alone. It was better that way. No one getting in his way, telling him what he should or shouldn't do. He wouldn't make that mistake again.

Ryan Cross stared up at the ceiling. "I screwed up man. I allowed a jackass to break into my home and sneak up on me."

Frankie saw shame written across Ryan's face. "I'm better than that," Ryan continued.

"Tell me about this mystery lady," Frankie said, changing the subject. Frankie liked Ryan, but he didn't give a crap about his ego. Frankly, it surprised him that Ryan felt the need to whimper like a bitch in front of him.

"There's nothing to tell. I never met up with her. She never told me anything. She called me from a payphone. No way to track it, I tried. Police have no footage from any cameras. No witnesses. She's a ghost."

"A ghost you say?" *That's an interesting way to put it,* thought Frankie.

"What?"

"Nothing. When's the last time you spoke to her?"

Ryan gritted his teeth. "The day before I got shot, she called and said she'd call me Friday and tell me where to meet her. She was paranoid."

"You're a detective. Why do you think she was paranoid?"

"Listen Frankie, I know you mean well. I already went over all of this with John, the police, the detectives assigned to the case, and I really don't want to keep repeating myself."

"Okay, Ryan. Let's start over. Hi, my name is Frankie and I don't give a rat's ass who you've spoken to and how many times you have to repeat yourself. I'm—"

He cut Frankie off. "That's—"

Frankie put his hand up. "Let me finish. I'm here to help find the man who shot you. Do you know why I care?"

Ryan glared at him. "Why don't you go ahead and tell me."

"Because I believe the man who shot you is the same man who killed the Stucker family."

Ryan swallowed hard. His face turned pale.

"I believe that your mystery woman, knows the man from your triple homicide case. The man who shot you—the man who killed Mabel's family—they're one in the same. Your mystery woman was about to name the killer from your unsolved mystery—but the killer found out and tried to kill you first." He paused to allow Ryan to take in what he'd said so far. This wasn't news to Ryan, but it was high-time he started acting like a detective again and stopped acting like a wounded bitch.

"Now I ask you again, Ryan, have you heard from this mystery woman since you've been shot? Has she called you even once?" He continued before Ryan could answer. "For instance. On that last Friday when she was going to call you and you were shot—did she try to call you? If yes, you didn't answer because you were fighting for your life. Did she leave a message? If not, why do you think that is? If she never called, why do you think that is? I have to ask myself, Ryan, is this mystery woman still alive? Have you asked yourself that? I would also have to ask myself, how much longer will it be before this bad guy comes back for you?" He stood up, walked to the window and scratched his head.

Ryan sighed. He was about to say something but stopped himself. "John's a good man. A smart man. He speaks highly of you."

"And he of you." Frankie turned to look at the man.

"I don't have to tell you . . . there isn't a day that goes by that I don't look over my notes looking for something I missed." He lifted himself to an upright position. "I should have asked you for help."

"I'm here now. With or without your permission. I've looked at your notes. I believe it's someone from Ben's accident. We thought that from the beginning. I saw that Bill White interviewed most of the victims involved. I'm going back through them all. There's a few that stand out. Of course, they all have alibis, but I don't give a shit. Now we have your shooter and a woman to find."

Doc poked his head in, gave Frankie a look of disapproval. "Ryan, you need anything?"

Ryan shook his head.

"How are you feeling pain wise—on a scale of one to ten?" Doc asked.

"I'm fine, Doc," Ryan replied.

"You didn't answer my question. You want me to send you back to Penrose-St. Francis?" he asked, deadpan.

"Nice, Doc, threaten to send me back to the other hospital," Ryan mumbled. Doc's expression didn't change. "No, Doc. I do not want to go back to Penrose," he responded, annoyed by the question. "My pain is at a four if I don't move and a seven when I do."

"That's more like it," Doc said, pleased with himself. "I'll be back to give you a little something to help ease the pain. I don't need any macho men enduring pain in my hospital." He looked at Frankie. "Try not to stress out my patient. You have five more minutes," he said, shutting the door behind him.

Frankie held his hands up in defense. He felt like a scolded child.

"She never called—the mystery woman—and she hasn't called since," Ryan said, answering Frankie's original question. "Your question on whether she's alive or not . . . that's a good question. I've been wondering the same thing."

"If she is alive, you won't hear from her now. You were in the paper."

Ryan shook his head. "I know. I'm not sure how it leaked. No one knows I'm here except the chief of police and the head detective. I'll be going home in a few days. I think Doc's trying to keep me here longer than actually needed—for my safety—but I need to get home to my wife."

"Do they have anyone covering your place?"

"No, because she's staying with her dad. They have an off-duty policeman watching her there."

"Good. If you think of anything, or you hear from the mystery woman—call me." He handed his card to Ryan. "Get better."

"Yeah, thanks."

Frankie said his goodbyes to Doc and Donna. The visit wasn't a complete waste of his time. He needed Ryan to trust him. He wasn't Ryan's favorite person, but he'd still call.

He walked out the door with a list of names and addresses.

TWENTY-SEVEN

WILBUR DIDN'T HAVE MUCH ENERGY ON Saturday. He was glad when Isabel spent the day reading the books she had picked out on Friday. But today, Sunday, he had to get her out. He couldn't keep her cooped up all day. He hadn't felt well for some time. He ignored the part of him that told him to go to the doctor. He didn't want to know.

If he went to the doctor and found out he only had three months to live, then he'd be miserable. Why would he do that to himself. He wouldn't. He'd keep living every day like it was his last.

He also knew that if Jimmy had any idea he was sick he wouldn't allow Isabel to be around him. Hell, he couldn't believe he had her now.

He'd enjoy it while he could.

Alcoholism is the second leading cause of cirrhosis, his doctor told him once. Heavy alcohol use over several years leads to fat and inflammation in the liver, which can lead to alcoholic cirrhosis.

Thanks for the information—after the fact.

Although, if he had known, he probably wouldn't have stopped drinking. At the time, he didn't think he was an alcoholic. The doctor had told him this great news the year *after* he quit drinking. It probably wasn't the first time he'd been told, but it was the first time he had heard the words.

He also learned that he could still die years after he quit. *Ha!* Punishment is a bitch. That's what he thought was going on with him now. He was no doctor, but he was one unlucky bastard.

"Grandpa, why does my dad not want me?"

Kill me now.

He was in his room, putting his shoes on. He looked at his granddaughter, her forehead furrowed. It was the same look she had given him when he tried to do things for her. Her serious, *I don't need help* look. Except this time, she needed his help.

"Uhm . . . Isabel . . .where . . .why would you say that?"

She studied him. "I miss my mom," she said, looking down. "I'm glad you're here, but now my dad is gone too. He told me . . . if I said he was there that day—they wouldn't take him away—but he's gone anyway."

She was right. His boy never thought things through.

He sighed. "Isabel, if there is one thing I know for absolute certain it's that your dad loves you very much. It's just that he's having a hard time."

"We are too, Grandpa!" she cried. "And we're here"

He gave her a hug, not sure what else to do. Everything this little girl said was right. When did she become so smart? "What do you want to do today, Isabel? Your choice."

She thought about it for a moment, was about to say something, reconsidered and said, "Can we go bowling and maybe watch *Twilight* later. I'm reading the books now. I finished reading the first one yesterday."

"Bowling and *Twilight*, it is. But first, church. Go finish getting ready."

Her excitement to go to church with him was bubbling up. She hadn't been since the last time he took her. Jimmy would most likely get upset, but he didn't care. Wilbur needed the good Lord in his life—and frankly, so did Isabel. And if Jimmy wouldn't take her, he'd do it himself.

"Can I call Daddy and see if he wants to join us?"

He grunted, "To church? I don't think your dad will want to go with us."

She laughed. Even she knew it was a ridiculous thought. "No—bowling, and then come here to watch a movie."

Anguish rolled over him in a sudden wave. He didn't know how much longer he could keep up the charade. How could Jimmy do this to her?

"I'll tell you what. I'll call him. I need to talk to him about a few things anyhow. After . . . you can talk to him, okay?"

She lit up, eyes beaming. "Okay. Deal."

His heart dropped. He put a smile on his face regardless. "Go on, get ready," he instructed.

He called his son as she skipped to her room. He smiled at her blonde, knotted hair.

"Hey Pops, what's up?" Jimmy answered, sounding tired.

"Hey Jimmy. What's your plan for today?"

"What's it to you, old man?"

Crap, crap, crap—is all that ever came out of his mouth!

"I have your daughter, Jimmy. That's what. Does that mean

nothing to you? She's wondering about her daddy. Asking why you don't want her."

"Shit."

That got his attention. Wilbur could hear ruffling around.

"I . . . I just woke up. You caught me off guard. You don't need to shit a brick."

"Isabel wants to go bowling and see a movie."

"Ahh man, really? I can't. Not today. Maybe dinner."

Well, that's something. She hadn't seen him since Monday. Even then, he showed up with one of his friends—one of those guys that reeks of trouble.

"How about five then? Don't be late."

"I said maybe. I don't even know yet, Pops. I gotta figure some shit out."

"Like what Jimmy? There ain't nothing to figure out. Except how to take care of your daughter. You hear me. She is *your* priority. Not your stupid friends."

"Look at you talkin' all big, like you ever gave half a shit about me when I was growing up. You were a shit-bag for a father—but you probably don't recall because you were too shit-faced to remember. Now you expect me to be perfect? Well, guess what, old man—I ain't. I'm trying here. I can't be around her like this."

Wilbur hated him sometimes. More than that, he hated the man Jimmy called Pops.

"Can I talk to my dad now?" she asked.

Crap! How long had she been standing there?

"Isabel wants to talk to you," Wilbur said, handing Isabel the phone before Jimmy could argue.

"Hi, Daddy," she said, smiling ear to ear.

Wilbur could hear Jimmy's voice on the other end but

couldn't make out what he said. Isabel's smile remained.

"Grandpa and I are going bowling and watching a movie later. Can you join us?"

Her smile disappeared, followed by a frown. Her eyebrows furrowed.

Wilbur shook his head in disgust. He could hear Jimmy talking again. Isabel was giving him the cold shoulder. Her frown and anger turned to sadness. She dropped the phone and ran off to her room crying.

Wilbur picked up the phone, thought for a quick second about hanging up, but instead said, "What did you say to her? She ran off crying. If you ain't here by dinner, I swear—"

"Swear what, old man? You better not be getting any crazy-ass ideas in that head of yours—because I'll tell them that you helped me plan it all."

"You're something else, you know that. Why do you make it so hard to help you? Be here for dinner at five." Wilbur hung up the phone before Jimmy could say anything else to get under his skin.

He felt miserable. Inside and out. All Wilbur cared about now was Isabel. His son, clearly, could not take care of her—love is not enough when your head isn't right—Jimmy proved that over and over.

TWENTY-EIGHT

JIMMY DUMEL HAD THROWN HIS PHONE against the wall, watching it shatter into pieces.

"How dare he talk to me like that," Jimmy mumbled to himself. *And hang up on me? Who the hell does he think he is?*

Head down, he paced back and forth like a raging bull, ready to attack, the steam building by the second. Everything was falling apart.

His mind drifted. The blood on Ryan's chest—he thought he'd bleed out.

Jimmy punched the wall. Rubbing his sore knuckles, he remembered the last time he punched the wall. It had been the worst day of his life.

Ryan didn't mean shit to him.

He found out yesterday the fucknut lived after all. Next time, he'd empty his clip on him. As if him living wasn't a good kick in the balls—the fucknut was a detective. Just Jimmy's luck. He hadn't seen that one coming.

Jimmy sat on his unmade bed, thinking. His room was a mess. Clothes thrown everywhere. He hadn't bothered cleaning since Robin . . .

Robin—what the hell was his wife doing cheating on him with a detective? He thought about it for a moment. The more he thought, the madder he became.

"Fucking Bitch!" he said to himself. How did he not see it?

I never cheated on you . . . her words rang in his ears.

His wife was ratting him out! And here he thought she was trying to save her worthless life. Any inkling of remorse he may have felt—Gone. Zip. Zero. Zilch. She deserved no sympathy. He was happy he took the snitch out when he did.

He needed a smoke.

He searched his room with no luck. Remembering where he'd left them, he headed for the living room. He fell back into his chair going through the motions, deep in thought. He couldn't say when he started smoking, one of his friends had gotten him into it. He tapped a cigarette out of his pack, placed it between his lips, fished out his lighter, and lit his cigarette. He ignored his shaking hands, inhaling deeply.

The possibilities of Robin telling this detective everything, before Jimmy killed her, was ruining his whole damn day. Not only would he be charged for the triple homicides, he would now be accused of his wife's disappearance. Murder when they found her body, and attempted murder of the detective.

He thought about it for a moment. Finishing his cigarette, he grinned. There was no way she got to the detective before Jimmy took her out. Jimmy would be behind bars already if that were the case. The news hadn't given a lot of information, but it gave enough.

The news played over in his head. They said the detective was shot multiple times, moved for his safety and was cooperating with the investigators. That meant Ryan lived and didn't know shit. If he had, Jimmy would have been arrested already. At the very least, he would have had a visitor by now.

Leave it to his dumbass wife. She'd tried to be careful by using a payphone, but all she'd done was help Jimmy—she'd left no trace behind that led to him.

Her departing gift to her once loving husband . . .

TWENTY-NINE

ISABEL SHOWED UP TO SCHOOL WITH RED swollen eyes—she'd been crying again. Mabel's heart went out to this little girl. Who did she have? Was her grandpa there for her like she needed? And where in the hell were her asshole parents?

Mabel shouldn't have thought that way. For all she knew, they were dead. The thought made her sick to her stomach. Isabel needed help, counseling, someone who loved her. Mabel wanted to take her into her arms and hold her, tell her everything would get better—in time.

She talked to Janet, the principal, and Lydia, the counselor that morning. They wanted to call Wilbur in to discuss Isabel. Mabel opposed. Mabel told them she'd only talked with her grandpa once and would like another opportunity. They agreed to give her another shot.

To her surprise, Isabel asked to stay in for recess. She didn't want to go out and play. She asked if they could talk. Mabel was ecstatic, at first. Isabel looked instantly regretful. Please don't take it back. Why did she have to be so freakishly overjoyed and scare the poor girl?

Recess couldn't come soon enough. Richard, the other fifth grade teacher, was more than happy to look over her class—again.

Isabel took Mabel's chair. She liked it. Spun around and around. She wore a gray sweater, blue jeans, and red canvas shoes.

"I finished reading *Twilight* on Saturday, and Grandpa and I watched the movie yesterday," she said matter-of-factly.

"How did you like the book?"

"I loved it," she said, with a small grin that disappeared quickly. She had something else on her mind. She was beating around the bush.

"Have you started *New Moon* yet?"

"Yep. And Grandpa said we can watch the movie on Saturday."

"Sounds like your grandpa loves you very much." She needed to know people loved her.

Silence.

"Isabel?"

Tears began to stream down her young pale face. She wiped them with the back of her hand.

"What's wrong sweetie?" asked Mabel, lowering her voice.

She sniffled. "My dad doesn't want me," she whispered.

Well, fuck me!

What does she say? The truth? He does, but he might be screwed up in the head. Mabel knew nothing about him. Does she lie? And say what?

She opted for more information. "What would make you say that?"

"I've only seen him once since my mommy . . ." she closed her eyes slowly as she said it, opening them as if washing away the thought.

"Since your mommy . . . what?"

Nothing.

"You don't have to talk if you don't want to, but it might make you feel better if you do. Sometimes talking helps."

"I'm not supposed to talk about it."

What the hell? What is she hiding? Or been told to hide?

Mabel worked to keep her tone steady. "Only talk about what you feel comfortable with and we'll go from there . . ."

She looked up. "I've only seen my daddy once since I moved in with Grandpa . . . and it wasn't for very long." Her eyes were reddening. "I invited him to go bowling with us yesterday, and watch a movie, and he said he couldn't."

What kind of an asshole . . .

"Grandpa said my dad loves me and wants me, but I don't think that's true. Him and Grandpa fight all the time. I heard them on the phone. Grandpa was yelling at him. Telling him he better come to dinner last night or else, but he never came. I knew he wouldn't."

"Sometimes adults don't understand how hard it is for kids and they think only of themselves. I'm so sorry you're going through this. It sounds like your grandpa loves you very much and he may be the best person for you right now. I know you miss your daddy and I'm sure he misses you, too." She tried to smile, but she wasn't feeling it.

Isabel rubbed her eyes. She had more to say.

"Is your grandpa picking you up today?"

"Yes."

"Would you mind if I spoke to him again?"

She looked at Mabel. Studied her. "Are you going to tell him I told you about my dad?"

"I wouldn't do that. I told you when you needed to talk, I would be here for you. I want to check on him, too, and let him know he can call me if he needs anything. As a matter of fact," she wrote down her cell number on an apple shaped sticky note and handed it to Isabel, "here's my cell number. For you and your grandpa. I'd still like to talk to him if that's alright with you, but the number is for you if you ever need anything, anything at all, even just to talk, you can call me."

She smiled a real smile. "I will. Thanks, Ms. Peters."

Mabel smiled back.

"My daddy told me to keep a secret."

Mabel's heart instantly beat faster. "What kind of secret?" she asked, keeping her voice steady.

"Me and Grandpa. He said not tell the cops or—,"

Ring, ring, ring.

Nooooooo!

The bell rang, recess was over. Kids started rushing in.

Cops?

Mabel turned back to Isabel. Saved by the bell. She was walking back to her seat. Their conversation played over and over in her head. The kids filed in, talking, laughing. She wanted to say something. Anything to get Isabel alone again.

Her dad must be in trouble, that's why she's with her grandpa. What about her mom? Where is she in all this?

Why does Mabel care so much? She knew why. It affected

Isabel. Isabel reminded her of herself. She needed to talk to her grandpa.

THIRTY

JIMMY BANGED HIS FIST AGAINST THE DARK blue door. It had fake webs in the corner and a skeleton in the middle. He listened for footsteps that never came. There were three carved pumpkins sitting on the porch. The largest had huge eyes, a large smile, and one tooth. The second was a ghost and the third a witch. He guessed Isabel's was the largest. He found it odd his pops was capable of such an activity. Something he never did with Jimmy when he was young.

He wondered where his old man was. He would have called, but he shattered his phone in a fit of rage. He blamed his pops for pissing him off. He looked down either side of the walkway, not seeing him.

Wilbur's car was in the driveway. He banged again.

Nothing.

He stepped off the porch and peered into the window overlooking the living room.

No movement.

He knocked on the window. "Pops," he yelled out.

The nosey old lady next door came out.

"Have you seen my pops today?" asked Jimmy. "He's not answering his door, but his car's here."

"Sure, I saw him. He had the little girl with him this morning. Pretty little girl."

Jimmy nodded. "Have you seen him since?"

She put her crooked finger to her mouth, thinking. "Nope. Can't say I have. But I took a nap—"

"Okay. Thanks." Jimmy cut her off. He ran to his truck and grabbed his key to Wilbur's house. Something he should have done to begin with. He regretted talking to the nosey neighbor who watched his every move.

"Pops . . . Pops . . ." he called out, after letting himself in. A groan came from the bathroom. "Pops!"

Panicked, he rushed in to find him sprawled out on the floor. He knelt next to him. "What happened?" Jimmy asked shaking him.

Wilbur moaned again.

Jimmy searched around the best he could for blood, not seeing any. He grabbed a towel, ran it under cold water and put it on Wilbur's head. He was winging it. Something his mom probably did when he was younger. He wondered if he needed to call an ambulance. With what? The smashed phone that lay on his floor? And Wilbur didn't have a land line.

He looked around for his pop's phone. "Pop, where's your phone?"

"I'm fine," moaned Wilbur.

The sound of his voice sent a wave of relief through him. "Like hell you are. What happened?"

"Stop fussing and help me up," Wilbur insisted.

Jimmy hesitated. He was talking, so he supposed his head must be alright. He watched a show once about not moving someone if they had a head injury . . . or was that a back injury . . . or neck. *Shit!* He didn't know.

Wilbur moved to get up.

"Hold on, Pops," Jimmy said. He took Wilbur by the arm, shut the toilet seat, and helped him sit down. "You feel alright?"

"Yeah," Wilbur said doubtfully, rubbing the back of his head.

"Let me see."

"I told you—I'm fine." Wilbur swatted his hand away.

"Listen, old man. Don't make me send you to an old-age home." He threatened. "Now let me take a look." Jimmy leaned over his shoulder. Not seeing anything, he reached out and touched the back of his head.

Wilbur winced.

"There's a bump, but no blood. Where's your aspirin?"

Wilbur pointed to the cabinet.

Jimmy handed him three and poured water into the glass sitting by the sink. "Here. Drink up."

Wilbur frowned, but took the offering and did as Jimmy said. "What are you doing here?" he mumbled.

"You're lucky I showed when I did. I came to pick up Isabel from school. Thought I'd surprise her today."

Wilbur's expression softened. "She'd like that."

"I was actually going to go with you, but you don't look up to it." He thought about his daughter waiting at school for her grandpa to show up, only to find out he had passed out in his bathroom. "You passed out Pop. Did you fall or something?"

"No. Well yes. After I passed out I guess."

"You guess?"

"I came into the bathroom to splash water on my face and next thing I knew . . . you were over me."

"How long were you out?"

"Uh . . . I can't really say."

"I was knocking on your door for a few minutes, took me another talking to your neighbor, maybe a couple more to get your key and come in and find you on the floor. That's five minutes there," Jimmy said.

Wilbur closed his eyes. "Help me to the couch."

"When is the last time you ate? You look . . . sick. You don't look well."

"I did just pass out. I'd imagine I wouldn't."

Jimmy clenched his jaw. "Listen. I only care because you have my daughter." He had to make that clear. He helped Wilbur to the couch, noticing how bony he felt. The man was definitely losing weight. "If you don't feel well enough to do it, I'll ask Susan."

"No!" yelled Wilbur.

"Then talk to me, old man," he demanded, sitting on the coffee table. "I don't need you passing out on Isabel . . . or worse." He wanted to say dying on her, but couldn't get the words out. As much as he hated his pops, he didn't necessarily wish death on him.

"Don't take her. She's gone through enough." An alarm went off on Wilbur's phone. "You need to go. She'll be out in ten minutes."

Jimmy stood to leave, turned back remembering his broken

phone. “Oh, I don’t have a phone. I . . . uh, . . . broke it.”

“I’ll be fine. Go. Don’t be late.”

She took one step forward and caught his eye. Instantly she froze. Jimmy could see her big blue eyes grow and her smile spread as pure excitement spread throughout her body.

“Daddy! Daddy!” she yelled, running toward him.

That’s my girl, he thought. A pair of lungs capable of shattering glass. She first introduced those lungs to the world eleven years ago. He held her in his arms for the first time. From day one, she’d shown him she was a force to be reckoned with. And all he could do was stare into the small shiny slits, exposing her bluish-gray eyes that eventually turned deep blue. He heard that babies don’t see much of anything when they’re born. But she saw him that day. She stared right back at him and till this day, she still saw him. Like Will. The only two people in this world worth anything. Even then he couldn’t believe she was his. She was part of him, his blood. His angel. How did he get so lucky?

“Isabella Rose Dumel,” he said, calling her by her full name.

She frowned. She hated when he did that.

“Look at you,” he went on, taking her in his arms and twirling her around. “I think you’ve grown a few inches since I saw you last.”

She beamed. “I have?”

“You definitely have. Is that a new sweater?” he asked. “It’s beautiful.”

She smiled. “Grandpa bought it for me yesterday.”

“That’s nice.”

She looked at his truck. “Where’s Grandpa?”

"He's home. I wanted to pick you up. How does ice-cream sound?"

"Good! Guess what we did today, Daddy?"

He opened the door of his truck for her, "Get in and tell me all about it." He turned and noticed a young woman watching him. She caught him off guard and he quickly looked away. He got in his truck and shut the door. "Who's that lady watching us?" he asked, turning the ignition. She made him uncomfortable. She looked familiar, but he couldn't place her.

"Oh, that's my teacher, Ms. Peters," she announced. "Oh Daddy, I want you to meet her. She's the best teacher ever . . . oh, no . . ."

"What is it?"

"I forgot she wanted to talk to Grandpa today," she said, disappointed she had forgotten.

That would explain her watching them. But why did she look familiar? He couldn't get her out of his head. There was something about the way she looked at him.

"Why did she want to talk to Grandpa?"

Isabel's happy mood took a sudden turn. "Uh . . . I don't know. I think . . . it's about the conferences coming up."

"Oh. When are they?"

"I think next week. Can you make it?"

"I'm not sure." He glanced at her. "That's still a week away. Let's have fun today, get ice cream, and watch a movie."

"We get to watch a movie, too?" she asked, bouncing in her seat.

"Sure, why not? Now, tell me about your day," he said, as he pulled away from the school.

He smiled at his daughter, who wore a permanent grin from ear to ear. It was good to see her happy. He did that. He'd forgotten how easy it was to make her happy.

She rambled on and on. He couldn't really say about what. He nodded and reacted when he thought he should, but he wasn't listening to the actual words coming out of her mouth. He was wondering what it was like for her to be without her mom and dad. He was wondering if his pops treated her good. She had dark circles under her eyes.

Without missing a beat, she said, "Daddy, are you listening?"

"Yeah, of course . . . you were talking about . . ."

"Daddyyy," she said, in a disappointed tone, carrying the e out an extra second.

"I'm sorry baby. I'll try harder. I have a lot on my mind."

"That's okay." Then without warning, she added, "Grandpa said they still haven't found Mommy . . ."

This was a bad idea, he thought. He wanted to see her. He needed to see her. But he wasn't ready to discuss Robin with her.

He didn't answer, and she didn't press.

He needed time to think of a response.

Jimmy fell down on his bed with all his clothes on, he was beat. He stared at the ceiling thinking how his pops had never answered any of his questions. He'd talked himself in circles not responding directly to a single one.

He'd left his daughter with an old man who had passed out and couldn't say for how long. What did that say about Jimmy?

He needed to settle his shit and quick.

Isabella Rose—what would he do with her as a single

father? Could he raise her on his own? He had missed taking her trick-or-treating—something Robin usually did anyway. Isabel said she'd had fun with Wilbur. He could see she had.

Would her life get better or worse once she found out her mother was dead? He didn't even want to think about what life would be like if she ever found out he'd killed her mother. . . .

The detective.

What the hell was he going to do about Ryan? He went to the hospital that day after he saw the news. Despite the news not releasing his name, they had said enough. He had to see for himself. If he had lived, Jimmy had to finish him off. It was stupid really. Thinking he'd be able to get to him. Wishful thinking was all that amounted to. Not from a lack of effort. He tried finding a way in without getting noticed. The media was everywhere. And the cops . . .

That's it!

He saw the teacher at the hospital.

He sat up, playing the day over in his head. He absently took out a cigarette and lit it. Inhaling, he recalled a young woman, long dark hair pulled up into a ponytail. Her hair was down today, but he wouldn't forget her pale beautiful face. She saw him drive by. Looked right at him, as if she was looking for someone and thought he might be the person whom she'd been searching for.

Who was she looking for? he wondered. And why was she there that day? She was a long way from home.

The opened side door at the hospital had caught his eye as he drove around trying to find a way in. And out came a doctor. He shook the older man's hand and hugged the young lady. He thought it odd. He drove right by them. Couldn't have been more than ten feet away.

The old man . . .

He's the one he thought looked familiar to him that day. He knew he'd seen him before. But where? He looked at his cigarette that had burned halfway through, tapped off the tip, and put it between his lips.

He tried to recall where he'd seen the old man. He sat back thinking. If the teacher was with him, maybe he knew her, too . . .

No, he didn't think he'd ever seen her before the hospital.

The doctor didn't look familiar at all. Forget the doctor.

He leaned over and put his cigarette out. Talking to himself, he said, "Okay, the old man and teacher were there at the same hospital Ryan was at . . ." he paused, thinking. "I shot Ryan Cross, I go to the hospital to finish him off and I see the old man who I know I've seen before—but where? The old man knows the teacher . . ."

What the fuck?

He stood up and started pacing. No way he's sleeping now. Why is this bothering him so much? There were a lot of people there that day.

His head hurt.

He found himself in his kitchen opening a bottle of aspirin. His mind drifted to Wilbur and the bump on his head. He removed a glass from his half-empty cupboard and filled it with tap water. He swallowed the pills thinking, *What if Wilbur died?* What would he do with Isabel? He hadn't been to a funeral since . . .

"Well, I'll be a monkey's uncle!" he shouted.

The old man—he looked familiar because he saw him that day—the day of William's funeral. That was what?—sixteen years ago—but he would never forget that family. The old man was the driver. Not just any driver, Ben's dad.

He thought about killing him, too, but Ben's wife and kids were so much better.

After all these years . . .

THIRTY-ONE

IN THE BARN, SHE PUNCHED AND KICKED THE heavy bag. Mabel had been thinking of her man in black for thirty minutes when Frankie snuck up on her. "Hey, you," he said, scaring the hell out of her.

"Oh my God! Uncle Frankie, what the fuck!?" she said, holding her heart from erupting out of her chest.

"Whoa," he said laughing. "I thought I taught you better than letting someone sneak up on you?"

"You did. I . . . I just . . ." she was lost for words.

"Who you beating up anyway?"

"What's the plan, Uncle Frankie?" she finally asked. "Because if there isn't one, then I'll make one myself. I can't wait any longer. Not while he's out there. We know he's the one that shot Ryan. Grandpa says to focus on Ryan, but they're connected. If we catch my man in black, we catch Ryan's shooter. What are we waiting for?" Tears welled up in her eyes. She turned so he wouldn't see.

"Hey. Hold on, Mabel," he said, grabbing her by the arm and pulling her in close for a hug.

She let him. It felt good and she needed the comfort. The security. She wouldn't let herself cry. She squeezed her eyes tight, took a deep breath and pulled away.

"I'm tired. I'm tired of waiting. I've waited sixteen years. Grandpa says we'll go after him together, but I can't wait any longer. I know his priority is protecting me, and I love him for it, but I'm not an eleven-year-old girl anymore. I need to do something. I'm ready to go after this bastard."

His eyes narrowed and a muscle in his jaw twitched. He lifted an eyebrow and looked her over.

She added, "You and me. Let's go get him." She put her hand on his muscular shoulder. "Let's do some sparring. You really bring it this time and see if I've maintained what you taught me. What do you say?" she kidded.

"Oh, hell, Mabel. You were kicking my ass the other day. If you held back—then, shit, girl."

She smiled, pleased with herself. Mabel wanted to make him proud, often feeling like an amateur next to him.

"But," he added, "your grandpa loves you and would do anything for you, and don't you ever forget that."

"I know," she said slowly, unsure where he was going.

"You can't just go out there willy-nilly by yourself and hope to catch a killer. That's just plain stupid."

Ouch.

"Your grandpa is trying to protect you, be thankful for that. If he would have said as much, would you have listened to him?"

She didn't say anything and neither did he. The branches scraping against the exterior of the barn sent chills through her. She wrapped her arms around herself.

"No, you wouldn't have." He answered for her. "And don't give me that look."

What look? Her mouth dropped. For the life of her, words would not come.

"Speak woman."

She blinked. "I . . . I don't know what to say."

"Listen, I love you. You know this, but it's high time you snap out of this." He sighed. "Sometimes I just want to . . . smack you on the head," he blurted out. "But I would never do that. Because I love you, and I'd never hit a woman." He shook his head. "But, girl . . ."

She snickered. She had tried keeping a straight face but failed.

"This is serious," he said. His deep voice took a higher pitch.

A smile spread across her face and a chuckle escaped her.

"This isn't funny," he continued.

She broke out into an all-out laugh.

"Mabel! Stop laughing," he demanded. As expected, he rewarded her with the deep belly laugh she loved.

She caught her breath. "I'm sorry, Uncle Frankie. I heard you. I just couldn't get the image out of my head . . . ," she giggled again, ". . . of you smacking me on the head."

"You found that funny? I thought you would be mad."

"No, no. You're right. I think I could use a good knock."

"I have something to show you," he said.

"That reminds me—where were you all day?"

"That's what I want to show you."

He pulled out some folded papers from his back pocket. As he unfolded them, Mabel could make out a list.

"What is that?" she asked.

"These are all the names of the victims in your dad's car

accident back in ninety-seven." He handed her the list. "The highlighted names are the names of the victims—people that were actually in the accident. Everyone was interviewed by either Ryan or Bill sixteen years ago. The circled names underneath the highlighted ones are the closest relatives, or anyone that could be connected. These people were also interviewed back then."

Mabel looked at the long list of names. "How about the ones that aren't circled or highlighted?"

"Those are the ones I added. Additional people of interest that were never looked at or questioned according to Ryan's files."

"Who are they?"

"They're siblings, cousins, aunts, uncles, girlfriend, boyfriend, friends, coworkers, bosses—anyone that had a connection."

"I don't understand," she said, confused. "Why would Ryan, or Bill for that matter, not have questioned them? Isn't that what detectives do?"

Frankie blamed Ryan. But Bill White was Ryan's superior at the time, so it wasn't all Ryan's fault. There are plenty of cases out there that go unsolved. Was Frankie being too tough on Ryan or was she being too soft?

"Mabel, I don't know why. All I know is—in my line of work—I pursue every angle. I look at everyone. Everyone's a suspect until proven otherwise." He handed her another list.

"There's more?" she asked, taking the papers.

"Well, yes. That list has the names of the three that died . . . including your dad. I'd like to start with this list and then move to the victims who lost the most; such as an injury that left them disabled or worse."

She opened the papers, afraid to see the names. She knew three people died that day, but she never knew the other two names. Maybe she'd seen them. She couldn't remember.

~~Ben Stucker.~~ ~~Margaret Stucker.~~ ~~Melodi Stucker.~~ ~~Peter Stucker.~~

A tear streamed down her cheek.

~~William Dumel.~~ Wilbur Dumel. Jimmy Dumel. ~~Joni Dumel.~~

"Oh my God!" shouted Mabel.

"What?"

"Do you have pictures of these people by chance?"

"Not on me. Why?"

"I think I know Wilbur and Jimmy Dumel," she said, pointing at the names, handing the paper back to Frankie. Her heart raced. The bad vibes she'd been getting were coming true.

Could it really be them?

"How do you know them?" he asked, skeptical.

She took two bottles of water out of the small refrigerator and offered one to Frankie. She sipped the other, her hands shaking. "I have a new student," she said. "Her name is—Isabel Dumel." The sound of her last name was surreal.

"Well, shit," Frankie said.

She looked at Frankie. "I met her grandpa, Wilbur Dumel. She's living with him now." She paused to let him digest the news. "And I saw her father today. I never got his name, but my guess is it's Jimmy."

"That's a stroke of fucking bad luck right there." He mouthed the words, *what the fuck*. Exactly how she felt. "Wait, what do you mean you saw? Did you meet him?"

"No. Wilbur picks her up every day from school. I don't think she expected her dad today. As a matter in fact, she had confided in me earlier that she thought her dad didn't want her. The girl's a wreck."

"How long has she been in your class?"

"Only a week. She started the Monday after someone shot Ryan."

"I don't like it."

"What would Ryan's shooting have to do with her switching schools though?"

"I don't know, but it seems odd."

"What's odd is her telling me her dad told her and her grandpa to keep a secret."

"What secret?"

"I don't know. She never told me. Now that her dad showed up, I don't know if I'll be able to get her to talk again. She was feeling rejected at the time. You should have seen her light up when she saw him. She was so happy."

"Where's her mom?"

"I don't know that either. She said she's not supposed to talk about it."

"Now that's odd."

"Tell me about it. There're a lot of red flags when it comes to this little girl. Something's not right. She's such a sweet little girl too."

"What does your gut tell you about Wilbur?"

"I've only talked to him once. He seemed nice enough. Protective, proud, and a bit standoffish. Kind of in line with her demeanor. I can't tell if Isabel's comes from Wilbur or her dad."

Frankie opened his water and chugged it, wiped his mouth, and stared at the paper in his hand.

"Why is Joni's name crossed off?" she asked.

"That's Wilbur's wife. She committed suicide a year after the car accident."

Mabel's jaw dropped.

"Weird right? The same day someone murdered your family. Wilbur was Jimmy's alibi and Jimmy was Wilbur's alibi. My guess is Bill believed the mom dying gave them a pretty good alibi. *I think* it would give someone all the more reason to go after someone's family—if they believed he was responsible for the death of their son and wife . . . or brother and mom."

"My God. Could my man in black really be right under my nose?"

Frankie held her gaze. "It's possible. Do you have any reason to believe he knows who you are?"

She saw Jimmy from fifty yards away. He didn't appear to know who she was, but she couldn't get past the look. "I don't think he knew who I was. But, I didn't get a good feeling about him."

"Watch yourself, Mabel," he warned. "This doesn't feel right. He could be using his little girl to get close to you."

She didn't get that feeling, but she'd take his advice.

THIRTY-TWO

THE CALL CAME AN HOUR BEFORE SCHOOL started. She'd spent the night at her grandpa's, making a detour by her house to throw a load of laundry in the wash. She heard a faint ringing as she neared her car. She touched her pant pockets—empty. She looked at her car and hurried to answer it, struggling to open the door.

Ryan? Lucas?

Finding her phone, she looked at the number she didn't recognize. "Hello," she said, her voice throaty.

Not Ryan or Lucas. A kid.

A kid crying uncontrollably and gasping for air. Panicked, Mabel blurted out, "Who is this? Who's there?"

"Is . . . is this Ms. Peters?" asked a soft voice in between sobs.

"It is. Who is this?" She had an idea but asked anyway.

"It's Isabel," she whimpered. "My grandpa, he . . . he won't wake up."

"Isabel—" her mind blank. She visualized her scared and

bawling for the man who was supposed to care for her. *Was he dead?*

"Ms. Peters? I don't know what to do."

Snapping out of it, she said, "You did good calling me. Have you called anyone else?"

"My daddy won't answer his phone," she whined. "I tried him three times."

Of course, he's not answering. Why would he? *Asshole!* She put her key in the ignition. "I'm on my way. Where do live?"

"452 Locust Street."

"Good job, Isabel," she said slowly, as she pulled out of her driveway. "I'll be there in less than ten minutes." She knew the area. It was near a park, not far from the school.

Isabel sniffled. "K."

"Is he . . . do you know if he's breathing?"

"I think so. He was making breakfast," she explained. "I was getting ready and I heard it," she was sobbing again. "I'm scared. I tried to wake him up."

"You did good. I'm on my way. I have to hang up now—"

"No!"

"I have to call 9-1-1 so they can send an ambulance for your grandpa."

"K."

"They might call you, so if the phone rings, be sure to answer it."

"K."

Mabel hung up, her head spinning as she dialed. A few minutes later she pulled up to a pale-yellow, one-story ranch style home. The early morning darkness brought temperatures below freezing for the first time this fall. A nip in the air, the way it felt before a storm. The weather lady had informed her there was a slight chance for snow, the first of the season. She shivered as she stepped onto the porch and rang the doorbell.

Isabel peeked out the window, panic written all over her face. Her eyes met Mabel's and disappeared—*click, click*—the door swung open.

Mabel took a step forward and was met with thin arms wrapped tightly around her waist, keeping her from the warmth of the house.

Isabel cried convulsively, each breath gasping for air. Attempting to talk, her voice caught in her throat. "He . . . he . . ." she cried. Tears soaked through Mabel's shirt.

Mabel held her tight, shushing her like a baby. "Shhh, shhh, shhh. I'm here. I'm here." Holding Isabel close, comforting her, she spotted legs sticking out from behind the couch. Gently pulling her away, she said, "The ambulance will be here any minute. I need to check on your grandpa."

Isabel nodded and followed Mabel, watching intently.

Wilbur lay on his side. Mabel rolled him onto his back, happy to not find the pool of blood she had imagined. His chest wasn't moving.

"Wilbur!" she shouted when his chest failed to give signs of life. "Wilbur!" she shouted again, louder, tapping his shoulder.

She ripped open his shirt and started chest compressions—one, two, three, four . . . she counted under her breath.

Isabel cried harder.

Despite being tired, she kept going. She couldn't stop.

The sound of the siren was music to her ears. Two men, wearing dark navy-blue, rushed through the open door. The first EMT, and most prominent one of the two, was named Chuck. The white lettering on his shirt said so. Chuck had a tribal tattoo on his muscular lower left forearm and she guessed him to be in his mid-thirties. But what stood out to her was his shiny bald head. She'd seen bald heads, but his was smooth and touchable. Frankie was bald, but his head didn't shine like Chuck's.

The other EMT looked like he'd just hit puberty. The white lettering on his shirt read, Mark. Chuck pulled out an AED and attached it to Wilbur.

Mabel made room for the two men, pulling Isabel close. She fought the lump in her throat. Isabel needed family not her teacher.

Mark flipped a switch; a shock went through Wilbur.

Nothing.

Chuck continued CPR. Mark asked how long he'd been out. Mabel explained the best she could.

To Mabel's surprise, Wilbur moaned. Without missing a beat, Mark and Chuck put him on the stretcher and wheeled him out the door and into the back of their vehicle.

Chuck shut the doors and told Mabel they were taking him to the Medical Center of the Rockies. She held on to Isabel as the ambulance pulled away and turned the corner. As they walked back to the house, she realized she hadn't called in to work. What would she say? No one at school could know she was with Isabel. She didn't need to tell them anything. She had an emergency, which was true.

Isabel stared out the big window. The ache in Mabel's stomach grew as she watched her. She put her hand on Isabel's shoulder. "Has your grandpa been sick?"

She shrugged. "He's been tired a lot." She spun around and hugged Mabel's waist. "I didn't know who else to call."

She cupped Isabel's cheek in her hand and moved her face up till she met her eyes. "You did good. I gave you my number to use when you needed it. I'm proud of you."

The next step terrified Mabel. The situation required Isabel's dad be notified. Then again, Isabel had already tried to call him.

"Is there anyone else we can call?" asked Mabel.

"My Aunt Susie. She's my mom's sister."

"Where's your mom, Isabel?" *No more secrets.*

"I don't know," she cried.

The last thing she wanted was to make things worse for her. But she had to know. "Is she—"

"She's missing . . ." she blurted out.

Nausea came over her. Without thinking, she pulled her close and stroked her hair.

"That's why I moved in with my grandpa. No one can find her."

"How long—"

"She's been gone eleven days."

Mabel hugged her tighter. She scanned the room for tissues and spotted Wilbur's phone. "Let's try your aunt. She can meet us at the hospital. Do you need anything before we go?"

Isabel bit her lip and her eyes drifted to her room. "Can I take my stuffed dog that my grandpa gave me?"

"Of course, you can. How about your grandpa? What will he want?"

"His phone . . . and maybe his new magazine." She ran to the kitchen and came out with a National Geographic still in its plastic sleeve. "He hasn't read this one yet."

"Good idea." Mabel followed her to her bedroom. Isabel pulled the covers back on her bed exposing a brown dog with fluffy ears. "What's your dog's name?"

"I named him Wilbur, after my grandpa," she said, managing a weak smile and clutching the stuffed dog against her chest.

"That's a good name. I bet he keeps you safe."

"Mhm."

Mabel found the house keys, locked up and left for the hospital. On the way she had Isabel call her aunt. Mabel learned Isabel's aunt lived near her dad. Susie said she would check his apartment and work.

"What's your dad's name?"

"Jimmy," she said, pulling her legs up on her seat and wrapping her arms around them.

Mabel drove in silence, lost in thought. The day had taken an unexpected turn. She woke up dreading work, wanting nothing more than to hunt for the man who changed her entire life. And now, to think, he may be coming to her.

Could Isabel's dad really be her man in black?

The thought terrified her.

Is this what she wanted? To be in the middle of Isabel's personal life? She had been a teacher for five years and had cared for all her students. She'd met many who had appeared to have personal problems, but none like Isabel. Isabel was different.

At several points in her life she had fantasized about confronting her family's killer. He wouldn't know her, but she would know him. She would have the strategic advantage. She would be stronger and smarter. And she'd only strike when she was ready. He would never see it coming.

Was she ready?

Mabel sat with Isabel in the cafeteria, while the doctors ran tests on Wilbur. On the outside, she appeared as a lady watching a girl eat her breakfast. On the inside, a storm brewed as Mabel imagined the shitstorm that would certainly come her way when Jimmy showed up. *What would she say?*

What would she do? How would she get him alone?

"I need to make a call. I'll be over there where you can see me."

Isabel glanced toward the window where Mabel said she'd be. She bit down on her lip, pushed her plate away and said she wasn't hungry.

"I'll be quick. Ten minutes most," Mabel added. "I've got to make two quick calls," she continued.

Isabel's eyes desperate, she blinked away tears. "B-but . . . ," she looked down at her plate.

"I won't be long. I promise. When you finish eating, if I'm still on the phone, you can come join me, okay?"

"K," she said, with a slight hesitation.

Mabel let out an involuntary moan as she walked away. She didn't want to leave her, but at the same time, she had to talk in private.

"Grandpa, you're never going to believe where I am and who I'm with."

"You're with Isabel, although I have no idea where you might be. The zoo?" he guessed.

"Yes, I'm with Isabel, but why would we be at the zoo?" she asked, annoyed. "We're at the hospital. Her grandpa nearly died this morning and she called me."

"For pete's sake, Mabel! Where's her dad?"

"Who the hell knows. She already called him, whose name is Jimmy by the way. He's not answering. Isabel got a hold of her aunt who lives near him. She's trying to find him."

"You need to leave as soon as you can. If Jimmy is who we think he is, it's not safe for you."

"I'm not going anywhere," she said defiantly. "He doesn't know who I am, and I can't leave her. At least not until she's with a family member."

"I can understand you want to protect the girl, but—"

"Where's Uncle Frankie?"

"Hold on," he said irritated. The phone went dead for a moment.

Mabel turned to Isabel, who was on Wilbur's phone. Her dad? She felt a flutter in her chest.

"Mabel, I got Frankie on the line."

"Hey Mabel! I hear you're at the hospital with Jimmy's daughter. That doesn't sound safe," shouted Frankie.

"Well, what can I say? Trouble follows me."

"No shit!"

She didn't have much time, she had to make her point. "Isabel told me this morning that her mom's missing. Has been for eleven days."

"What do you mean—missing?" her grandpa asked.

"Wait . . . that means she went missing the same day someone shot Ryan," Frankie said.

"I did the math, too."

"Son-of-a-bitch!" shouted Frankie.

"Franklin Dowdy! Watch your language in my house," shouted Grandma in the background.

"Sorry, Kat."

Mabel smiled. "Remember the secret . . . I'm thinking this poor girl knows something about that day."

"I think you're right," Frankie agreed.

Frankie and Grandpa were discussing what to do. Should Frankie find Jimmy and follow him or keep an eye on Mabel.

"I'm done, Ms. Peters," Isabel said from behind.

How long had she been standing there?

"Isabel," Mabel announced into the phone, looking at the stealthy blue-eyed girl who now stood before her. Mabel glanced at the table where she'd sat. "Did you get enough to eat?" she asked.

She nodded and smiled.

"Good." Mabel spotted a bench nearby. "Let's sit here. I'm almost done."

"K." She shrugged her shoulders. A shade of pink back in her cheeks.

"I have to go," Mabel said. "Can you two finish discussing this and I'll call back. Better yet, text me and I'll call back when I get a moment."

"Will do," said Frankie.

"Be careful," Grandpa added.

"Are you carrying?" Frankie asked.

Damn. She left it in the car. Not like she could have brought her gun inside the hospital anyhow.

"Mabel? Are you?" Grandpa asked.

"It's in the car. I'll be safe," she said, her heart racing like a freight train.

THIRTY-THREE

HERE WE GO AGAIN, THOUGHT JIMMY. PEOPLE screwing with his day. He had planned on finding the fucknut detective. He learned a little secret about Ryan Cross searching the web. Detective Cross had investigated a triple homicide sixteen years ago and come up empty-handed. Poor little detective.

Could it be a coincidence his bitch of a wife was snitching on Jimmy to the same detective that investigated his misdeeds? He hadn't given her enough credit. She knew exactly what she was doing.

Bitch! What the hell is it with his family?

Then Susan, of all people, called him at work to tell him about his pops. She offered to pick up Isabel. Hell no, no way would he let that shit happen.

Jimmy called his pops to find out what was going on and Isabel answered instead.

"Where are you?" A question he shouldn't have to ask.

"I'm here at the hospital with Grandpa and Ms. Peters," she replied, coolly.

He felt the steam boil up to his ears. Susan left out the hospital and the fact that his daughter was with some stranger. "Who the hell is Ms. Peters?" Jimmy asked, fuming.

"Why are you yelling at me, daddy? I tried to call you."

The thought occurred to him that he never gave Wilbur his new number. She called his old phone. The phone still in pieces on his floor.

"I'm sorry, baby, I didn't mean to get upset. I'm just worried about Pops and you."

"She's my teacher from school. I pointed her out to you yesterday. I called her when you didn't answer."

The lady from the hospital.

His mind raced. Why would she call her teacher? Surely there were other alternatives.

"How did you call her?"

"What you mean?"

"Did you call her at school?"

"No. She gave me her phone number."

Holy fucking shit! Why would a teacher give a student her personal phone number? That was about the creepiest fucked up thing he'd ever heard. His breathing heavy, fists curled into balls, his chest elevated and dropped. Up and down, up and down.

"Daddy? Are you mad at me?" she whispered.

"Yes! No!" *Why would she call her teacher?* All this was her teacher's fault. "Isabel, who is this teacher? Why did you call her?"

"She's nice, Daddy. She gave me her number to call if I ever needed her and . . . and I didn't know who else to call. It scared me."

He had questions about this teacher.

"Where is she now?"

"She's on the phone, by the window."

"What's her first name?" He tried to think. Her teacher was with James Stucker at the hospital on the day he shot Ryan. Why? He'd tried finding James after he killed the Stuckers. And he vanished—only to show up the day he shot Ryan—and with Isabel's teacher . . .

"Mabel Peters. She's nice Daddy."

Stop saying she's nice!

"What has she told you? Who is she? Where does she come from?"

"You're scaring me."

"Isabel," he shouted. "Listen to me very closely," He lowered his voice. "This ain't right. Nothing about it is right, you hear me?"

"What do you mean?"

"Teachers just don't go around giving their personal numbers to kids. She's up to something. Did she try to touch you . . . you know, in your private parts?"

"No, Daddy. Never."

"Good, good. That's good baby." He'd cut her head off if she did. "Now tell me—who is she. What do you know about her?"

"She said her grandparents raised her, that her parents died when they were my age."

"Holy fuck! It is her," he said, under his breath.

"She just moved back here, to Colorado."

"You did real good baby," he said, smiling. "I'm proud of you." He couldn't be more proud.

"Are you coming? I'm scared. I don't know what to do. I

don't like being alone. I called Aunt Susie, too."

"Yeah, baby. I'm coming. I'm on my way. Watch yourself—and stay in the hospital."

"K, bye Daddy," she said. He could hear the uncertainty in her voice.

"And Baby?"

"Yes, Daddy?"

"Don't tell her we spoke or that I'm coming. I want to meet her. I don't want her scared off. She needs a talking to. I promise I'll be nice. I know you like her."

"K."

His damn kid was too trusting. He'd fix that. It was about time she learned to take care of herself. She was old enough. He had to toughen her up. That's what she needed.

THIRTY-FOUR

AS IT TURNED OUT, WILBUR COULD NO LONGER ignore his waning health. The doctor told him his granddaughter and her teacher had saved his life. He had gone into cardiac arrest this morning. If she hadn't performed CPR on him, he would have died.

He remembered feeling faint and hearing voices and then waking up in the hospital. He later went into shock due to his varices rupturing. Basically, his cirrhosis is blocking the flow of blood to his liver. He had the godforsaken disease. The blood flow must find a new way, which forms in the upper stomach and esophagus, which are likely to burst. That explained him coughing up blood.

He never realized drinking alcohol could do so much damage to his insides. Wasn't the human body supposed to break down the foods and beverages he put into it? His body absorbed the alcohol giving him the feeling he craved—silenced his past, numbed the pain, simply took away his ability to think.

For the longest time it had been his miracle drug. It healed him. And he drank it again and again, ignoring the part of him that said he drank too much. He silenced that part with more scotch—his miracle drug of choice.

Now as he looked back at all the years wasted, he wondered why.

Why did he do it? Why did anyone else for that matter?

Why did he put the so-called miracle drug into his body day after day, night after night? He could see clearly now. It's no miracle drug. It's a silent killer.

Hey dumbasses, wanna die? Oh, you do? Maybe not today or tomorrow. Drink some of our cool refreshing booze, become dumb and stupid, maybe smack your wife and kids around—that would be a bonus, wouldn't it? And then suffer and die of cirrhosis, maybe cancer if you're lucky.

He was being dramatic, feeling sorry for himself. No one forced him to start drinking. No one forced him to keep drinking.

He had regrets.

Things he would do over—if he could.

If he could, he would have said no to his first drink, at fourteen, when his dad offered it to him. But Wilbur didn't blame his dad, even if he was an alcoholic. Jack Dumel never laid a hand on his wife or kids. Wilbur could only guess that his dad drank because he simply wasn't happy with the life the good Lord handed him. He saw it in his eyes. The disappointment, the shame.

If he could, Wilbur would never have gone to her house that night. If he could, he would have died too. He took the wrong path and now he's paying his debt.

Some things you never forget.

He shut his eyes, ready to die.

The doctor's words ran through his head—*Bleeding from varices is life-threatening. Your liver cannot remove toxins effectively. This leads to accumulating toxins in your blood which can impair your mental function, lead to personality changes, and possibly a coma.*

An image of Isabel appeared. Her smile, her laugh.

"I need a little more time," he whispered.

How would he care for Isabel?

He couldn't. That's all there was to it.

His boy wasn't ready to take her back. No matter how much he wanted Jimmy to be a good father, he wasn't ready—

He may never be.

THIRTY-FIVE

"MY GRANDPA WANTS TO TALK TO YOU," Isabel announced. Her red eyes were becoming a permanent look. "He asked me to wait here till you send me in."

Without hesitation Mabel jumped up, her butt sore from the uncomfortable chair in the waiting room she'd been sitting on. She glanced at her watch. Jesus, three hours had passed, it seemed more like a lifetime.

No sign of Jimmy yet.

She couldn't help but feel nervous. She didn't know Wilbur. For all she knew, Wilbur could be a killer. As she made her way to door 211, she reminded herself this man cared for Isabel, when her good-for-nothing father couldn't.

She opened the door and a sudden gust of pungent hospital smells, mixed with the stench of urine, overcame her. The odor reminded her of pain, agony, and death. Shivering, she closed the door behind her.

"Ms. Peters, is it?" muttered Wilbur.

"Yes, but please call me Mabel." She scanned the room. He had a heart monitor and IV hooked up. She made herself comfortable in the god-awful, multi-colored, striped chair. "How are you?" she asked.

"That's what I wanted to talk to you about. I owe you a huge thanks," he said. "From what I'm told, you saved my life."

Should she say *you're welcome?* That didn't seem appropriate. She thought of Isabel. "You gave your granddaughter quite a scare. All I could think of . . ." she hesitated, thinking of her own grandpa, "was saving the man who's the center of her world."

"Yes. Well, there's another reason I wanted to speak with you. She thinks very highly of you, Ms. Peters."

Mabel smiled. "She's a sweet girl." She wanted to say how much she liked Isabel, how she'd do anything for her, but she thought he wouldn't understand.

"Thank you for being there for her."

"Absolutely," she said, searching his face. His black eyes tired, somber.

"She adores you," he continued. "I've never seen her this way with anyone, beside . . ." he looked away, "beside her mom."

"I'm happy to help any way I can."

"She told me you also lost your parents when you were young."

She licked her lips, her mouth dry. She wondered if he could hear her heart banging in her chest. She took a deep breath. "Yes. Isabel has good and bad days in school. She needs someone to talk to and I know all too well what she's going through. I hope I didn't cross the line."

"No, not at all. I'm glad she has you," he said, grabbing Mabel's hand.

She flinched, immediately regretting it, as she caught the shock in his eyes.

"I'm sorry, I didn't mean to—"

"I'm sorry," she interrupted. "I guess, I'm a bit on edge. I'm worried about her. She can't get in touch with her dad.

She watched his reaction. His face hardened the moment she said *dad.* For a split second, she thought she went too far.

"That boy makes it hard on everyone around him. Most recently his daughter," he grumbled. "I haven't spoken to him since yesterday. He showed up unexpectedly at my house saying he wanted to pick Isabel up from school. I think he was trying to make amends for not showing up for dinner the night before."

"I'm sorry." His story aligned to what Isabel told her.

"I haven't been straightforward with you. Jimmy, my boy, he loves Isabel. I have no doubts about that. But he ain't so smart that one. He's made a lot of trouble for himself."

That's putting it lightly, she thought, straining to keep a straight face. She kept quiet, patiently waiting for him to keep talking.

A dark shadow came over his face. This man knew more than he wanted to—just like Isabel. What if he was as demented as his son? Don't they say '*like father, like son, or the apple doesn't fall far from the tree?*'

After a minute, he took a deep breath and looked at her. "Jimmy," he snorted, "he did the most terrible thing and can't be, shouldn't be," he stressed, "around Isabel. I convinced him it would be best if she lived with me until things calmed down."

"Isabel's mom, where is she?"

"Let's just say I don't think she's ever coming back," he said, looking away.

Jesus Christ, what was he getting at? Her skin crawled. He was going to say what she'd been thinking all along. She waited for the words to come out.

The door opened and a nurse in blue scrubs walked in.

No! Not now.

"Hi," said the obtrusive nurse, smiling at Mabel.

Her very bad timing was not worthy of a smile. Instead, Mabel threw daggers at the nurse. Regardless of her immaturity, she didn't care.

The nurse, most likely uncomfortable, turned her attention to Wilbur. "Mr. Dumel is due for his medication," she said. "It won't take long," she reassured, glancing at Mabel, displaying pure compassion.

Mabel sunk back into her chair and gave a quick half-smile, all the while feeling like crap. Here this lady was, doing her job, clearly a natural, and all Mabel could think about was getting information from a sick and possibly dying man. She watched the nurse closely—Kristine, according to her badge. She chatted with Wilbur the whole time. Kristine had dark hair and no makeup, and though she could have used a little, she obviously cared more about her patients than she did about looking good for them. *An innate beauty,* thought Mabel.

Mabel stepped out to check on Isabel and found her reading a magazine. Why hadn't she suggested she bring one of her books?

"Hi. You doing okay?" Mabel asked.

"Just tired. Can I see my grandpa yet?"

"The nurse is checking on him now. We're almost done talking. Can you give us a little more time?"

"Sure," she said, looking down at the magazine.

"How about I have one of the nurses bring you an actual book you can read? I'm sure they have some here."

"Sure, okay. This magazine is dumb anyway." She tossed *Taste of Home* on the chair next to her.

Mabel chuckled. Of all magazines for an eleven-year-old to choose. She asked one of the ladies at the counter for any children's books that a tween might like. The lady beamed, said she had just the thing, disappeared, and came back with *Wonderstruck.* She said one of the nurses found it last week and no one ever claimed it. It hadn't made it over to lost and found yet.

Mabel handed the book to Isabel and searched for water, thinking she should have asked for some to begin with. Finding it opposite the nurses station, she helped herself to one and another for Isabel. Isabel was reading her new book when she returned, so she decided to check her phone. She gasped when she saw she had several texts and a few missed calls.

CALL ME! Frankie.

Her phone lit up, she had another message from Frankie.

Mabel . . . Are you safe? Call me. First, get out . . . then call.

Not yet. She didn't hear everything Wilbur had to say. He wanted to talk, and she needed more time with him.

"All done," said Kristine the Nurse, coming out of Wilbur's room.

Shoving her phone into her pocket she grabbed her purse. "I won't be long," she said to Isabel.

Mabel scurried back into Wilbur's room. "How are you feeling?" she asked.

"I'm dying," he blurted out, his face pale.

"What?" she whispered. That was the last thing she expected him to say.

"I don't have much longer. I have cirrhosis. I've had it for a while now and I'm in my later stages."

"But aren't there treatments? Drugs, a transplant—"

"Listen Mabel, I made my decision a long time ago. Truth is, I haven't felt well for some time. I made my bed . . . but now . . ."

"Isabel?"

"Yes. That was before Isabel. But it's too late for me now. I can take drugs to help with the confusion I've been having, but it's only going to get worse. I'm too far gone. I don't trust myself with her, not after this morning." Tears welled up in his eyes. "My boy, Jimmy, he . . . he just ain't right. I don't trust him with her either, but for different reasons."

"Why? Tell me why!" she demanded.

"She's not safe with him," his voice wobbly. "God forgive me," he prayed. His right hand wiped away tears from his eyes. He looked like a man getting ready to go to confession. He knew he didn't have much time and wanted to get his sins and the sins of his son off his chest.

Mabel wasn't Catholic, but she had friends who were. She remembered her friend Rachel telling her about the sacrament of penance when she was a senior in high school. Her friend had just gone to confession and told her all about it. Mabel had sins she thought she needed to confess and asked her grandpa why they never went to church. He said he believed in God, considered himself a Christian, but didn't feel the need to put it on display. If the Lord Almighty loved everyone, he would surely be forgiven for not showing up to church every Sunday or Saturday or whatever day he chose to pray. Believing is all he needed.

She asked him if she could go to church with Rachel, to see what it was about, and he let her. He said he would never keep her from learning or making her own decisions when it came to the Lord. She went with her friend the following Sunday and never went back. She researched different religions and realized what her grandpa had already decided long ago. She, too, believed in God, probably because her grandparents spoke of him and taught her basic prayers, but she was certain about one thing: She didn't need a building and people to tell her what to believe.

Even so, she wondered if Wilbur was Catholic.

Bless me father, for I have sinned. It's been sixteen years since my last confession . . .

That's when Mabel imagined Wilbur last went to confession. And then Wilbur would confess all his sins and place his trust in God, a merciful Father who wanted to forgive him.

Wilbur would finish . . . *For these, and all my sins, I am truly sorry . . .*

"Wilbur." She put her hand on his arm. Head dizzy, heart hammering, she told herself to hang in there. She licked her lips and took a deep breath. "Please tell me. Isabel must be with someone who can keep her safe. What did her dad do? What did Jimmy do?" Her voice steady.

"She won't understand. She loves him too much." His eyes were already closed.

Was he falling asleep? She glanced at the clear bag the nurse left, almost empty now, dripping medicine into Wilbur's IV. Did the medicine make him sleepy?

"Wilbur," she said, gently shaking his arm.

He opened his eyes slowly. He *was* getting sleepy.

"Tell me what Jimmy did," she demanded desperately, leaning over him.

Mabel's head turned slightly toward a commotion outside the room, in the hallway. Isabel? The nurse spoke to someone.

"He killed Robin."

Mabel's head snapped back, her attention on Wilbur's face—his words ringing in her ears.

"Jimmy killed Robin and I covered for him," he confessed. A single tear fell down his face.

Mabel's heart jumped. Even though she had a hunch, somehow hearing it from Wilbur's mouth surprised her. She was glad he confessed—but at the same time, she resented him for covering for him.

"And it wasn't the first time he killed," he continued.

HE KNEW! He knew and didn't say anything.

THIRTY-SIX

WHEN HE HAD RECEIVED JOHN'S CALL THE week prior, he jumped at the opportunity to catch the asshole who turned Mabel's life upside down. Frankie Dowdy could finally scratch the itch that had bothered him for years. He wanted nothing more but to shoot the motherfucker. Once in the head for Margaret, once in the back for little Pete, and once in the chest for Melodi. That would about do it.

But that isn't who he is.

Frankie prided himself on preparedness, perfection, vigilance, the whole nine yards. Why he didn't follow Mabel this morning was plain stupid on his part. He was already on his way down to Jimmy's work that morning when he got the call from John. He flipped his car around. His speedometer got up to ninety and he didn't care. He had ways of getting out of tickets in Oregon, and he hoped it would work in Colorado, too.

Frankie stepped on the pedal. He didn't trust the murdering psycho.

He didn't trust him at all.

THIRTY-SEVEN

SHE DIDN'T EVEN HEAR THE DOOR OPEN. ALL she heard were Wilbur's words . . .

Jimmy killed Robin and I covered for him. And it wasn't the first time he killed someone.

Lost in her head, as Wilbur's words ran through it—

"He killed that family—the Stuckers . . ."

She was well aware what he had done. Who he killed. Who he tried to kill.

A familiar voice echoed in the distance. For a brief moment, she thought she might be dreaming again.

"What have you done old man?" asked the familiar voice. "I thought I could trust you," the familiar voice continued.

Mabel tried to clear her thoughts. She looked at Wilbur, his already pale skin turned another shade of white, as if all blood drained out of him. Eyes bulging out of his head, she turned to see what he was looking at.

Too late.

Jimmy stood over her, gun pointing to the back of her head. She moved to get up. He pushed the barrel into the back of her skull.

She should have known better. One mistake after another. All those years of training gone. Like dedicating years of your life to a law degree or doctorate only to fail in the end. Various split-second opportunities lost that she would never get back. Split-second decisions, that if made differently, like Mabel had been taught, would have changed the outcome—but instead she froze. She froze just like that night in the woods, at the edge of the creek. She tried to tell herself, that it all happened too fast. But in the end, she was unprepared.

"Don't move," Jimmy said coolly. "What's wrong, Pops, cat got your tongue? You were flapping your lips not five seconds ago."

"Leave him alone," Mabel said. All she could think of was her grandpa.

"Who in the hell do you think you are telling me what to do? You're not my teacher. Which reminds me, we have some talking to do," he scolded. Turning his attention to Wilbur, "I'll deal with you later. This one's on you old man," he said, pointing the gun into Mabel's temple. "You left me no choice."

Mabel started coming to her senses. She considered her options. She could scream, but he would not only shoot her, he'd most likely shoot Wilbur too, and anyone else that came into the room. She could fight him for the gun, but he'd most likely get a shot off, hit her, or miss and hit Wilbur. As the options ran through her head, he pulled her out from behind him.

Mabel hadn't seen her. She'd been there the whole time. Silent.

Mabel instinctively moved toward her.

"Uh-uh," he said to Mabel, pointing the gun at his daughter.

He wouldn't!

Mabel couldn't take the chance.

"Let's go," he said. "We're taking a ride."

"Where're we going?" she asked, as if he would tell her his plan.

"Don't you worry your pretty little head. Now, I'm only going to say this once. You're coming with me and you're going to do it quietly. We're going to walk through that door and you won't notify anyone. You hear me?"

Mabel nodded.

"If you do, I blow your fucking head off and anyone else around me." He pointed the gun at Isabel—again. "THAT will be on you. You understand me?"

Mabel nodded.

"Walk," he demanded.

She did.

"Don't forget your purse," he said.

She clutched it and walked toward the door.

"That's better." He held her by the arm and put his gun into his right jacket pocket.

Mabel would buy her time. She had to get out of the hospital. That was the only way. She couldn't risk Isabel's life or anyone else. If she didn't take him down and do it quickly, he would shoot as many people as he possibly could, just to prove a point.

She wasn't afraid.

She wasn't the same eleven-year-old girl he chased sixteen years ago.

She opened the door a crack and he whispered in her ear, "My wife is dead and you're next. You'll pay for what my father did."

My father . . . He didn't say, *your father.*

The words rang through her just the same, like hot lava in her veins. He sparked a fire within her that had lain dormant for years. Her head down and eyes on the floor, the door cracked open an inch, she closed her eyes. His hot wet breath blanketed her ear. Opening her eyes, he remained on her right, his left foot slightly behind her right.

She'd make her move.

A small soft hand touched hers, "I'm sorry, Ms. Peters," the small voice whispered. "I didn't know."

Mabel's head shifted left, looking at Isabel. She stared straight into her dark blue pleading eyes, full of remorse. Her father was a monster—her suffering had only begun.

"It'll be alright," she whispered back, so low she wasn't sure if Isabel heard.

"What are you waiting for?" he asked.

She opened the door and led the way out, holding Isabel's hand. The nurse behind the counter smiled at her. She thought of giving her a sign—mouthing, call 9-1-1. But Jimmy dug his fingers into her arm and she smiled back, thinking she couldn't risk it.

At one point, Wilbur was convinced his son would shoot him. Wouldn't that be something. Hell of a way to go out. It would almost come full circle.

Wilbur couldn't distinguish if it would be a good thing or bad thing. A gift or punishment. It was hard to tell.

He watched Jimmy take Mabel and his granddaughter. His son, pointing the gun at his own daughter's head. That part was clear as day. Punishment.

It was his fault. Jimmy said so.

He had that feeling again. The feeling where he might pass out.

Holy shit! Not again.

The heart monitor went off.

And everything went black.

THIRTY-EIGHT

AS MABEL OPENED THE DOOR THAT READ 'first floor,' she hesitated to walk through. Seeing her grandpa step into the elevator didn't surprise her one bit. Seeing him gave her hope, gave her courage. It reminded her how strong he had been and how strong she needed to be.

This is what she wanted. *This* is what she waited sixteen years for.

The time had come.

"Hurry up," Jimmy threatened. "What the hell you waiting for?"

"A security guard just stepped into the elevator," she lied. "Do you want him to see you pointing a gun at me?"

"Just get moving," he said, shoving her forward.

Her heart pumped harder when she noticed the gun was pointed at Isabel's head. *Bastard.* Isabel didn't notice, she'd been looking at Mabel. *In time,* she thought.

Jimmy using his daughter to get to Mabel proved him to

be more twisted and heinous than she'd imagined. She could handle Jimmy, it was Isabel she had to protect.

The parking lot was mostly full. He watched her like a hawk as she walked slowly.

Isabel whimpered.

"Stop crying. Everything's going to be fine." The man with the gun was oblivious to what could possibly be going through his daughter's mind.

"Why do you have a gun?" Isabel asked her dad.

"Safety," he said. "I don't know this woman. I told you, it ain't right the way she is with you. She's up to something."

Now or never.

"Why don't you tell her the truth Jimmy. Why are you lying to her?"

"Shut the fuck up teach, or . . ."

"Or what? You'll shut me up?"

Jimmy clenched his jaw, clasped his fingers tightly around her arm. It hurt. She didn't care. Isabel had to see the monster for what he was.

"Like you shut up the Stucker family," Mabel added.

His eyes widened.

"What is she talking about Daddy?

Smack! Right on the side of Mabel's head.

He just hit me. Stunned at first, she felt no pain.

Isabel screamed.

There were bright flashes of light. Mabel blinked to clear her sight.

"You have anything else to say?" he asked, bobbing his head to look into her eyes.

Feeling woozy, he looked funny, sounded funny.

Was she bleeding? Her hand went to her head. She looked at her hand. A little. Not much. It felt numb. The pain would come later.

Isabel sobbed, grabbed Mabel's arm and hugged it tight. She felt her breath and tears. Mabel needed to keep Isabel on her side.

For some reason Lucas popped in her head. "*Not a good time,*" she whispered to Lucas, who, of course, was hundreds of miles away. Had he been thinking of her right now, too?

"What did you say?" scowled Jimmy, pushing her through the parking lot. He stopped in front of a black truck, grabbed his daughter, and held the gun to the back of her head.

Mabel's skin crawled. The cold, heartless, black soul it must take to do that. She glanced from the frightened girl and back to the demon, forcibly softening her features.

"Jimmy, just listen to me. You don't want to do this. I know you love Isabel."

"You don't know nothing about me" he hissed.

"You love her more than anything or anyone in this world. Am I wrong? You'd do anything for her."

"You think just because you're a teacher you know everything. Well, you don't."

Should she bring up his brother? She better not. He killed her family over it. "I know your dad is lying in a hospital bed fighting for his life."

"What are talking about?"

"He's dying, Jimmy. Wilbur doesn't have long. Please, don't—"

"He told you that?" His voice softened.

"Yes. He has cirrhosis. He's had it for years and went into shock this morning. Isabel only called me because she couldn't reach you. She's scared. She loves you."

"How did she get your number? You better not have touched

her."

"I'd never. Your daughter is remarkable. She gets that from someone. I know you have to be good—to raise a daughter like her." The words burned in her like hot molten rock.

She looked down at Isabel.

This remarkable little girl didn't get any good traits from him—if he had any.

He had the gun pointed at his daughter's head again.

It wasn't working.

"If I'm so good, Teach, tell me then—why did I kill my wife?"

Mabel froze, keeping her gaze on Jimmy, afraid to look at Isabel.

"Why did I kill your family?" he continued.

He knows who I am . . .

Mabel clenched her jaw for a brief second. With a straight face she imagined ripping his heart out. Breathe, she reminded herself. She'd been so stupid. How long had he known? Does it matter?

"No surprise to you, is it?" he smirked. "Why is that? Oh yeah . . ." his voice became louder, "because my father—who is lying on his death bed—ratted me out!"

Isabel sniffled, Mabel's eyes dropped to see her holding back her tears. She knew now. She knew her father was a monster. She wondered if he even realized what he'd said.

"You're a monster," Mabel said.

The corner of his mouth turned up, into a disturbing grin.

Time kept passing by. She felt like she'd been here before. A nightmare that had come true. She couldn't keep allowing her opportunities to pass her by.

She thought of her grandpa. He blamed himself for not protecting her family. For not getting to her sooner in the woods. But he did. He saved her life. He'd spent the last sixteen years protecting her, caring for her. She had spent the last sixteen years thinking how she'd been wronged. That wasn't fair. Not to the man and woman who gave their lives for her. She fantasized saving lives when she was young. This was her chance.

Save Isabel. This didn't have to be all about her.

"Get in the back and get down. We're going for a ride," Jimmy said in a firm voice.

"Daddy, what are you doing?" Isabel cried.

"Quiet," he demanded, between clenched teeth.

Like a deer caught in headlights, her eyes brimmed with tears, chin shivered. She looked at Mabel—her nightmare getting worse by the second.

"It'll be okay, Isabel," assured Mabel, with a weak smile. Mabel got in and laid down as instructed.

"Give me your purse," he demanded. "There's a cable tie back there. Tie your wrists together."

She threw her purse in the front seat, grabbed a cable tie and said, "I can't do this myself."

Hatred swimming in the black storm of his eyes, he glared at Mabel. "Isabel, help her."

"But Daddy, don't—"

"Stop whining and do as I say." He glanced at her and changed his tone. "Baby, I need your help. I don't know if I can trust anyone besides you right now. There are too many people after me. Please baby. Help me."

He kept the gun pointed at Mabel. She wondered what kind of childhood Jimmy had had to turn him into the monster who stood in front of her today. Into the monster that killed a family, his wife, and held a gun to his own daughter's head. She thought of Wilbur, who appeared to be a good man. She didn't believe people were born bad.

Isabel did as her dad asked and tied Mabel's wrists. "It's alright Isabel. I'm fine," she said. "See," she held up her hands,"it doesn't hurt."

"You're not in school anymore, Teach. You don't get to talk to her anymore. Now, where's your phone?" he asked, looking through her purse.

Mabel glared at Jimmy. She thought for a second. "I must have left it in Wilbur's room." He didn't look convinced. "On the chair."

Please don't pat me down.

He looked at Mabel, then to Isabel. "Now her ankles."

She did as she was told.

Releasing the air she'd been holding, she regretted not grabbing her gun from her car. Or a knife. Something. She had left herself completely exposed.

He handed Isabel a piece of duct tape. "My favorite part," he said grimacing. "Now shut her up."

Confusion crossed Isabel's face.

"Awe, c'mon. Don't tell me you've never wanted to shut your teacher up. It's for her mouth," he said sarcastically. "Just me?" He laughed. "You need to loosen up girl."

She gave him a dirty look and took the tape.

Satisfied, Jimmy started the truck and drove off.

"Where's Aunt Susie?" asked Isabel, a hint of anger in her voice.

"Don't you worry about Susan."

She cried at the thought. She was learning quickly what her

daddy was capable of.

When we get to where we're going, I'm going to make you pay asshole, thought Mabel.

THIRTY-NINE

WHEN JOHN PETERS STEPPED ONTO HIS deck earlier that morning, the sun was shining bright, with all indications of it being a glorious day. Now it was bitter cold, with snow in the forecast. John had missed the snow. He'd put in a heated deck for that reason. He planned to spend his snow days and evenings reading. Or hell, maybe he'd add a TV back there and watch some football. Better yet, he and Kat would cuddle up and watch a movie.

But now, as he pulled into the hospital, there was a dark cloud, thick and ugly. He rushed through the front doors and pushed the button on the elevator repeatedly. He thought of taking the stairs after waiting a whole three seconds.

Ding. Never mind.

The doors slid open and he stepped in. As he did, he got a weird feeling he may be too late. When the elevator reached his floor, he immediately heard commotion coming from down the hall. Rushing out he pushed the couple waiting to get in. Rude, something he usually was not, but he only thought of Mabel.

He sprinted down the corridor dodging a nurse and family.

A lady, coming out of room 211, stopped him. "I'm sorry, you can't go in there."

"Is Wilbur in there? Where's Mabel?"

"Are you family?"

He shook his head no, trying desperately to look over her shoulder. "Where's Mabel?" he repeated.

"Who's Mabel?"

"The lady with the little girl. She was just here," he said, annoyed. Why was this lady arguing with him? He met her eyes, finally seeing her. A doctor? "She's the one that called the ambulance for Wilbur. She came here with his granddaughter."

"Sir. There's no one in there besides doctors and nurses. Are you family?"

"No. What happened?"

"Are you a friend?"

"Yes, sort of. I'm the grandfather of—"

"He's very sick. He barely made it. Do you know how we can reach his family?"

"They should have been here. They were just here."

"I'm sorry," she said again and walked away.

Maybe she's in the cafeteria. He walked up to the nurse's station. "Excuse me, ma'am. Did you see a young lady, dark brown hair, visiting the patient in room 211, with a little blonde girl?"

"Oh, yes. She just left, right before Wilbur went into

cardiac arrest. Both of them left with a man."

"Man? What man?"

"I saw him talking to the little girl first and then he and the little girl went into Wilbur's room. Next thing, I saw all three of them leaving. Then Wilbur goes into cardiac arrest. It was the darnedest thing. Are you a cop?"

"No. I came here for Mabel. The young lady."

The old uncomfortable feeling engulfed him like a blast from an AK-47. He struggled to breathe. He leaned forward, arms and head on the counter. His chest tight, he couldn't get enough air.

"Sir. Are you okay?"

Flashback. He hadn't had one in . . . he couldn't remember how long.

"Sir!" the lady yelled. "Can you hear me?"

He heard her, but her voice sounded far away. He couldn't get the words out. Breathe, he told himself. From experience, he knew it would pass. Breathe. Slow. In. Out. He lifted his head, her face shadowed with worry.

"I'll be okay," he managed.

He pulled out his phone, dialed Mabel.

No answer.

Reaching over the counter, he grabbed a paper and pen. "Call the police. I think the lady I'm looking for was just abducted," he said, handing her the paper with his number.

"Are you serious?"

"Just do it!" he demanded. "That's my information if they need to contact me." He disappeared down the corridor, deciding on the stairs. Quicker.

He dialed Frankie.

"John," Frankie answered.

"She's been taken."

FORTY

JIMMY TURNED INTO THE FAIRGROUNDS. HE could have dumped his truck plenty of other places, but here his truck wouldn't be found for a while. He didn't go far, parking on the south east corner of the massive lot.

His pulse quickened at the thought of his pops giving him up. Jimmy should have known he couldn't trust him. Why now? After all this time. And to her, of all people.

His pops screwed him. He couldn't go home now. He couldn't go anywhere, for that matter. And now he had to ditch his truck—his baby, his pride and joy.

Fuck! He slammed his palm into the steering wheel.

Isabel jumped. He could feel her eyes on him.

He'd find a way to get it back. He had to. Might as well get a new phone too. All because his pops couldn't keep his trap shut. So much for taking care of family. *Two-faced bastard!*

He threw on his baseball cap and sunglasses.

"Be right back. Don't move," he told her.

She nodded.

He walked away from his truck, lighting a cigarette. His hands shook. He regretted bringing Isabel. There was no way he could have left her with his pops. He'd fill her mind with shit.

He needed to get this over with. He still hadn't programmed any numbers in his phone. Good thing he had a good memory.

Jimmy punched the numbers in and instantly he picked up. "Hey fucktard. Come get me."

"What the hell am I, your chauffeur?" Anthony asked.

"You are today. And come alone. I'm in a bit of trouble, if you know what I mean. Got a job to finish. I got my little girl back, too. So watch yourself."

"Whatever."

And just like that, the fucktard came through, like usual. Hell, he had nothing better to do. Lucky for Jimmy, he lived only ten minutes away. Jimmy met the loser seven years ago when his pops had moved to the small town. He met him at a bar of all places. Jimmy never drank. He went to find some bad dudes to run deals with. Anthony was as bad as they came. They'd been causing trouble ever since.

FORTY-ONE

"JOHN HERE." HE PICKED UP BEFORE IT finished ringing. He didn't recognize the number but hoped it was Mabel or the police.

"John Peters?" asked a male voice.

"Yes."

"This is Detective Corneal, Loveland Police Department. I got a message from the Hospital about a possible abduction."

He had been digging in his pocket for his car key. "Yes," he responded. Finding it, he unlocked the door. "Mabel Peters, my granddaughter. She's a teacher at Northridge Elementary. She got—"

"Can you come down to the station?" he asked.

"No, I can't." He sat in his car. Irritated the man had cut him off. "You need to move now. We're out of time."

"Okay, Mr. Peters. Tell me why you think she's been abducted."

"She got a call this morning from one of her students—Isabel Dumel. Isabel told her that her grandpa, Wilbur Dumel, who nearly died and is at the hospital—"

"Slow down."

John was a patient man, but at that moment his patience was slipping away quite quickly. He didn't have time for this bullshit. He started his car. "Listen, Detective. I know you're trying to help but stop interrupting me and keep up. Wilbur, the grandpa of Isabel Dumel, is in the hospital. Mabel, my granddaughter, is the one who called 9-1-1 and brought Isabel to the hospital. Wilbur went into cardiac arrest right after Isabel and Mabel were last seen with some man." He paused to let him catch up. "Isabel's dad, Jimmy Dumel, wouldn't answer his phone this morning. I think he's the one that Mabel and Isabel were seen with at the hospital. That's the last I heard from her."

"How do you know she was abducted?" Corneal asked.

"Listen closely. I believe Jimmy, Isabel's father, may have done something to his wife, Robin Dumel. When Mabel called earlier, she told me that Isabel's mom was missing, has been since October 24. This is the same day Detective Ryan Cross was shot. I believe they're connected. When I got to the hospital, not ten minutes ago, the nurse tells me Mabel left with a man and the little girl. I can't say for sure it's Jimmy, although I believe it is. Mabel would have called. She isn't answering her phone. It's not like her."

"That's a lot of speculation, John."

"I have to go. You have my number. Just look into it. I have to find Mabel."

"Now, wait a minute. You can't go after this guy if he's dangerous like you say he is."

"Try to stop me," he challenged, hanging up.

John sped away. He had already lost too much time. Either the detective believed him, or he didn't.

FORTY-TWO

THE SOUND OF ISABEL WHIMPERING IN THE front seat slowed to an erratic gasp. Hearing her misery took Mabel back to her own losses. Her dad. Her mom. Her brother. She had lost her dad in a snowstorm. Life wasn't fair. His life put him in the wrong place at the wrong time. He'd driven in many snowstorms prior to that day. He couldn't have known that day would be his last. She understands that now.

But her mom and brother died before they were meant to. Their lives were cut short. Jimmy did that. He made the horrible decision to end their lives.

Now he made the decision to end Isabel's mom's life. Tried to take Ryan's. Tried to take Melodi's and wanted another shot at it. Who does he think he is?

He's playing God. Only he's the Devil.

Wilbur claimed Jimmy loved Isabel. She clearly loved him. The man she thought to be the center of her world had broken her heart.

Fuming, Mabel tried to get Isabel's attention. *"Mmmm—mmmmm—mmmmm."*

Please turn back and look at me, Mabel willed Isabel.

Isabel sunk deeper into her seat, pulling her legs up onto the seat and wrapped her arms around them.

It was hard to move, but Mabel managed to kick the back of Isabel's seat.

Isabel's eyes shot back, wide open and scared.

Mabel whined like a puppy and batted her lashes, sending subliminal messages to her. *Please Isabel, take this tape off my mouth. I need your help.*

Isabel's eyes flooded with tears.

Mabel shook her head, whining more.

She glanced out the window, Mabel guessed to her dad. Looking back at Mabel, she slowly peeled the tape back.

"Oh God. Thank you. We don't have much time. I'm sorry I got you into this." Her words came out fast and hoarse. Mabel swallowed, trying to clear her dry throat.

Isabel blinked to hold back more tears. "I didn't know. He said he wanted to talk to you." Her voice quivered as she spoke.

"Sweetie, it's okay. It's not your fault. I need you to reach into my back pocket. Hurry. Take my phone. Hide it. Don't show your dad. When he's not looking—I need you to call my grandpa, John . . . and Frankie. Tell them where we are. Tell them where we're going. Tell them whatever you can."

"He's coming," she cried.

"Quick. Take it!"

She grabbed the phone and shoved it in her front pocket.

"My tape."

Reaching back, she rubbed the tape back on her mouth and hunched into a ball in the front seat.

Slow your breathing, Mabel thought. She could hear her from the back.

Jimmy climbed into the truck, breathing heavy himself. He gave Isabel a once over, looked back at Mabel, turned and scrutinized his daughter. “What’s with you?” he asked her.

“I’m scared,” she said.

“What are you scared of? She’s tied up. You got nothing to be scared of anymore. I’ll make sure of that.”

She didn’t reply.

FORTY-THREE

IT SHOULD HAVE TAKEN ANTHONY TEN MINUTES to get to Jimmy, but ten minutes passed five minutes ago. Isabel whined the whole time. He didn't know if he could take it much longer. She needed to know life wasn't all sunshine and daisies. Her momma made her all soft and mushy. Maybe he did too. He couldn't imagine laying a hand on her, after what his pops did to him. He'd have to think of other ways to toughen her up.

When Anthony finally did arrive, Jimmy jumped out of his truck, "What took you so damn long?" he demanded.

"Shut the hell up. You're lucky I showed up at all," Anthony challenged.

Asshole, thought Jimmy. He wondered if Anthony knew what Jimmy was capable of.

"Let's go baby," Jimmy reached his hand out to her. "Get in the Bronco."

Isabel glanced back at Mabel. Damn that girl needed a

talking to.

Turning back to Anthony, Jimmy added, "Help me move her."

Anthony walked over to Jimmy's truck and peeked into the back seat. "Damn dude. This just gets better by the minute," he said with too much excitement.

"Throw her in the back."

Anthony glanced around, dropped his tailgate and grabbed the teacher's legs. "She's nice looking."

"Don't even think about it."

They tossed her in the back, rolling her in.

"Where to?" asked Anthony, lighting a cigarette.

"I need a car."

"What's wrong with your truck?" he questioned.

"My old man squawked. I can't be seen in it." He motioned for Anthony to give him a cigarette.

"Shit man. That sucks. Take mine," he insisted.

"I can't. He knows you. They'll come knocking on your door soon enough."

"What the hell, man! Are you shitting me? Why didn't you say anything sooner? I have shit all over the place," he said, throwing his hands in the air like a drama queen. "Fuck!"

"I'm telling you now. I just found out."

It would serve you right for disrespecting me, Jimmy thought. He lit a cigarette and took a long drag.

Anthony cursed under his breath, jumping in the driver seat. "Get in. I gotta go get rid of some shit."

"I know, I know. Drop us off at that old, abandoned sugar mill."

"Don't be messing with my mama."

"I ain't going to be messing with your mama. You deaf or

something? I said I was going to the sugar mill. Your mama living at the sugar mill now?"

"No."

"What an idiot. *'Don't be messin' with my mama.'* Where's your head at? You smoking too much of that weed?"

"No—Yes. Shut up."

"The car—I need it tonight. Don't steal it though. Can you do that? A phone too."

"I got you. You owe me though."

"I know," Jimmy grunted.

"Daddy," Isabel pulled at his arm.

He almost forgot she was with them. She was so quiet. She'd finally stopped crying.

"What, baby?"

"I have to go pee," she said nervously, her gaze focused on his gun.

"We're almost there." He hoped there was a bathroom there. He would hate to make her go in a corner.

"I can't wait. I have to go really, really bad. I'm about to pee my pants." She wiggled in the seat and stared at him until he looked away.

"Seriously? Why didn't you ask to go when we were at the hospital?" Jimmy asked.

"I didn't have to go then."

Of course, you didn't. Why would you? he thought, shaking his head.

"There's a gas station up ahead," Anthony offered.

"Goddammit," Jimmy said under his breath.

"Don't be mad, Daddy," Her voice faltered. "But I really have to go."

"Fine. Pull over."

Anthony did.

"Give us five minutes," he said to Anthony.

Jimmy was thankful they were the only customers in the store and the man behind the counter was nice enough to ignore them when they walked in.

"I can go by myself," Isabel said, when he followed her to the bathroom door. It's not like he planned on going in with her.

"Just hurry up," he said.

"Daddy?" She looked at him with the saddest, sweetest eyes.

"Yeah, baby?"

"Please don't hurt my teacher. You're just going to talk to her, right?" Her voice soft as lemon meringue, his favorite.

This made it hard for Jimmy to breathe. Why, why, why did he bring her with him? She doesn't understand. She will though. He'd make sure of it. "It's either her or me, Isabel." His voice unsteady. He didn't look at her. He couldn't. He clenched his jaw and tilted his head, tightening his left fist.

She didn't respond, closing the door behind her.

How did he get here? All these years. He put it all behind him. Moved on. Never got caught. Now here he was. No going back now.

Would Isabel ever forgive him? How would he run with her?

"Goddammit!" he muttered. He had meant to think it, but the words came out anyway. The clerk looked his way.

Might as well get a drink. He pulled out three sodas from the cooler and threw down a five on the counter. The clerk rang him up, giving him a funny look as he gave him his change.

"Have a good day." The words may have been nice, but they came out rude. He scowled at the clerk. Asshole speaks after all.

He glanced at his watch and looked toward the bathrooms, growing more and more impatient. He tapped on the door. "Isabel, hurry up," he said.

"I'm trying," she yelled back.

He paced back and forth. A couple minutes passed. "What are you doing in there?" he growled.

"Dad! I'm going number two!" she shouted, loud enough for the rude clerk to hear.

Ew. Jimmy felt his face get hot. *What the hell!* he mouthed to himself. "Fine. I'll be outside."

Anthony stood by his Bronco smoking a cigarette. He offered one to Jimmy. They leaned against the door, neither one of them said anything. They never spoke of their bad deeds more than once. The version Anthony knew was that Robin cheated on Jimmy, attacked him, and Jimmy killed her in self-defense. He dumped the body because no one would have believed him. He left out the detective. Jimmy knew Anthony had done plenty of bad things himself and told his own version. But he didn't think Anthony had it in him to kill anyone. Just last week, Anthony had held a gun to a black kid's head and robbed him. He never would have shot him though.

Jimmy had just finished his cigarette when Isabel came out. He tried to gauge her expression, but she strolled right past him and hopped in the Bronco.

He rolled his eyes. Robin was better at these things.

FORTY-FOUR

THE MOMENT HE HEARD HER VOICE, HE pictured Melodi as she lay motionless, life draining from her small body. Vivid as his memory was, he had to remind himself that Mabel was a twenty-seven-year-old woman. Strong, resilient, and smart. She was no longer the four-ten, seventy-pound, skinny little girl he called Melodi.

Mabel didn't feel like just his granddaughter, she felt like more. She did, and she didn't. He loved her like he loved Ben—maybe more—if that was possible. Maybe that's just how it was with grandchildren. Especially grandchildren you raised as your own.

Hearing her voice on the phone confused him. For a short moment he thought he was dreaming. She sounded just like Melodi.

"Is this John?" He attempted to turn up the volume that was already at its highest setting. He could barely hear her small voice.

"Who is this?" he asked, his breathing getting heavier.

"Isabel. Ms. Peters told me to call you."

Oh, Lord!

He swerved, taken by surprise, nearly hitting the car in the lane over. The man in the red car swerved into the shoulder and blasted his horn, flipping him off. John deserved it.

"Isabel . . . thank God. Is Mabel all right?" His voice shaky.

Silence.

"Isabel, dear girl . . . please tell me."

"He hit her . . . my daddy . . . hit her in the head," she whimpered.

Exhaling, he closed his eyes briefly to keep the tears from coming. He needed to keep it together. If this girl was calling him, she was taking a risk and couldn't have much time.

"He tied her up . . ." she continued, "I'm sorry . . . I didn't know."

His heart sank, ached. He couldn't get Melodi out of his head. He swallowed the lump in his throat. "But . . . she told you to call me?"

"Yes." She paused. "I heard my dad. He told his friend to take us to the old sugar mill."

"Oh my God. Where are you now?"

He heard banging and a male's voice. *Her dad!*

"I'm trying," she yelled.

"You don't have much time. Where are you?" he blurted out. He had to get her talking and fast.

"In the bathroom."

"Where's the bathroom?"

"At a gas station . . . but, I don't know where."

"It's okay . . . it's okay," he repeated. "Why are you there?"

"We waited for his friend, Anthony, to show up. But we're

leaving."

"Okay. Quickly describe the car you're in."

"My dad's truck is black. But we're in Anthony's car."

"What does he drive? What does it look like?"

"I don't know, but it's black too."

"Truck or car?"

"Neither."

Not a car or truck? Semi? Work vehicle?

"Does it have any writing on it?"

"No. It's about the size of my dad's truck, but it has a cover on it."

Better. "What's Anthony's last name?"

He heard the male's voice again.

"Dad! I'm going number two!" she yelled louder this time. "I have to go. My dad is getting mad."

"You're so brave. Do you know Anthony's last name?

"Shea"

"Anything else you can tell me?"

"I don't want to be with my dad anymore. I'm scared. I want my grandpa."

Oh, God! Not that. What if he doesn't make it.

"Your grandpa's in the hospital. Is there anyone else I can call for you?"

"My Aunt Susie," she paused, then added, "Susan Brevens."

"I'll find her. Thank you, Isabel."

And just like that she was gone.

John used to have feelings of remorse. When he started caring for Mabel, his life changed. He didn't have time to regret what he could have or should have done. He only had time to live. So that's what he and Kathryn had done.

This time, his granddaughter needed him again. And he would give his life to get her back.

FORTY-FIVE

JOHN WAS THE MOST STUBBORN PERSON FRANKIE had ever met. John wanted to go to the sugar mill and they didn't both need to go. Truth is, Frankie didn't want to worry about John. Not that he thought John couldn't take care of himself. He just knew Mabel would never forgive him if anything ever happened to her grandpa. And Kat would probably shoot him.

"This is what I do, John. Let me do this," Frankie repeated himself. "You're too close to this. Head over to Mabel's, call Ryan and fill him in so he can work with Loveland PD." John wasn't budging. "Doc's already on his way. We need you two close, but not in the middle—yet."

"You're right," he said. Frankie knew his friend. He wasn't sitting still. "Ryan is going to have to make the decision on whether or not he wants to reveal that Mabel *is* Melodi."

Frankie knew the questions would come up. There was no way out. At this point, it probably didn't matter if Jimmy knew.

They hung up. It didn't take long for John to call back. Frankie had just exited I-25, answering his phone.

"They found Jimmy's truck off I-25, at the fairgrounds. No Jimmy."

"We didn't think they would find him," replied Frankie. "Anyone see anything?"

"No. Nothing is scheduled there today. The landscape crew noticed the truck and called it in."

"How about his friend Anthony? Any luck there?" asked Frankie.

"Anthony Daniel Shea from Windsor, Colorado, drives a black 1993 Ford Bronco. He has a rap sheet ranging from aggravated burglary and felony theft, to weapons, drugs, battery charges and everything in between."

"A real Boy Scout, huh?" Frankie ridiculed.

"PD is on their way to his place now."

"How about the sugar mill?"

"They might just beat you there."

"I'm close John. Call you back."

He wanted a crack at Jimmy. He wouldn't get that if the police got there first. But, if they beat him there, that meant more of a chance Mabel wouldn't be hurt.

He could live with that.

FORTY-SIX

HE SAID THEY WERE GOING TO THE SUGAR mill, but she didn't trust him or his friend. Mabel made mental notes of the turns, skyline, and timeline. As they turned onto a dirt road, she spotted a smokestack and three large white silos, and knew exactly where they were. If Isabel called Mabel's grandpa, which she's certain she did after her little stunt to get them to stop at the gas station, then they were right where Jimmy said they would be. The old abandoned mill.

Most of the windows were boarded up on the top level, while the bottom level had old broken shutters. She'd never been this close before but saw the smokestack and silos every time she ran down the dirt road to the east. Her path was only a hundred and fifty yards away. The thought sent a chill through her. To think he had been so close to her as she ran by.

"Get out," he hissed, pointing the gun at Mabel's head. He glanced up at Isabel for a quick second and said, "Let's go, baby."

Isabel opened the door and watched Mabel struggle to inch her way out. Mabel offered a wink to let her know she wasn't afraid. Confused, Isabel responded with a nervous glance toward her dad.

"Thanks," he said to his friend. "I owe you."

"And don't you forget it." The man, Jimmy had called him Anthony, got back in his Bronco and drove off.

Mabel skimmed the area before turning to Jimmy. She raised her eyebrows to Jimmy, offering a—*happy now?*—signal to him.

Jimmy's nostrils flared as his anger welled up like a wild animal. He nudged her with his gun, ripping the tape off her mouth. The bite of the adhesive made her cringe. She licked her sore lips.

Something hit her hard, causing her knees to buckle and lose her balance. She couldn't grasp anything to keep from falling—her hands and feet still tied—she hit the ground, like a tree crashing—*timber.* A cloud of dust bubbled up around her.

"Asshole!"

He laughed. Pleased with himself. He'd kicked the back of her knees. Juvenile is what he was.

"Ms. Peters!" screamed Isabel. "Are you okay?"

Isabel was by her side, tears streaming down her face. "Daddy. Stop. Don't hurt her."

"I'm fine," she said, blinking. Glancing at Jimmy, she added, "Why don't you untie me? I won't run." No, she wouldn't run. She would stay and fight. She never should have let him tie her up. He's not letting her go, she knew that.

He scrunched up the duct tape that he'd pulled from her mouth and threw it at her. Then, without warning, he yanked her to her feet. Lightheaded and nauseous, she swallowed hard. It took everything for her not to fall over.

To her surprise, he put his gun in his pocket and pulled out a knife. Surely, he wouldn't stab her in front of his daughter—would he?

"Fine," he grunted.

Mabel shuddered, as his breath fluttered through her hair when he spoke. Moving around Mabel, he sliced through the cable ties on her ankles.

She peered down at him as he started to rise. She could kick him right in the groin.

"Move and you never have kids," he threatened, reading her mind. The knife pointed below her belly button.

The side of her head throbbed from smacking the ground. There was a sharp pain in her right knee. She glanced at Isabel who wiped tears from her eyes.

She ran up to Mabel and hugged her.

Jimmy looked confused at the sight of his daughter running into the arms of the woman he gagged and bound. *What a dumbass,* thought Mabel. He removed his cap, turned it backward and pulled it down. His brooding eyes burned into Mabel.

For a brief second, she saw a man who could have been someone's loving husband. His years of hatred took a toll on his face, but Jimmy was not a bad looking man. If he didn't have such a piss-poor demeanor about him, she imagined he got his share of women. Until they saw the wicked side of him. She questioned what kind of woman Isabel's mom had been. Isabel had to get her admirable qualities from her mother. Her mother had to be a respectable woman. Why she married a man like Jimmy—

"What are you looking at?" he asked.

"How about my hands?"

"I'm not stupid—*bitch.*"

"What are you afraid of?"

"You got a big mouth, you know that? How would you like me shut you up for good?" He held the knife pointed at her mouth.

"If that's what gets you off."

"Shut the fuck up!" he shouted, spit landing on her face. His heavy breathing smelled of cigarettes. She was getting to him. "Now walk." He pushed her toward the old abandoned building.

She knew once she got inside, it would be over. She figured he would most likely shoot her. Stabbing wasn't his thing. She looked down, noticed his hand with the knife by his side. Isabel was a couple feet off to the side.

Now or never.

She took a step back, bumping into him, hard—catching him off-guard. Violently, she threw her head back into his face.

Jimmy cried out in pain. The blunt force of her hitting him caused him to drop his knife.

"Run, Isabel, RUN!" Mabel shouted.

Isabel froze. Why wasn't she running? Her eyes reminded Mabel of visiting the animal shelter—the animals frightened and desperate.

"Isabel!" The girl looked at Mabel. "You have to run. Go! Go NOW!"

Mabel turned to find Jimmy touching his bleeding, and most likely broken, nose. His dark eyes full of hate. Realizing Mabel had struck him, he reached for his gun.

Quick like the Tasmanian devil, she spun counter-clockwise. One swift kick to the chest. He grunted, stumbling back. Attempting to catch his balance, he fired, missing by a mile.

Before he could regain his balance, she stepped forward, another spin and kicked him again. This time in the face. Blood spattered from his already broken bleeding nose. His body twisted away from her. He fired his gun as his body turned away.

Missed again.

His head whipped back in her direction. Eyes wide, bloody teeth showing, nostrils flared—Jimmy was one pissed-off killer—a wild animal getting ready to take out its prey. The time it took him to puff his chest, gave her the momentum and force she needed to kick the gun out of his hand. It went flying before he knew what was happening.

The animal pounced, his fist struck her jaw before she saw it coming. Dazed, she licked her swollen aching lip and tasted blood. She wished she had her hands. Fighting without them proved to be a challenge.

He glanced away searching for the gun and she ran for cover. She couldn't risk it. She had to get away and get her hands free.

Isabel! Her eyes did a quick scan—she didn't see her.

Relief surged through her as she ran. Isabel got away. Now it was just her and the man in black.

FORTY-SEVEN

THE SOUND OF SIRENS COULD BE HEARD AS the sugar mill came into view.

Frankie dialed John. "Less than a minute away, I see lights. The police beat me."

"That's not a bad thing. Detective Corneal should be there too. Ask for him, Ryan gave him your name. Corneal's keeping me updated. They found Anthony home, along with his Bronco. The guy claims he hadn't seen Jimmy all day—which we know is bullshit. They found a small amount of fresh blood in the back of his Bronco."

"Mabel's," Frankie said.

"They arrested him," John continued. "Ryan's confident they'll get him to talk."

"I'd like to get my hands on—"

"We don't have that luxury," John said, cutting him off. "He's in Corneal's hands now."

"He better hope he stays there," he added. He didn't have

to say it. He was sure John felt the same way. "I'm here now. Call you back."

Turning the car around, he parked the crackerjack car on the side of the road. The entry for the sugar mill was blocked off. The officer standing guard, casually put his hand on his firearm.

Frankie realized what the officer was seeing. An enormous black man, in a freakishly small car, parked outside a barricade. Danger! Danger! Send the police! Oh, wait—you are the police.

He laughed at the thought and shook his head.

The officer greeted him, suspiciously. "Can I help you?"

"Is Detective Corneal here?"

"Who's asking?"

"Frankie Dowdy."

"Hold on." He spoke into his shoulder. "Corneal, there's a Frankie Dowdy out here for you."

"Send him in," a voice said over his speaker.

"You got ID?"

Frankie handed him his driver's license.

"Go on in." The officer motioned.

No pat down? What kind of barricade was this? All the better for Frankie, he was packing: two guns and a knife.

He had no idea what Corneal looked like. He spotted a man that looked like he was in charge. "You Corneal?" he asked.

"No. He's over there," the man said, pointing.

Frankie looked in the direction he pointed. "Thanks man."

"Corneal? I'm Frankie Dowdy."

Corneal was not in uniform, his back to Frankie. He was talking to an officer who snapped photos. Corneal turned.

"Frankie—John said you'd be coming. I hear you were a

Green Beret."

Frankie's eyes dropped to the little girl that lay before him. His mouth fell open. Speechless, he looked at Corneal. *The dead girl didn't bother him?* He could never get used to seeing a dead kid. He cleared his throat. No time to get emotional.

"Yes, sir," he replied. "What happened? Is that Isabel?"

"Couldn't tell you for sure until we get DNA back," Corneal said. "She had this on her." He held up a cell phone in a bag. "John said Isabel called him on Mabel's phone. Is this it?"

"No. Mabel has an iPhone. Was that the only one on her?"

"Only one we found. Nice phone for a kid."

"Could be her grandfather's."

"Possibly. It's locked, so I can't tell you what's on it right now. Damn shame." He shook his head, referring to the little girl that lay lifeless. "You have kids, Dowdy?"

He didn't want to get into it with him. "I guess you can say Mabel's like a daughter."

"Me, I have two," he said, eyes fixated on the dead girl. "One girl, one boy. They're both older now, and I have three grandkids. The oldest, a boy, he's about her age." Corneal pointed to the girl on the ground. "I just don't understand what . . ." he trailed off, not finishing what he was about to say. He didn't have to.

Frankie thought of Ryan. Corneal seemed sharper than Ryan. He missed nothing. He was older, with silver streaks in his almost black hair. He looked to be in his early fifties.

"How long has she been dead?"

"Waiting for the coroner to tell us that. She wasn't breathing when we arrived. Couldn't tell you how long. We tried to resuscitate her. She took a shot to the chest."

Jesus Christ. Melodi took a shot to the chest. He had to force himself to stay focused.

"Where's Mabel?"

"Couldn't tell you. There's a scuffle over there." Corneal looked in the direction he referred to. "My guess is Mabel and this Jimmy character fought. No sign of either one of them yet. It's a big place. We're still searching."

"Fuck!"

"Tell me about it," Corneal replied.

Frankie had to go find her, but he knew Corneal wouldn't let him get in the way.

"Mabel's tough. She got away. If she could have, she would have called." He spoke mostly to himself, looking around. "There's no way she would have left Isabel like this. She didn't know about her."

"You're getting ahead of yourself. We haven't confirmed who this girl is. Was Mabel carrying?"

"No."

"How can you be sure?"

"I asked her . . . when she called us from the hospital this morning. She does carry, but she left her damn gun in her car at the hospital. You can check it out if you haven't already."

"We did, and we found a gun in her car."

"This wasn't her," Frankie said, raising his voice as he pointed at the little girl. "And if she had her gun, this would have never happened. Jimmy would be the one on the ground, not this poor helpless little girl."

"Why do you say that?" Corneal wasn't stupid. He only gave Frankie the time of day with the intentions of solving a crime.

"Because Mabel just doesn't let someone kidnap her or harm one of her students. She can fight. If he has her, she's tied up."

"Funny you say that. We found some zip ties over there," he pointed, "and blood."

"Mabel's?" asked Frankie.

"Don't know. But it wasn't a lot. There's blood over there, too."

Frankie handed him his card. "You can reach me if you have any questions. I'm going after her."

"No, you're not," Corneal informed him, fuming.

"I wasn't asking. I only told you out of courtesy."

Corneal held his eyes for a second, opened his mouth to retort.

"Listen, Corneal," Frankie continued, before he could get a word out. "I'm sure Ryan filled you in on the Stucker case."

He nodded, "And your point is?"

"Then you know. I stood by the side once before. I'm not making that mistake again." Frankie darted off without looking back. He could feel Corneal's eyes burning into him.

"Frankie!" Corneal yelled.

Damn. He shouldn't have been so goddamn cocky. He stopped, refusing to turn around.

Corneal caught up to him and handed him his card. "Call me if you find anything," he demanded.

Frankie liked him, as long as he didn't give him any reason not to. Corneal's eyes said the unspoken words, *don't fuck up.*

They shook hands.

Pleased with himself, Frankie rushed off.

FORTY-EIGHT

YOU'RE AS WHITE AS A GHOST, JOHN. YOU feeling alright?" Doc asked, standing in Mabel's doorway.

"Am I feeling alright? I about shit my pants!"

"That sounds like a medical issue. I can prescribe you something for that," he joked, pushing John aside to let himself in.

"Ha-ha. Why didn't you call or text me when you got here? And where's your car?" John asked, looking outside.

"You're wound tight, John. I'm parked on the other street. You okay, buddy?" he asked, patting John on the shoulder.

"No. Not at all. I'm going nuts here. It's my . . . it's Mabel," he shook his head. "I can't lose her."

"You're not going to lose anyone. Especially Mabel. Do you mind?" Doc asked pointing to the refrigerator.

John shook his head.

"Want one?" he asked, pulling out a bottle of water.

"No, thanks. How's Ryan doing?"

"He's good. Donna and Lillian are with him now. He's

recovering like a champ. It took Lillian threatening his life to keep him away today."

"I bet."

"He blames himself," said Doc, taking a sip of his water.

"I know he does," John said at last. There was a time when John blamed him too.

"He's a good man," added Doc.

John turned his back to Doc. He picked up a picture of Mabel and Lucas. She deserved to be happy. She wouldn't be until Jimmy rotted in prison or was in the ground. John much preferred the ground. The state didn't deserve to pay to house that lunatic. He struggled with the death penalty. He believed in God, yet he believed people should pay for their sins. Some sins should not be forgiven.

Did that make him a sinner? Probably.

John knew he was always better at information gathering and Frankie was better on the ground, executing. But when Frankie called and told him a little girl was found dead at the scene and Mabel was MIA, he panicked.

He needed to go. Why did he let Mabel out of his sight? He found himself helplessly frozen.

"John?" Doc asked, who was now by his side staring at him. "You need to sit down."

"I'm fine," he said, suddenly winded.

"No, you're not. You look horrible."

He felt horrible. This day was taking a toll on him. "I'm leaving."

"What? Where?"

"Where do think? The mill. I can't stay here. At least I'll be closer. Maybe I can help."

"You're a stubborn fool, John. You need to rest. You don't look so good."

Rest? What's he talking about?

How could he be there for Mabel if he was resting?

"I'll be fine," he decided.

He left Doc standing in the doorway.

FORTY-NINE

JIMMY LOOKED OUT TO THE ORANGEY GLOW of the sun as it settled in for a nightcap behind the mountain. A reminder he needed to hurry before he lost all light. The temperature had dropped twenty degrees. No snow yet. He had hoped for snow. Damn weather lady never got it right.

How the teacher escaped him all those years back was a fucking miracle. He saw her go down with his own two eyes. Her tiny body, he shot her in the chest, and she went flying into the freezing water. It took her away. How on earth did she live? Someone or something was looking out for her that night.

He turned his head at the sirens. *Damn.* He was running out of time. They'd be closing in on him soon. Maybe he should lay low for a while. His original plan was already shot to hell.

He ducked low into a ditch and scanned the field. He knew she was out there and when he found her, he'd put an end to her once and for all. He puffed his chest, his ego feeling a bit deflated, and scurried toward the building he'd spotted.

He also knew if she wasn't there, he'd steal a vehicle and get the hell out.

Wait. He stopped breathing.

Sure as shit, the ballsy bitch ducked behind the building. He's not quite sure how he even saw her. Maybe her luck was running out.

He bolted in the direction he saw her go.

FIFTY

CERTAIN JIMMY WOULDN'T BE ABLE TO KEEP up with her, she slammed up against the cold metal building trying to catch her breath. Mabel ran all the time. It wasn't the running that wore her out, it was the cold in her lungs and fact that a crazed killer was after her all while her hands were tied.

She took a moment to soak up her surroundings and realized how quickly the sun had fallen. A ray of hope shot through her, as her eyes fell on three work trucks. One quick scan around her and she bolted to the first one.

Locked. Same with the second and third.

Running back to the warehouse she tried the door. Also locked. *Didn't anyone work around here?*

She found herself back at the trucks searching for anything to help her situation. *Jackpot.* A treasure of tools under an old tarp. Her eyes lit up as she lifted a metal bar. Strong enough to whack Jimmy with and maybe . . . break into the truck.

The thought of bashing the window and hot wiring the truck dissipated. Why didn't she know how to hotwire? She could kill someone with her bare hands—but she couldn't hotwire a measly truck?

She wondered if Frankie could. Most likely. She could probably Google how to do it. Apart from Isabel having her phone, she didn't exactly have time for a YouTube video right now.

Looking around for something to free her hands, she spotted a sharp edge and ran the cable tie along the makeshift knife. Her hands broke apart and she rubbed them mindlessly.

Back at the warehouse, she broke the padlock with one good whack. Letting herself in, she quickly found what looked like an office. She felt for the light switch, thought better of it, and instead reached for the phone and dialed Frankie.

"Uncle Frankie, it's me."

"Mabel!" he shouted in her ear. "Where are you?"

"Some warehouse. Not far. Maybe a few fields to the east."

"Half way there. Oh, it's good to hear your voice. Are you okay?" Frankie asked.

"Yes." She searched the room as she spoke, both by touch and as her eyes adjusted. God, where did the little bit of mysterious light go when she entered? She found keys in a metal box attached to the wall. "Wait, I think I may have keys to the trucks outside."

A noise from outside prompted her to stop talking. She listened but heard nothing. Quietly, she picked up the cold metal bar, squeezing it tight. The sound returned, closer.

"He's here," she whispered. "Hurry." She set the phone down softly.

FIFTY-ONE

JOHN PETERS WAS ALREADY LOSING HIS MIND when he left Mabel's house. Seeing all the emergency vehicles as he pulled up to the sugar mill nearly put him over the edge. It reminded him of that night long ago. Frankie had told him to stay away. He thought it was for other reasons. He should have known better.

It was for *exactly* this reason. Flashing lights, the scene closed off, men in various uniforms—everywhere . . . *oh my God . . . the dogs.*

"John Peters?" asked the officer holding him back.

He nodded. He couldn't speak.

"You have ID?"

He pulled out his wallet and handed his license to the officer. John made eye contact with him for the first time. He had dark hair, brown eyes, and a medium build. He looked fresh out of the police academy.

"Go on in. Corneal is waiting for you," the young officer said.

He nodded.

"John." A man, who he could only guess was Corneal, waved him over. "I take it you haven't heard from her?" he asked. Corneal wasn't at all like he'd imagined. He wore a button-down shirt and jacket, no tie, and jeans with boots.

John wore pretty much the same, minus the jacket. They could have been twins. "No," he replied.

"Good work, Hudson," Corneal hollered to the woman he'd been talking to. She walked away and stopped at a body. A dead body.

The waiting, wondering, not knowing—was utterly terrifying. Be that as it may, John remained confident Jimmy was no match for Mabel. Still, he'd trade places with her in a heartbeat, if she'd allow him to. He may not be as tough as he used to be, and he certainly was no Frankie, but he could hold his own. He patted the gun he always carried with him.

Corneal must have noticed John staring. "That's Officer Hudson, she's a Crime Scene Investigator." Corneal said.

"Have they identified the girl yet?"

"Not yet. Did you ever meet Isabel Dumel?"

"No. She was in Mabel's class, fifth grade. She would have been ten or eleven, I suppose."

"This one could be her."

"Corneal!" yelled a man running up from one of the police cars.

"What?"

"Call."

"Why the hell they don't call my cell is beyond me," he said, walking away. "I'll be back."

John's phone rang. It was Frankie. "Tell me you're with Mabel," John said.

"John?" asked a voice that sounded like Frankie, but he could barely make it out.

John turned to hear him better, as if that would help. "For crying out loud Frankie. I can hardly hear you. Where are you?"

"Mabel called, said she's at a warehouse. Maybe a mile east of the mill. I'm coming up on it now. Tell Corneal." And he hung up.

Son-of-a-bitch! He mumbled under his breath. He had questions. Like *was Jimmy with her?* He guessed not since she got to a phone and called him. *Was she hurt?*

He looked around for Corneal in the direction he'd gone, but he'd disappeared. He found the officer who had informed Corneal of his call. "Where did Corneal go?"

"He and Officer Mickeals left. Got a tip."

"What do you mean? What tip?"

"And you are?" asked the officer.

"Someone with a tip. I need to talk to Corneal—now!"

FIFTY-TWO

HE THOUGHT FOR A BRIEF MOMENT—CLIMB on top of the wooden crates, try to make his way through the window, catch her off guard—then Jimmy remembered how uncoordinated he was. It would be just his luck that he'd fall and break his neck.

He heard a voice coming from inside. If he was quiet enough, she wouldn't hear him coming. When he and William were kids, they had played cops and robbers. Will told him he needed to be stealthy if he wanted to be a good cop—which Jimmy never cared to be. Will was a perfect *good* cop, and Jimmy naturally made a good *bad* guy. Jimmy always played the robber, the convict, the guy running away. But Will found him every time, because Jimmy never could get the stealthy part down.

He pulled on the front door, expecting it to open. It didn't. He moved around the side, eyeing his surroundings. *Ah*—another door, open, inviting him in . . .

He peeked inside, not seeing her or anything else for that matter. It was dark and quiet. He couldn't hear her anymore. Did she hear him?

He was being paranoid. He had the gun, not her. He stepped into the warehouse. It felt open, airy.

Where in the hell was she? Left? Right?

He felt his way along the wall, stopping, giving his eyes time to adjust. Not quite what he planned, but it was kind of fun. His heart raced. He found himself sweating, even in the cold temperatures. He had had the same feeling that night long ago.

He remembered the little girl, running up the stairs, hiding in her room, playing hide and seek like he didn't know where she was. Then surprising him and climbing out the window. It had been so much fun. Making him chase her. Ballsy little shit.

Now she's all grown up and here he is again. Chasing her. Playing hide and seek. If he wasn't having fun, he'd be pissed.

Was he fooling himself?

No . . . this was fun. If he didn't hate her, he just might date her. His throat let out a noise, *hawk,* like a laugh he tried to hold back.

His eyes adjusted a smidge, but basically, he couldn't see his own hands. The place smelled of diesel.

He stepped closer along the wall and around whatever got in his way. When he got to the back wall, near what looked like another room, an uninvited light suddenly blinded him.

BAM.

What the fuck?

The bitch took him by surprise. Hit him with some big ass steel bar. He was bleeding—again. And maybe seeing stars.

Gun? Where's my gun?

"Looking for this?" she asked, dangling the gun from her finger, as he tried to clear his foggy mind.

It took him a split second to realize she *had* been tied. Fucking Houdini. "I see you freed yourself," he said, dragging himself up.

"Guess I didn't hit you hard enough if you can still see."

Her eyes wide, mocking. He hadn't expected her hands to be free. Stupid really. How else did she get inside the building?

He took a step toward her.

She didn't move. It was amusing how brave she was.

A laugh escaped him. He didn't mean to laugh. Melodi, he thought. Not so little anymore, are you? No fear this time.

"I'm going to kill you—*Teach*," he said sardonically. "Like I killed your family." He paused, watching her reaction. He might have seen her pupils get bigger. Hard to tell. "You should have died too. You're like a fucking cat, except you don't got nine lives. I'd give you a freebie—but you already used it."

"And you say I have the big mouth."

He snickered. She was too much fun. He hated to end it. He kind of liked the dog and cat chase. Too bad he just recently found out about her.

His eyes drifted to his gun. Her finger, now on the trigger. She didn't want to kill him, if she did, she would have done it by now. He saw fear under the hate in her big brown eyes. She was pretty, like her mother.

"What are waiting for?" he asked, inching closer.

"For a clear conscious."

He grinned.

"Nothing to smile about asshole. You've given me plenty.

You're already going to spend the rest of your life in prison. It's your choice. Concrete and metal bars or dirt and maggots."

FIFTY-THREE

DESPITE CALLING JOHN, FRANKIE DIDN'T SEE any lights or hear any sirens as he approached the warehouse. Frankie considered calling Corneal himself, but the last thing he needed was sirens. He may have liked the detective, but could he trust him? He didn't know him. In fact, there was a small circle of people he trusted, and it didn't include people he'd met only once.

He studied the building for another entry point as he ran toward an open door with a light shining though. Not seeing anything immediate he settled for the easy access point. No real tactical advantage charging through an open door, but he didn't have time to run around the whole damn building. They'd see him, but he'd see them as well.

As he came up to the door, he heard mumbling inside. He raised his gun, the Kimber 1911, Custom II TLE. He owned a lot of guns, but this one was one of his favorites. If he could get a shot off from a distance, he'd take it.

Slow and steady, he stepped inside. Before his foot made it over the threshold of the door, the warehouse went dark. He couldn't see.

"Well, why didn't you just say so?" he heard a man say.

He heard a loud crash come from the back, followed by a clatter and Mabel swearing.

Grunting—not Mabel. Banging, thumping, crunching, more swearing.

Frankie turned quickly looking for a light switch. Flicking it on, the harsh bright light took over the space, blinding everyone but Frankie. He'd expected it.

Frankie raised his gun to fire, but Mabel got in the way.

In one quick move, Mabel disarmed Jimmy.

Not giving up, Jimmy's right hook aimed for her head.

Ready for it, she blocked his weak attempt and struck him in the neck. Stunned, Jimmy staggered back.

Snake hand—good girl, thought Frankie.

She glanced back at Frankie and he fired. His subconscious mind took over. Jimmy didn't deserve to live.

Jimmy fell to the floor like a limp rag doll.

Mabel's eyes glanced from Frankie to Jimmy and back to Frankie. She didn't say anything. Her face softening as she realized it was over.

"Hey," Frankie said to Mabel.

"Hey, yourself," she replied. They shared an awkward laugh.

"Are you okay?" he asked.

"I've had better days."

He looked at Jimmy and back at Mabel. "This is a pretty good day for me."

She smiled. "You didn't have to shoot him, you know."

He looked at her, surprised. "You're too soft, Mabel. On the inside. All that man ever brought you was pain."

"You're right."

"And just so you know, if I meant to kill him—he'd be dead. I spared his miserable life because I knew you didn't want to kill him."

She looked away, a hint of shame. "I wasn't thinking about what I want." Her head snapped back. "Isabel," she cried. "Where is she?"

FIFTY-FOUR

AS IF ON CUE, THE CAVALRY ARRIVED—CARS screeched to a stop, doors slammed in unison, footsteps beat the ground. Uniformed men with guns appeared in the doorway. All guns pointed at Frankie.

"Ah, shit . . ." Frankie dropped his gun and his hands flew up.

Two men ran up to Frankie, grabbing his hands and cuffed him. He's a big man. It took two to handle him. Not that he fought anyone. Another officer stepped on the gun he had dropped.

Mabel froze, hands up, but no one came to arrest her. She didn't know what else to do.

Two more ran to Jimmy. "He's been shot," one shouted.

The officer holding Frankie glared at him.

"Self-defense," Frankie said.

The man started reading him his Miranda rights. He didn't get through his first sentence before a man, who Mabel assumed was in charge, took over.

"I got him," said the man with silver streaks in his hair.

"Corneal. Am I happy to see you," said Frankie, flashing him his pearly whites.

"I'm sure you are. You shoot him?"

"You're damn right I shot him. He had a gun pointed at Mabel."

Corneal eyed her.

"She's my niece." Frankie continued.

"Sure, I see the family resemblance," he remarked. "I thought I told you to call me?"

Frankie shrugged.

"Don't go anywhere," he said to Frankie, as he uncuffed Frankie's hands. He looked at the officer with his hand still on Frankie's arm. "Make sure of it."

Frankie rolled his eyes.

Corneal joined the men hovering over Jimmy. A big part of Mabel hoped he was dead. She wanted to shoot him herself but couldn't find it in herself to pull the trigger. She'd beat his ass down—no problem—but couldn't pull the damn trigger.

Frankie pulled out his buzzing phone and put it on speaker.

"John, it's over. Come pick us up."

The officer—who'd been watching the crew who were attempting to save Jimmy's miserable life—snapped his head back to Frankie's smiling face.

"How's Mabel?" John asked.

"She's perfect," His smile grew, putting his arm around Mabel.

"Isabel? Where is she?" she asked again.

"Ah man, I'm sorry Mabel . . ." He didn't want to be the one to tell her.

“What? Why?”

“They couldn’t identify the girl . . . so I’m not certain, but there’s a dead girl at the mill. She was shot.”

“No,” she whispered. “She can’t be.” Her eyes darted to where Jimmy lay. Before he could stop her, she was gone.

“You fucking psycho! You killed her! You killed her!” she screamed, charging at him.

Corneal, who’d been close, lunged to stop her. It took three men to keep her away from Jimmy.

“What are you talking about?” Jimmy barked, his voice hoarse.

“Your daughter, you asshole. You killed her!”

“NO!” he protested.

“Mabel! Mabel!” yelled Corneal. “You need to come with me.” His voice firm, he pulled her away.

“I should have killed him—when I had the chance. I should have killed him,” she gasped, tears streaming down her face.

“I got her!” Frankie growled.

Corneal led them into the claustrophobic office and shut the door. Mabel’s hand went to her jaw.

“It wasn’t Isabel,” Corneal said, standing by the door.

Mabel’s lips twitched as she thought about what he said. “But you said . . .?” Her voice wavered looking at Frankie.

“There’s a dead girl, yes. But I got a call from a lady that lives nearby,” Corneal explained.

“I told her to run . . .” her hands were trembling. “Is she alive?”

“Yes. Isabel is alive,” he said. “She’s with her aunt.”

She walked to the window, staring off into the darkness. “Then who’s the girl? I didn’t see anyone else.”

We’re guessing wrong place, wrong time,” Corneal added.

Tears began to pour down as her hands covered her face, not wanting to look at anyone. She didn't pull the trigger, but Frankie knew she blamed herself.

FIFTY-FIVE

GRANDPA!" SHE YELLED, HER HAND GOING to her jaw robotically, as the piercing pain reminded her how careless she'd been.

"Mabes," he gushed, "I was out of my mind with worry." He held her tight. "Tell me everything," he said, pulling her away, studying her eyes. "You've been crying," he accused. He spotted her swollen bruised lip. "Dammit, Mabel! What happened?"

"I'm fine," she said, attempting to smile. It hurt to smile.

He let out a sigh.

"You worry too much. We fought. I won, and Uncle Frankie shot him." She shrugged.

"Where's Isabel?" she asked.

Grandpa nudged her and pointed. She followed his finger.

"Who's that?" she asked.

"Susan."

Aunt Susie!

She ran to the door where Susan was being kept from entering. As soon as she stepped outside, she spotted Isabel, a small ball matted to the building.

"Are you Ms. Peters?" Susan asked.

Mabel nodded.

"I can't calm her down," Susan said. She was pretty. She looked like Isabel. Which meant Isabel looked like her mom. Susan had shoulder length blonde hair, like Isabel. And sort of resembled Heidi Klum.

As Mabel got closer, she could hear faint murmuring, "No, no, no."

Mabel's right hand instinctively covered her heart, letting out a heavy breath.

Was she in shock? Isabel was shaking, her hands covered her ears and her head was buried between her knees. Mabel glanced at Susan, speechless.

"She said she heard shots and ran. She thought you were dead. She's scared out of her mind," Susan explained. Mabel had seen that look before. Parents coming in to talk to her, at their wits end, not knowing what to do with their child.

He won't listen to me . . . does he listen to you? I can't get her to do her homework. I can't get her to eat breakfast. I can't get him to eat his lunch. He's fighting with his sister non-stop . . . does he fight with the girls in his class?

Mabel didn't have kids of her own. But what she did know about kids was they needed time and space. And someone who cared. Not an overbearing, in-your-face kind of parent. But a, 'I'm here when you're ready to talk' kind.

"Isabel?" Mabel said in a low voice, moving Isabel's golden mess of hair away to expose her face.

Isabel peered up, exposing her blue, red-rimmed, defeated

eyes. They registered Mabel was before her and a trace of hope crossed her face. Confused, she glanced at Susan. "I thought my daddy shot you," she said, looking back to Mabel.

"No," Mabel said, shaking her head. "See." She stood up to give Isabel a clear view. "I'm fine," she added.

"My daddy? Is he dead?" Her lip quivered at the thought.

"No, he's hurt, but he'll be okay."

"I'm sorry I lied to you," she sniffled. "I didn't know . . ."

"Shhh, it's okay. I know you didn't. You were very brave today."

Shouting and commotion could be heard from inside. An officer appeared in the doorway startling the already frightened child.

Isabel threw herself into Mabel, knocking her off balance. Steadying herself, Mabel wrapped her arms around the terrified girl.

"She's out here!" the officer shouted into the doorway. "With a child."

Isabel squeezed Mabel tighter when she heard Jimmy screaming.

The snow started falling. Millions of pure white crystals—cold and bittersweet—washing away the day that had been laid to waste.

No. Not the whole day.

"Wait," Mabel told the officer, keeping her eyes on Isabel. She held her blue eyes for a second. "Can you give us a minute?" she asked the officer.

He hesitated with suspicious eyes, nodded, and stood outside the door.

"Is my daddy going away now?" she asked, white crystals falling on her long lashes.

"He is," Mabel answered. She examined her face for signs of distress. At eleven, she seemed to understand if you did something bad you paid the price. "You want to say goodbye to him—before he goes away?" she asked. The words came easy.

Isabel considered the offer and looked at Susan, whose telling eyes did not approve. She may not see her father for a long time and this would be her opportunity to say goodbye—goodbye to the dad she thought she knew. Turning back to Mabel, she nodded, "mm-hmm."

Over her shoulder, as she moved toward the door, Mabel heard Susan *tsk*, unhappy with Isabel's decision. Mabel did it for this child, who no one else would stand up for, not for Jimmy. She certainly didn't need Susan's approval . . . or did she?

Not yet, she told herself. Susan didn't have custody of her yet.

She would not deny Isabel the good-bye she never had.

"What can I do for you?" asked Corneal, clearly annoyed he was called out.

"This is Jimmy's daughter, Isabel. She'd like to say goodbye to her father, before you take him away."

"Are you shitting me? Didn't this dirt bag just try to kill you?" He had a point there.

"Can we *not* do this now?" Mabel challenged, agitated by the lack of sensitivity toward Isabel. Without missing a stride, she moved Isabel in front of her and led her to her father.

"Looks like he needs to keep his niece on a leash," mumbled a rookie to Corneal.

"What did you say, maggot?" Frankie said.

"He didn't say anything," Corneal said. "Shut up jackass." Corneal smacked the *maggot* in the back of the head.

Frankie shook his head in disgust, turning his attention back to Mabel and Isabel, giving Mabel a nod of approval. Mabel watched as Isabel walked up to Jimmy and reached for his cuffed hand. The man who lay shackled, got to say good-bye to his daughter. A gift her mother never received. One she never had. He didn't deserve it, but she couldn't think about him. So she pushed the hate she felt for him down deep and smiled when Isabel smiled.

"Baby, you listen up now. I have to go away. Like I told you." Jimmy said.

"I know."

"You need to stay with Aunt Susan now. You come see me, as soon as you can."

"That's enough," said one of the officers. "Let's go." He led Isabel away by the shoulders.

"Hold on now," screamed Jimmy.

Isabel threw herself over Jimmy's chest. "Bye, Daddy."

The officer pulled her away, parking her in front of Mabel.

Jimmy kept his eyes on Isabel. "I'll write to you. I'll write you every day."

Isabel ran toward her dad, but an officer caught her before she got to him. "I got her," said Susan, who came from nowhere.

Mabel did a double take. The officer that caught Isabel looked familiar. He glanced up at Mabel and half smiled. *Dad Mike! He's a policeman.*

Mabel followed Jimmy out. "Officer, may I?" she asked, signaling to Jimmy. "Just a minute?"

Jimmy turned to look at her. "Stay away from my daughter, Teach. Don't you go near her."

"You made your choice Jimmy."

"You tricked me. You set me up."

"Have you heard the quote by Bob Marley?" she asked. He stared at her blankly. "*'Every man gotta right to decide his own destiny.'* You chose yours. Now it's you that can't see Isabel."

"Fuck you!"

The officer, Dad Mike, smiled ever so faintly.

"You always have a choice Jimmy. You always have a choice," she said, walking away.

"It's Mabel—right?" asked Dad Mike.

"Yes. And you're Mike?"

"Good memory. Fancy meeting you here," he said, looking confused. "I have to go, but you okay?"

"I am now," she replied, staring at Jimmy as they shut the ambulance doors.

"We really need to get that drink," he said. "This is really bad timing, but here." He handed her his card. "Call me." And he was off.

"What was that about?" asked Frankie, sneaking up on her.

"The little bit of redemption I could get—for my decision not to put a bullet through his skull." She smiled.

"I would have done it for you."

"I know."

"That's not what I was talking about though."

She looked at him blankly, no clue what he was referring to.

He tilted his head. "The handsome officer," he said, like she should have read his mind.

"Oh," she chuckled. "That's nothing. I know him. Well, kind of. It's sort of a long story."

"Okay, don't tell me."

"Uncle Frankie, it's nothing . . . really."

"Corneal's waiting for you," he said, changing the subject.

She turned to see Corneal staring at her.

She took a step forward, stopping for just a moment. Closing her eyes, she inhaled deeply—appreciating the feeling of air expanding through her—then exhaled heavily, in an attempt to rid herself of the days negative energy.

After all this time, she was free.

Acknowledgments

THANK YOU TO MY FAMILY. NOT JUST FOR your support while I wrote my first book, which I will forever be thankful, but for all the days after till the day of publication. For putting up with my ups and downs, and most of all for keeping me around after learning who I truly was. You thought me weird before, but writing unleashed the beast in me and you all stayed by my side.

Thank you to my first reader and friend, James Brown. Your insight, feedback, and expertise in the police department helped me more than you know. What I appreciated most was your encouragement and belief in me as a writer when I needed it most. Thank you for everything.

And to my beautiful daughter, Marisa Holbrook—they said don't have family be your beta readers, but you, my dear, gave nothing short of valuable feedback. Feedback that helped shape the book into what it is.

Heidi McCarthy, The Librarian—you are an amazing person

who didn't know me from squat, but you took the time to read my manuscript at its worst stage and gave me feedback. Thank you for being there for me and continuing to offer your help.

Tom Schiola—thank you for being a wonderful teacher to my daughter, and for lending your expertise when I had questions.

Shauna Burd—you were one of the many wonderful people I got to work with in my previous life. Thank you for making time to read my manuscript, offer feedback, and edit the complete mess it was. I am forever in your debt.

Kimberly Peticolas, my editor—thank you for taking me on when I was lost. I knew my goal was to self-publish, but you helped make the journey an easier process. Not only did you catch my mistakes, you made my book better and answered every question I threw at you. Thank you for all you do.

About the Author

LAURIE HOLBROOK GREW UP IN A SMALL TOWN in southern Colorado, where she spent an excessive amount of her time playing make believe and watching movies. Her debut novel, *Still Out There*, was inspired by her love of thriller movies and the average everyday kickass heroine. After spending twenty plus years in the retail industry working in various managerial positions, she decided to pursue her lifelong dream of storytelling. She now lives and writes in the northern suburbs of Denver with her husband, children, and dogs. Find out more about Laurie by visiting www.laurieholbrook.com.

Author photo by Amy K Wright.

Enjoyed the Book?

If you enjoyed this book, please consider leaving a review on Amazon or Goodreads.

Want to know more about Lauire Holbrook or her next book? Make sure to visit www.laurieholbrook.com and sign up for her newsletter.